"Turn toward me, slowly."

The man complied. But as he did, Bolan saw the face of a demented, self-righteous radical.

"What will you do?" the man asked in Spanish. "Will you shoot me?" He looked at the burning match in his hand. "If you do, this will fall."

"You come up the stairs now, I'll let you live."

For a moment, a look of indecision crossed the man's face. "How can I be certain you're telling the truth?"

"You have my word," said the Executioner.

Suddenly the man shook his head. "I don't believe you," he said simply, and let the match fall to the gasoline-soaked floor.

MACK BOLAN ®
The Executioner

DON PENDLETON'S
EXECUTIONER®
THE
KILL RADIUS

BOOK II

THE BORDER FIRE TRILOGY

A GOLD EAGLE BOOK FROM
WORLDWIDE®

TORONTO • NEW YORK • LONDON
AMSTERDAM • PARIS • SYDNEY • HAMBURG
STOCKHOLM • ATHENS • TOKYO • MILAN
MADRID • WARSAW • BUDAPEST • AUCKLAND

First edition November 1999
ISBN 0-373-64251-2

Special thanks and acknowledgment to
Jerry VanCook for his contribution to this work.

KILL RADIUS

Every act of rebellion expresses a nostalgia for innocence
and an appeal to the essence of being.

—Albert Camus

It doesn't matter how many men you have as long as you
have a strong battle plan.

—Mack Bolan

THE
MACK BOLAN®
LEGEND

Nothing less than a war could have fashioned the destiny of the man called Mack Bolan. Bolan earned the Executioner title in the jungle hell of Vietnam.

But this soldier also wore another name—Sergeant Mercy. He was so tagged because of the compassion he showed to wounded comrades-in-arms and Vietnamese civilians.

Mack Bolan's second tour of duty ended prematurely when he was given emergency leave to return home and bury his family, victims of the Mob. Then he declared a one-man war against the Mafia.

He confronted the Families head-on from coast to coast, and soon a hope of victory began to appear. But Bolan had broken society's every rule. That same society started gunning for this elusive warrior—to no avail.

So Bolan was offered amnesty to work within the system against terrorism. This time, as an employee of Uncle Sam, Bolan became Colonel John Phoenix. With a command center at Stony Man Farm in Virginia, he and his new allies—Able Team and Phoenix Force—waged relentless war on a new adversary: the KGB.

But when his one true love, April Rose, died at the hands of the Soviet terror machine, Bolan severed all ties with Establishment authority.

Now, after a lengthy lone-wolf struggle and much soul-searching, the Executioner has agreed to enter an "arm's-length" alliance with his government once more, reserving the right to pursue personal missions in his Everlasting War.

1

The man cautiously approached President Don Juan de Fierro Blanco's summerhouse. Dressed in desert camouflage battle dress, matching floppy boonie hat and tan combat boots, he moved stealthily from rock to rock three hundred yards from where Mack Bolan stood guard. In the man's hands, Bolan saw a long black object—a rifle of some sort. From the distance, it was impossible to determine what type.

Bolan stood at the shore of the Gulf of Mexico. Wearing a swimsuit and sandals, his trademark .44 Magnum Desert Eagle and 9 mm Beretta 93-R were both hidden beneath a loose extra-large T-shirt. But the M-16 he had taken a few minutes earlier from the incompetent federal sentry assigned to that post hung over his right shoulder. He had no doubt that the man in the camouflage would have seen it—even from the distance. In spite of his tourist beach garb there would be no mistaking that Bolan was guarding that side of the president's estate.

Which meant the intruder would have to kill him to get by.

Bolan pretended to stare out into the water, toward the spot where he and Mexican federal Captain Juanito Oliverez had watched the dolphins play earlier. The intelligent sea mammals who had followed the two men as they walked down the beach to the sentry post had returned just off the coast. Bolan knew they were his only advantage; to the camouflaged man approaching, he would look as if he were intent on watching the stripe-flanked dolphins cavort through the waves. But while his attention was eastward, his peripheral vision was glued to the intruder.

Known to the world as the "Executioner," as "Striker" to the other counterterrorist warriors who worked out of America's top-secret compound known as Stony Man Farm, and by a dozen other aliases when the need arose, Mack Bolan was on special assignment by direct orders of the President of the United States. Mexico was in turmoil; on the brink of a new civil war that would make the revolution of 1919 look like a rich ladies' bridge-club party. Mexican President Don Juan de Fierro Blanco, himself suspected of being behind the assassinations of journalists and political opponents and possibly aligned with the drug cartels and terrorist organizations currently operating south of the Rio Grande, had made a desperate call to his American counterpart for help. Fierro Blanco no longer knew whom he could trust. He suspected everyone, even his own bodyguards.

Did his paranoia come from the fact that he had sold out his own country? Bolan wondered. Or from the fact that he actually was honest and being set up as the fall guy for someone else's plan?

The Executioner didn't know. But his mission, in addition to keeping the president breathing, was to find the truth. The U.S. President was about to make a decision whether or not to recertify Mexico as cooperating with antidrug efforts, and the Man in the White House was worried about that decision. If he made the wrong one, his own political future was nonexistent.

Still facing the dolphins, Bolan saw the approaching man crawl from behind a boulder and go facedown in the sand. A few moments later, he began a slow belly-crawl forward again, pausing every few feet to observe the Executioner. Bolan lowered his eyebrows in thought. Whoever the man was—he could be a member of the communist-based *Partido Revolucionario Marxista,* the ultraright-wing *Ciudadano para Democracia Mexicana Legitima,* or even a gunner for one of the drug cartels—he wasn't particularly skilled in clandestine approach. Although his camouflage clothing blended well with the terrain, he had foolishly chosen a web belt cinched at the waist by a steel buckle. The bright Yucatán sun beating down over the peninsula caught every movement he made, sending beams of light streaking across the sand and allowing the soldier to keep tabs on the man as easily as if he had been using the most sophisticated radar tracking equipment.

The stalker was still a good 250 yards away when Bolan turned away from him and moved toward the walkie-talkie resting on a stone. Using his body to block the man's vision, he lifted the radio, pressed it to his lips and thumbed the transmission button. "Protection One to Two," he whispered into the transmitter.

Almost immediately, the voice of Oliverez, perhaps the only man in Mexico the soldier trusted at the moment, came back. "Two to one," the federal captain said simply.

"What's it like on the home front?"

"Quiet. I've sent a man—Sergent Delgado—to relieve you. *El presidente* and his family are planning to go fishing later. As soon as the boat arrives."

"You have radio contact with this Delgado?"

"Affirmative. Why?"

"Call him back," the soldier ordered. "I've got an intruder sneaking up from the east. I don't want to spook him off." He took a breath, then went on. "Contact the other sentries to see if any of them have noticed anything. I can't believe this guy would be alone."

"Yes, Belasko," Oliverez said, using the name by which the Mexicans knew Bolan. "I'll get back to you as soon as possible."

The Executioner grinned as he set the radio back on the

rock. Oliverez had proved to be a good, dependable and loyal man—a rarity, the Executioner was finding, in current Mexico. Poverty and governmental corruption were tempting many of the federals, police and other officials to betray their country. The financial offers from the wealthy cartels and the twisted patriotism put out by the revolutionary groups were simply too strong.

Bolan straightened and stretched his arms over his head as if bored with his assignment. To the man in the camouflage behind him, his use of the radio should look like a routine check-in. Rolling his neck around his shoulders several times to make it obvious that he was about to turn again, he finally stepped away from the rock and made a quick 360-degree scan of his post—the same as any reasonably well-trained sentry would do.

The Executioner's eyes swept past the glittering belt buckle without pausing. But they didn't miss the fact that the approaching man had taken advantage of the Executioner's back being turned to rise and move faster. A small cloud of dust was proof that the man in the camouflage gear had just dropped back to the ground.

Taking a seat on the rock, Bolan turned his face toward the dolphins again. The stranger had gained a good hundred yards while the soldier contacted Oliverez, and was now within firing range. Bolan could finally see that it was an assault weapon of some sort, a long box magazine hanging in front of the trigger guard. Would the man soon raise the weapon and try to take him out? Maybe, but he doubted it. The gunshot would be heard by the other guards at the house, and the Executioner could see little the man could gain from such action. Risking another slow scan, Bolan paused for a split second when he got to the man's position, squinting briefly at the rifle. AK-47. Reliable, but hardly the most accurate of weapons. More importantly, he could see no type of sound-suppression device on the barrel which furthered his suspicions that the man was there as a sniper.

Bolan's eyes continued, falling on a row of rocks perhaps ten yards to his rear. Again in his peripheral vision, he saw the belly-crawling man change course slightly, and what the man had in mind suddenly crystallized in the Bolan's brain.

The stalker was circling toward the rocks. He planned to secrete himself behind them, then eliminate the soldier by either making a last-minute dash with a knife or with a sound-suppressed pistol still too small for Bolan to have seen at that distance.

Turning to the sea once more, the Executioner continued to watch out of the corner of his eye but let his mind wander briefly to the other problems currently plaguing Mexico. Ronnie Quartel, an American movie star who had recently risen to become the number-one box office attraction, had been visiting his friend, Scott Hix, in Tijuana. Both men, along with the Tijuana mayor and several women, had been kidnapped from a party at Hix's house by members of the *Cuidadano para Democracia Mexicana Legitima*—the Citizens for Legitimate Mexican Democracy. The *Legitimas*, as they were commonly called, had announced they would issue their demands for the hostages' release shortly. Bolan suspected those demands would be more financial than political. Revolutions, whether Communist or democratic, were costly affairs, and the CDML was rumored to be running short on funds.

Meanwhile, the man in the battle uniform crawled closer. Bolan thought back briefly to the reason Fierro Blanco and his family were now at their summerhouse, rather than back at *Los Pinos*, the presidential mansion in Mexico City. Led by an unidentified leader in a ball-fringed straw sombrero, a combined force of *Marxistas* and Mayan Zapatistas—another socialist-backed revolutionary group operating in the south—had attacked the president first dur-

ing a speech at the Bosque de Chapeltepec, then agitated
mob violence throughout the city. One such mob, again led
by the man in the colorful hat, had overrun the presidential
mansion with the president and his family narrowly escaping away through a tunnel.

The walkie-talkie screeched quietly next to Bolan and he
lifted the radio to his lips. "Go ahead," he said.

Oliverez's voice came over the airwaves. "Two of the
other sentries have now reported suspicious sightings," the
captain said.

Bolan scowled but didn't answer. The sentries should
have noticed these sightings without having to be specifically instructed to look for them. Just another example of
the incompetence, unprofessionalism and perhaps outright
corruption with which he was being forced to deal.

When he heard nothing from Bolan's end, Oliverez came
back on. "I await your orders, Belasko," he said.

Bolan pressed the walkie-talkie to his lips again. "Tell
the sentries to hold for the time being. Get Fierro Blanco
and his family into the house, then take them to the basement and bolt the door." He let up on the transmission key
for a moment, then pushed it again. "Assign ten men to
them, and you stay down there, too. No matter what you
hear above, don't open the door for anybody but me." He
paused again. "Understand?"

"Yes," Oliverez came back. "Is it an assassination team
approaching?"

Bolan shifted slightly, now in a better position to watch
the man belly-crawling through the sand. "Maybe," he
said. "Something tells me it's not that simple. But whatever
it is, it isn't good. Now get Fierro Blanco, his wife and
kids inside." He dropped the radio to the rock next to him
again.

The Executioner saw the man crawl out of sight. But just
before he disappeared, Bolan caught sight of the grips of a
semiautomatic pistol to the right of the sparkling belt

buckle. Its holster extended almost to the man's knee—too long for anything but a weapon equipped with a sound suppressor.

The man was no more than fifty yards away now, and since he had disappeared from view he could afford to step up his pace as he snaked through the sand. Soon, he would be directly behind Bolan. Then, hoping his prey continued to keep his attention focused on the dolphins romping in the sea, he would draw his sound-suppressed pistol and put a bullet in the back of the Executioner's head.

A grim smile curled the corners of Bolan's mouth as he finally turned to face the oncoming threat. He couldn't see the man behind the rocks. But that also meant the man couldn't see him. Resting the M-16 in the sand, he drew his own sound-suppressed Beretta 93-R and dropped to the ground. Quickly, he executed his own tactical belly-crawl to the boulders separating him from the man in the camouflage.

Bolan didn't know who the man was, or which group he represented as he reached the rocks, but as he rolled to a halt against the sun-heated stones, an old expression came to him and his grin widen.

The Executioner knew he was indeed between the devil and the deep blue sea.

IN THE DISTANCE, Calvin James could see the DEA's Suburban still parked where they had abandoned it as his black stallion descended the slope out of the hills toward the desert. It was surrounded by the aged cars and pickups that Mexican *bandido* leader Victorio Vega and his men had driven before switching to horses for their escape into the hills.

James grinned. Luck must be on their side. The fact that the Suburban, or any of the vehicles for that matter, was still there was a minor miracle in itself. While James, Rafael Encizo and Drug Enforcement Administration-U.S.

Military Border Task Force Director Winston "Pug" Nelson had killed Vega and his band of cutthroats a few hours earlier, they were hardly the only bandits taking advantage of the current confusion in northern Mexico. James had half expected to return to find the Suburban gone or at least stripped to the bare bones.

"Damn!" Pug Nelson said as his palomino whinnied. "I'd have never believed it."

James's grin widened at the man he had known briefly years before when they had both been Navy SEALs. "You're gonna come out smelling like a rose, Pug," he said. Now a ranking DEA special agent, Nelson had been worried about his job, having willfully violated orders not to penetrate farther than ten miles into Mexico.

Nelson frowned, the scar tissue above his eyes—souvenirs of his days as the U.S. Navy's light-heavyweight boxing champ—lowering almost to his nose. "Maybe, maybe not," he said. "I've still got to come up with some scam on where we've been the past two days."

Encizo sat astride a spotted mare. "No problem," he said. "Just tell them we had a flat tire."

The horses hit flat ground as they left the hills. James looked over his shoulder at the woman who trailed them. She was the reason Nelson had violated his orders and the reason he and the two Phoenix Force warriors had pursued the *bandidos* into the hills. Vega and his men had ambushed the party of Mexican peasants of which she and her husband had been part as they attempted to cross the border into the U.S. She had been kidnapped, and the trio of Americans had barely had time to save her from being raped and murdered. Now dressed in filthy pants and a shirt taken from dead men, she had stared ahead silently during most of the return trip.

James caught Encizo looking at him as they approached the Suburban. The Cuban Phoenix Force warrior glanced briefly over his shoulder at the woman, then whispered,

"She hasn't asked yet. But she will. Even if she doesn't, sooner or later, one of us has to tell her."

Calvin James didn't have to ask what his fellow soldier meant. They had come across the party of Mexican pilgrims right after the attack and abduction. The woman's husband had been shot in both the lung and lower abdomen. Although they had radioed for medical help before pursuing the bandits, James figured the man stood a slim chance of surviving.

Nelson dropped out of the saddle and hurried to the Suburban. Opening the unlocked door, he checked inside, then stuck the key in the ignition and fired the engine. Leaving it running, he got back out and slammed the door. "I don't even think anybody's been by here," he said, shaking his head. "This is enough to make a man believe in God. I might just start praying." He glance to the sky. "That's a promise."

James and Encizo dismounted and helped the woman down. James turned toward the vehicles the bandits had driven, then back to Nelson. "If I can get one of these things started, we'll drive your unit back inside the ten-mile limit, then switch to this."

"What good's that going to do?" Nelson asked.

"It's going to save your job, Pug."

"How do you figure that?"

James shrugged. "I haven't worked out the details yet." He grinned. "But I usually get creative while I drive." Turning, he jogged to the nearest pickup and slid behind the wheel. The keys weren't in the ignition but it took only seconds to reach under the dash and connect the wires. As soon as he did, the ancient engine sputtered into a reasonable facsimile of life. Driving to the Suburban, he saw Encizo riding shotgun with the woman in the backseat. James leaned out the open window. "I'll follow you," he told the DEA man.

A few minutes later, the two vehicles were racing back

across the desert toward the border. When they reached the spot where the ambush had taken place, they saw remnants of the slaughter. But the men, women, children and dead bodies were gone. Whether the emergency medical staff they had summoned to the scene had evacuated them into the U.S. or to a hospital in Mexico, James had no idea.

Well inside the ten-mile limit, James got out of the truck and joined Encizo, Nelson and the woman who were examining the scene. The sudden realization that they didn't even know the woman's name crossed the Phoenix Force warrior's mind. He turned to her and started to ask but stopped when he saw her kneeling on the ground next to a torn and bloody shirt. Tears filled her eyes but she held them in check.

James recognized the shirt as the one her husband had worn. The medics must have cut it off him at the scene. "Ma'am," he said in a soft voice, as he walked slowly toward her.

The woman held up a hand for silence. James noted that even after all she had been through, in the disheveled shape she was in and wearing the baggy blood-caked clothes of dead bandits, she was still one of the most beautiful women he had ever laid eyes upon.

Apparently getting a grip on herself, the woman stood, still holding the shirt. "Is he dead?" she asked.

James shook his head. "I don't know," he said. "He was still alive when we left."

"How bad was he?"

James glanced to Encizo, then back to the woman. There was no use giving her false hopes. "Pretty bad," he said.

"Then he will be dead by now?"

Calvin James hated saying these words more than anything else he could ever remember doing. But he did. "Yes ma'am. I'm sure he must be."

The woman nodded, hugged the shirt to her breast, and got back into the Suburban.

Nelson slid back behind the wheel, but this time Encizo rode with his partner. James led the way. By now Nelson had a plan and pulled over. He was hurriedly unscrewing the bolts that held the DEA radio in place on the dashboard by the time James and Encizo noticed, and drove back to the Suburban. They dismantled the antennae and took it with the radio to the pickup.

"Task Force One to Base," Nelson said into the microphone as soon as the unit was operational. "Task Force One to Base. Come in, Base."

A moment later a surprised voice came on. "Task Force Base to One," it said. "What's your 10-20? I repeat, 10-20?" There was a moment's pause, then throwing radio procedure and the FFA to the wind, the voice said, "Where the fuck are you, Pug?"

"Not far from yesterday's scene," he said. "My vehicle was disabled, then we were pinned down."

"How did you—"

Nelson keyed the mike to block the transmission, then keyed it again and said, "Look, it's a long story and we'll tell you when we get back in. In the meantime, get a helicopter to pick us up."

"Roger that, Task Force One," the voice said. "It's on the way."

Encizo and the woman had stood next to the pickup while Nelson had transmitted. James had held the radio in his lap. Now he got out, set the radio on the seat and walked to the Suburban. Drawing his Beretta, he fired several rounds into the side of the big vehicle, then took careful aim and put one into the gas tank.

Liquid began to trickle through the hole as the pungent odor filled the air.

"You know, there are more holes in this story than there are in the vehicle," Nelson said. He had jammed one of his cheap cigars into his mouth and was lighting it with a match.

James nodded. "We'll fill them in later," he said. "I don't think they're going to investigate too closely, though."

Nelson picked a piece of tobacco from his teeth and flicked his fingers to get it off. "Oh really?" he said sarcastically. "When did you become such a big authority on DEA procedure?"

James's grin didn't fade. "I'm not," he said. "But I've come to understand how politics works in federal law enforcement. And if your superiors get told to drop the case, they will."

"Who's gonna tell them that?" Nelson asked.

"Would the President be okay?"

"You're shitting me. You got the ear of the President?"

James thought of Hal Brognola, the director of sensitive ops at Stony Man Farm. Besides the Farm's personnel, the President of the United States was the only other human who knew of the Farm's existence. "No, Pug," he said. "I don't have the ear of the President. But I know the guy who does."

The distant sound of helicopter blades filled the air. A few minutes later, the chopper had landed and a DEA agent wearing a gray suit helped them board. As they flew over the site where Vega had waylaid the Mexicans heading for the border, James leaned forward and said, "What's the word on the survivors?"

The fed had to shout to be heard over the chopper's noise. "The ones who weren't hurt were turned back," he said.

"How about the injured?"

The man shook his head. "Only one survivor," he said. "He's still in ICU but the doc thinks he's gonna make it."

"What's his name?" James asked.

The DEA man pulled a notepad from the breast pocket of his suit and flipped it open. "Mena," he said. "Fernando Mena."

When James turned, his head struck the woman who, unbeknownst to him, had been pressed directly behind him. She didn't seem to mind, however. Her beautiful face was now more lovely than ever, and radiated a joy that made her literally look like an angel.

James couldn't help but smile back. Then he remembered he had never asked her name.

He might ask her first name later. But for now, just knowing her last one seemed enough.

THE FIRST PART of the plan was no different than any other undercover drug deal—the bad guys would bring the dope to the good guys who would be pretending to be bad guys themselves. Only the location and what would happen after the deal went down were unique.

Carl Lyons pulled the strings tight in the collar of his light windbreaker. The temperature in Nome, Alaska, was usually in the high forties or low fifties this time of year, but a cold front had passed through and he found himself chilled as he led the other two members of Able Team down Front Street to the Glue Pot restaurant. He looked across the Bering Sea as they neared the small eatery. He didn't know if the Russians had come by sea or air. But they should be there by now.

And they were, the Able Team leader saw, as he opened the door and ushered Hermann "Gadgets" Schwarz and Rosario "Politician" Blancanales inside the restaurant. Half-dozen burly, Slavic-looking men, who might as well have had "ex-KGB" tattooed across their foreheads, sat around a pair of steel and linoleum tables that had been pushed together. With their cheap shoes, white shirts and broad shoulders threatening to burst the seams of their tight brown suit coats, all six looked like they'd been fashioned by the same wide cookie cutter. Twelve eyes looked up from grease-drenched cheeseburgers and French fries when the door opened, but the men went on eating.

One of the Russians, with sandy-blond hair, a low sloping forehead and bushy eyebrows nodded toward the three vacant chairs facing him.

Lyons led his fellow Able Team soldiers forward. A portly waitress ambled over and the three men ordered burgers and fries too. As soon as the woman had left again, Lyons said, "Have a good trip?"

The sandy-haired Russian—Demitri, unless Lyons missed his guess, the leader he had spoken to over the phone the day before—merely grunted.

"Did you come by plane or sea?" Schwarz asked pleasantly.

The Russian looked at him but didn't answer. He obviously had no intention of giving up any more details about his operation than was necessary. The conversation died then and there.

Three more green plastic baskets filled with cheeseburgers and French fries arrived, and the men of Able Team began to eat. Lyons kept his eyes on his food but watched the other men out of the corner of his eye. Demitri's organization—which was made up primarily of former KGB officers, agents and snitches, had been operating for several years. During that time, with the help of a few crooked Alaskan cops and a Seward Peninsula-based faction of the Vancouver Mafia, they had smuggled literally tons of cocaine and heroin across the Bering Strait. The division of labor was simple: the Russian Mafia delivered the dope to Alaska where dirty state police officers escorted it to the more traditional Mafia in Canada. From there, it filtered down the pipeline, finally ending in the bloodstreams of American and Canadian youths.

Able Team's mission had been simple. Break up the game and eliminate the players. Blancanales, a master of psychological warfare, had accomplished the first part of that goal by creating the illusion that the Alaskan troopers were skimming money from the mobsters. One hell of a gunfight between the two contingents had taken place at Beaver Creek, the point of exchange on the Alaskan-Canadian border. All of the dishonest law enforcement officers, and many of the mafioso, had died. With a hole in the network that left the Russian without contacts on this continent, Able Team had used a surviving member of the shoot-out to introduce them over the phone as U.S. Treasury agents willing to step in and take the cops' places as safe escorts.

Lyons watched a piece of lettuce caught between Demitri's gaping teeth bob up and down as the man smacked his lips revoltingly. The agreement they had come to was that both he and Demitri would bring only two men to the point of exchange. The Russian had already violated that agreement. And Lyons suspected that violation was only the beginning.

The Russian glanced around the otherwise deserted café and then looked at Lyons. "You have brought the money?" he whispered.

Lyons set his half-eaten cheeseburger back in the basket. "Back at the room," he replied in a low voice. "You've got the..." he did his own 360-degree scan "...product, I presume?"

Demitri opened both lapels of his suit coat. "It's a little large to carry around with me," the Russian said. He closed his coat again.

But not before Lyons had seen the grips of the 9 mm Tokarev pistol jutting from his waistband. The Able Team leader's hand moved slightly closer to the Colt Python stuffed into his own belt beneath the windbreaker. "Then I suggest we go our separate ways and meet at the room," he said. "Then both of us will have what we want."

Demitri gave him a wolfish smile that Lyons suspected had been carefully practiced over the years to inspire terror in men who faced the Russian. While it had no such effect on the Able Team leader, it did serve to remind him that the men around the table with him, Blancanales and Schwarz, were not only drug smugglers, they were killers.

The nine men stood as if on cue. Lyons dropped a hundred dollar bill on the table and smiled back. "Dinner's on us."

The Russian nodded toward his men, then led them out of the café.

Schwarz walked over and stood next to him as Lyons watched them go. As soon as the glass door had swung closed again behind them, Able Team's electronics wizard said, "You know they're planning to rip us off, don't you?"

Lyons nodded.

Blancanales moved in with them. "So," he said. "Have we got a plan?"

The Able Team leader nodded again.

"And it is...?" Schwarz said.

"Same as before," Lyons answered. "Kill them."

2

Bolan lay faceup in the sand, the grips of the Beretta encircled by both hands and pressed into his belly. His shoulder against the rocks, he heard the man on the other side of the barrier slither the final few feet to the stones. The man planned to kill him. The soldier's counterstrategy was simple: Wait until the man's nose peered over the edge.

Then shoot it off.

Bolan took a deep breath and let it out slowly and quietly. As soon as the man was dead, he would rise from cover and search the body. Clues as to what organization he represented might turn up. But before he could search the man, he had to make sure he didn't get killed.

Distant gunfire changed the Executioner's plan.

As shots began to ring out on the other side of Fierro Blanco's estate, a dark-skinned face leaned over the rocks above the Executioner. Bolan squeezed the trigger twice, sending a pair of 9 mm Glaser Safety rounds upward. The blue-nosed bullets entered their victim's brain, sending the dead body flopping across the stones.

More gunfire roared down the beach as the Executioner rolled to his feet. He had no time to try to ID the stalker—like he had suspected, the man who had attempted to creep up on him wasn't a lone assassin but part of a larger assault; one intended to take out the president of Mexico and maybe his wife and children as well. Picking up the M-16 by the strap, Bolan raced toward the house.

The gunfire, which had sounded as if it came from the outlying area of Fierro Blanco's summerhouse before, now appeared to be closer to the house. That meant that at least one or more of the other sentries had been taken out by the attack party.

Bolan ran on, the adrenaline of upcoming battle surging through his body to mix with disgust at the incompetence of the other men. He had notified them. They'd had plenty of time to prepare.

But they hadn't.

Rounding a curve in the shore, the Executioner saw the house in the distance. With its Spanish architecture and the chaos surrounding it, it looked like a scene from a painting by Goya. Flames leapt from the half-dozen automobiles and buses that had brought the bodyguards to the house. Around them, men were falling as the attackers advanced. The foray was one-sided and the outcome looked almost as if it had been predestined.

Bolan dashed on, his eyes scanning the area for the ball-fringed sombrero of the leader. He didn't see it. Still, his heart—his very soul—told him the man who had led the charge at *Los Pinos* was somewhere nearby. The attackers wore the same white peasant garb that he had seen in the earlier attacks in Mexico City. There was little mistaking who they were—*Marxistas*.

Searching around the house, he saw no signs of the president or his family. But then that was to be expected—they were safely locked away in the basement. He had ordered Oliverez to take charge of them himself, and the captain had proved his skill over and over since the Mexican campaign had begun.

He was fifty yards from the house when the attackers finally saw him. Bolan dived forward, hitting the sand in a shoulder roll. A firestorm of 7.62 mm rounds cut rivets through the sand, sending bursts of the fine white grains over the Executioner as he rolled to a kneeling position.

Slamming the M-16 to his shoulder, Bolan tapped the trigger and sent a short burst down the beach. A round of .223-caliber hollow point slugs took out the nearest white-clad rifleman and sent him sprawling across the sand in a flurry of crimson.

Swinging the assault rifle slightly to his right, Bolan sighted down the barrel at six attackers who had grouped together to take him out. The M-16 in his hands was of the older A1 variety, with full-auto capacity rather than 3-round burst. The Executioner took advantage of that feature now, pulling the trigger back and holding it. The Colt-made weapon emptied itself at the rate of 800 rounds per minute but the elapsed time of the torrent lead was only seconds.

When it ended, a half-dozen more of the white-clad *Marxistas* lay dead in the sand.

His rifle clicked empty, the bolt locking back. Bolan dropped the weapon and drew the big Desert Eagle from under his shirt. A .44 Magnum Glaser Safety slug—similar to the 9 mms but bigger, louder and more powerful, claimed the Executioner's eighth casualty as he neared the house. Stopping to grab the AK-47 the man had wielded, Bolan dived to the side as a volley from other rifles sailed his way. Again he rolled from harm's way, the rounds pounding the sand only inches behind him.

A flash of color appeared in his vision. He saw a ball-fringed sombrero disappear around a corner of the house. The same mysterious man he remembered? Maybe. But like Oliverez had said earlier, such hats were common in Mexico.

Many of the guards had fallen around the house but a few had fled successfully inside. Now return fire from the windows drew the attackers' attention away from the Executioner. Bolan rolled to a halt on his belly, rising just high enough to get the AK-47's banana clip out of the wet sand. The onslaught in his direction halted as the men who had previously fired at him now concentrated on the house.

Dropping the rifle, Bolan drew the sound-suppressed Beretta from beneath his shirt and lined the sights on the back of the nearest *Marxista*. Another of the quiet 9 mm Glaser projectiles bisected the man's spine, folding him backward as if he'd been struck by a club. He fell awkwardly to his knees, then his head hit the sand behind him as his blood piped from his body.

Several of the peasant-dressed attackers sprinted into the house. Gunfire erupted in the rooms nearest the Executioner. Muzzle-flashes could be seen through the windows of the semidark interior.

Bolan swung the sights to the side, sending another round of exploding slugs into the next man from the rear. He could only hope that Oliverez had gotten Fierro Blanco and his family down into the cellar where a steel door would barricade them from the attack. If he and the guards fell, the remaining *Marxistas* would eventually blow the door, then carry out the assassinations at their leisure.

Turning his attention to the immediate threat, Bolan continued to move the Beretta's barrel across the sand. Each new semiauto shot began to diminish the enemy force. He had barely had time to wonder about the sombrero again when a loud voice from the other side of the house echoed through the explosions. A second later, a *Marxistas* relayed the orders shouted through a window of the house. As soon as the words had left his mouth, the men in the yard began beating a hasty retreat in the direction from which they had come. As they ran they were joined by the attackers from the other side of the house.

That included the man in the ball-fringed sombrero. Bolan took aim. But before he could fire, a gunman appeared in the doorway. Force to switch his attack, the Executioner dropped the man on the doorjamb with a pair of slugs, then turned the Beretta back down the beach. He took a deep breath, lining up the sights in front of the jogging *Marxista* leader again. Letting half of the air escape from his lungs, he waited for the man to enter his sight picture. A split second later, he squeezed the Beretta's trigger.

The quiet cough of the 93-R met the Executioner's ears. The pistol jumped slightly in his hand. Bolan smiled, knowing, feeling that his aim had been true. But as he looked across the sand, he saw the colorful hat still making its way toward a transport truck in the distance. Turning to the spot of his aim, he saw another of the white-clad men lying in a pool of blood.

The soldier cursed silently as he leapt to his feet. One of the other *Marxistas* had stepped into the line of fire at the last second, taking the bullet meant for the man in the ball-fringed hat.

Inside the house several heads were now visible through the windows. Bolan said a silent prayer for the Beretta's sound suppressor, then squeezed the trigger again, then again and again.

The heads in the windows disappeared beneath the sills.

Grabbing the AK-47 once more, the Executioner shoved the Beretta back into his waistband next to the Desert Eagle. Cautiously, he crept toward the house. When no rounds came his way, he started to sprint. Pausing at the doorway, he peered around the corner.

The living room looked like a scene from a bad B-grade "slasher" movie. Dead men—federal and *Marxista* alike—carpeted the floor.

In spite of the attack, the stereo wasn't damaged and played on. The sounds of Margarita Felice, currently Mexico's number one sex symbol and the president's favorite songstress, sang out a lively song entitled "That Magic First Week of Love." Her words seemed to mock the butchery in the room.

Bolan stepped over the man in the doorway and waded through the blood. Had Oliverez gotten the president, his wife and children safely barricaded before any of the men could make it down the steps to the basement? The question haunted him as he silently made his way through the carnage to the stairs.

As he neared the open door to the basement, the soldier heard movement below. Setting the rifle quietly against the wall, he drew the more maneuverable Desert Eagle. He paused just outside the door, listening. What sounded like water splashing on concrete met his ears. Then the distinct odor of gasoline drifted up the steps and told the Executioner exactly what was going on below. Horror filled his soul as he realized that whoever it was who had made it to the basement was about to set it on fire. The steel door had stopped the *Marxistas* from entering the safe room. But they could still carry out their assassinations, in one of the most barbaric ways possible.

The secure room was constructed of concrete. That fact and the steel door, would stop the flames as well as it had the men. But it couldn't stop the heat. President Don Juan Fierro Blanco, his wife and children would all be baked alive in the steel-and-concrete oven.

Bolan ducked through the door to see several gasoline cans on the floor. Three of the cans already lay empty on their sides. Two were still full and stood upright. A lone *Marxista*, wearing peasant garb and a white straw cowboy hat, had just struck a match. As he backed toward the steps he used it to ignite the rest of the matches in the book.

The Executioner dropped the Desert Eagle's sights on the back of the man's head. But the flames of twenty matches already leapt from the gunner's fist. To shoot him now would mean the matches fell to the floor and ignited the inferno.

Bolan knew he had only one chance. "Don't move!" he shouted down the steps.

Still facing the other way, the man froze in place.

"Turn toward me, slowly," Bolan ordered, and again the man complied. But as he did, the Executioner saw the face of a demented, self-righteous radical.

"What will you do?" the man asked in Spanish. "Will you shoot me?" He looked at the matches burning in his hand. "If you do, these will fall."

"Start up the steps," Bolan commanded. "You drop them and you're dead."

The fire in the revolutionary's hand was burning down now. In another few seconds, it would extinguish itself. Even if he didn't come up the steps as ordered, if only the Executioner could keep the man preoccupied for a just a little longer....

The man in the white peasant shirt grinned crazily. "No, I don't think so," he said. "I think I have two choices. I can die as the man who killed *el presidente*, or I can die as the man who only tried." He paused as the flames continued to burn down. "I think I would like to be remembered as successful."

"You won't be remembered at all," Bolan said. "And you don't have to die. You come up the steps now, I'll let you live. I'll even let you go free."

For a moment, a look of indecision crossed the *Marxista's* face. "How can I be certain you don't lie?" he asked.

"You have my word," said the Executioner. The fire had almost burned out. Another second or two and the threat would take care of itself.

Suddenly, the revolutionary shook his head. "I don't believe you," he said simply, and let the matchbook fall to the gasoline-soaked floor.

Bolan's Desert Eagle erased his face a second later. But before the big hand cannon's roar could die, the basement had burst into a fire worthy of Danté's *Inferno*.

The soldier was forced away from the doorway as the fire shot upward, singeing his face and neck. He backed into the living room as flames lapped out of the opening after him. Below, he heard one of the full gas cans explode, and a second later a fiery ball blew up the steps to ignite the upper floor.

Bolan had no choice. Turning, he sprinted out of the house toward the beach as another explosion sounded. As he turned, the entire structure went up in flames. Staring at the holocaust before him, his mind flew to the people below.

Mexican President Don Juan de Fierro Blanco.

The man's wife and twin sons. A teenage daughter. Oliverez. And whatever other guards the brave captain had with him.

Bolan thought of the man in the sombrero and the rage that burned through him became hotter than the fire itself. Whoever the *Marxista* leader was, he would pay—with his life.

RONNIE QUARTEL DIDN'T FEEL like a movie star who had just signed a contract for twelve and a half million dollars. He didn't feel like the tough L.A. detective he was going to play, nor like the tough sheriff he'd been in Satan's Sixgun, the movie he'd just finished. In fact, with his hands and feet bound with duct tape, and more of the itchy, sticky stuff covering his eyes, he didn't feel much like any of the action heroes he had portrayed during the last three years of Hollywood megastardom.

Quartel felt another wave of fear seize his chest as the mobile home hit a bump in the road. He'd been told that he had been kidnapped by the CDML, and was being held ransom for ten million dollars, and he might get killed if they didn't get their money. But there was nothing he could do about it. His best friend and a bunch of other people were also kidnapped but there was nothing he could do about that, either. Once the money was delivered, then everybody would go free.

A sudden thought washed the fear from Quartel's chest and replaced it with excitement. When this was over, he realized, he'd be an even bigger star.

Quartel listened blindly as the hum of the motor home

quieted slightly. He felt the vehicle turn a corner, then pull to a halt. Then Jesus Hidalgo, the man who had identified himself as the leader of the *Cuididano para Democracia Mexicana Legitima*, said, "Ladies and gentlemen, we have arrived at our final destination." The door that led from the living room of Quartel's hijacked mobile home opened and the movie star listened as the steps were unfolded to the ground. "You will be taken out one at a time," Hidalgo said. "Please be patient. I regret that you must remain blindfolded until we're inside."

Whispers from the other bound and blindfolded hostages began around the room. Quartel heard the four blond Hollywood starlets—the ones he had brought along for Hix's amusement and in whom his former college roommate had shown no interest whatsoever—begin to titter like frightened hens. The sound angered him but it also brought on a quick twinge of guilt.

Yes, if it weren't for him the bimbos wouldn't be in this mess. Neither would the mayor of Tijuana or Normandi West, the assistant director of Satan's Six-gun—the blonde with the brains in whom Hix *had* shown interest. The fact was, if it weren't for him, Hix, the mayor of Tijuana and the TJ whores who'd been at the party would be in bed safely sleeping off their hangovers that very moment.

Guilt had never been a long-suffered emotion with Ronnie Quartel; he turned his mind to other things. Speaking of Hix, where in hell was he and what was the man doing right now? The last Quartel had seen of his former roommate, he'd been sitting quietly in the mobile home, passively letting his hands and feet be taped. So, Quartel thought sarcastically, what's wrong with this picture? Hix was the one who'd been the Gulf War hero after college.

So why in hell wasn't Scott Hix doing something about this?

The blondes' voices grew louder. Then another voice, the one Quartel knew belonged to Hidalgo's foul-smelling sidekick, Pablo Huertes, boomed about the clamor. "*Silencio!*" Quartel doubted that any of the bimbos spoke Spanish, but they got the message and closed their mouths.

Quartel listened to the sounds of someone being guided down the steps. Maybe one of the high-class Tijuana call girls? They'd been seated closest to the door last time he'd been able to see. Of course that could have changed—the crazy-ass driver had driven them from Hix's house into the country and then twirled circles in the middle of the road until Quartel thought he'd be sick. The purpose behind the stunt, he had overheard Hidalgo tell Hix, was so the former intelligence officer couldn't count turns and time and know where they'd gone. That hadn't been good news at all. The fact that the kidnappers knew who Hix was meant they'd keep a closer watch on him.

Another blindfolded hostage was led outside. Then a groan sounded in the living room somewhere to his side. Quartel guessed it was the mayor. The man groaned again and Quartel heard feet shuffling across the carpet then down the stairs. He sat waiting his turn, trying to keep his mind occupied. How would he play this role if he were, say, back in Acting 1113 at UCLA? Easy—concerned but in-control hero. The way he always played his roles.

Quartel's mind drifted to the gun and gun-belt he had worn during the last film. He'd brought them along to amuse the Mexican women at Hix's party the night before. One of the whores had entertained them all by parading around wearing nothing but the gun belt and a lewd grin. Then Quartel had stashed the rig in a drawer in the mobile home's bedroom. So far, he didn't think the kidnappers had found it.

Could Hix put the gun to use? It held only the blank ammunition they'd used on the set but he remembered the technical advisor telling him not to point it directly at anybody or shoot too close. That must mean that even blanks did something.

A sour-smelling mixture of body odor and stale tequila suddenly filled Quartel's sinuses. A second later rough hands hauled him to his feet. He heard the duct tape around his ankles being cut. "Move," the voice of Pablo Huertes commanded. Rough hands shoved Quartel forward and he stumbled into the arms of another man. He sensed a face directly in front of his but this man had no odor about him.

"Stop!" Hidalgo said.

Quartel obeyed the voice, freezing in place, needles of fear prickling his neck and shoulders.

"You're shoving around ten million dollars," Hidalgo went on, and Quartel realized the revolutionary leader's order to stop had been meant for Huertes, not him.

With unseen men now guiding him by both arms, Quartel was helped down the steps. His legs were cramped from the long ride and felt sluggish as he made his way forward. A door opened ahead, and he was led inside, then down more steps and through another door. A moment later, he was forced again into a sitting position on the floor.

Handcuffs were placed around his wrists. He heard the clank of a heavy chain. Then an unseen knife cut through the duct tape around his hands and waist. Somewhere to his side, he could hear more chains and cuffs, and tape being sliced through. One of the starlets next to him suddenly shrieked.

A moment later, the tape was ripped away from his eyes and with it Quartel suspected went half of his left eyebrow. He was embarrassed to realize he had let out his own involuntary shriek as the tape came off. That kind of thing, he knew, had to stop.

As his eyes adjusted to the light, Quartel looked around the room. The only illumination came from a low-watt light bulb hanging from the stone ceiling. The walls were of the same stone, and at the other end of the room was an open wooden door. Through it, he could see nothing but the shadowy stones of another wall. The place looked like a wine cellar. Except for the chains leading from everyone's handcuffs down to the steel rings embedded in the stone floors. The chains, along with the stone walls, made it seem more like a medieval dungeon, and that thought brought the prickly fear to the back of Quartel's neck again.

The shadowy figures of the blondes were lined along the wall. Across the small room sat Normandi West, the Tijuana whores and the very frightened-looking mayor.

Scott Hix was nowhere to be seen.

Quartel looked up as two men, as filthy and sour-smelling as Huertes, dragged Scott Hix into the room. Hix, Quartel noticed, still had his ankles bound. The terrorists were taking no chances with a man of his abilities, and Quartel's former roommate was forced to shuffle along as the men pulled and jerked. A few moments later, Hix was chained to the floor like the others. But, except for his eyes, the kidnappers kept the duct tape on him.

Quartel watched his friend sit still until the filthy terrorists had walked away. As soon as they'd disappeared through the door again the former military intelligence officer's eyes darted around the room, taking inventory of his situation. Hix checked the cuffs and chain, then began looking around the room once more. His eyes fell to the floor beneath him and only then did Quartel realize they were all seated on cushions. Looking down, he saw a frayed pad that had once been part of a cheap divan. He remembered Hidalgo telling them that he regretted what he was being forced to do.

Bullshit, Quartel thought. The man's either a crazed zealot or on some personal power trip or both. He loves every second of this shit, cushions or not.

Quartel looked up in time to see Hix's and West's eyes lock. The beautiful blond assistant director looked frightened but composed. She looked like she knew Hix would get her out of this somehow, and for a brief moment Ronnie Quartel wished he was Scott Hix. Plenty of women had looked at him with lust or with awe, but no woman had ever looked at Quartel the way Normandi West was looking at Scott Hix. Were they in love? They had only met the night before. Quartel's thoughts suddenly turned to anger and jealousy.

This was one hell of a time for something like that to get in the way of Hix's thinking. Get your mind off her and back on business, Hix, he thought. Get us the hell out of here!

Jesus Hidalgo's shadowy form appeared suddenly in the doorway and stopped. Quartel waited for another speech from the radical loony, but it didn't come. Instead, the *Legitima* leader walked quietly around the room. Seemingly satisfied with security, he disappeared through the doorway.

A moment later, Hidalgo and Huertes both came back through the door. Hidalgo walked swiftly to Quartel, bent at the waist, and unlocked the handcuffs from the chain. "Mr. Quartel," he said politely. "If you would be so kind, we're ready for you to make your call." He offered his hand.

Quartel took the hand and let it help him to his feet. Okay. Show time. He was on. Time to do what Ronnie Quartel did best—act.

IT HAD BEEN A LONG TIME since Westerners were welcomed in Iran, and David McCarter knew that he, Gary Manning and Thomas Jackson Hawkins weren't going to pass as Mideasterners if anybody looked too closely. So he had opted not even to try. All three had dressed in simple Western business suits, and kept conversation to a minimum. McCarter relied on his gift for mimicking accents. For the people he couldn't avoid, he had spoken in Russian-inflected English, and it had gotten them by. Eventually, that accent had led him to the military base near Shiraz in southern Iran, where several companies of Iranian special forces troops were practicing maneuvers for what appeared to be an upcoming invasion of Oman and the United Arab Emirates. Their goal was to take control of the Strait of Hormuz and set the international price of oil to suit whichever ayatollah happened to be in power when it was all over.

McCarter dug in deeper behind the rocks a mile from the fenced-in base. He pressed the infrared binoculars to his eyes and watched as the complex geared down for the night. As soon as he had learned where the training was taking place, he, Manning and Hawkins had begun reconning the site. They had found that only a skeleton crew guarded the perimeter each night after 2200 hours. Even though they were planning a major invasion, the Iranians felt secure near Shiraz—they were close enough to shore to move quickly across the Persian Gulf and the Gulf of Oman but still far enough inland not to worry about being noticed.

Indeed, the Phoenix Force leader thought as he dropped the binoculars to the end of the strap around his neck and closed his eyes, had it not been for the satellite photos the U.S. had picked up, no one would have known about the operation. The photographs had led intelligence agents to the plan to invade the strait, which in turn had brought Phoenix Force to where they were at the moment.

Hawkins slithered across the rocks on his belly, closer to McCarter. "Are we still hitting them tonight, David?" he whispered, his accent retaining a touch of a Southern drawl.

McCarter nodded. "Unless unforseen circumstances arise, it's still a go." He paused, cleared his throat, then added, "Bolan's still shorthanded in Mexico. I'd like to go help him as soon as we can."

"Me too," Hawkins said, nodding. "Never a dull moment when you play the game with the big guy."

The Phoenix Force leader smiled. Hawkins, or T.J. as the other members of Stony Man Farm called him, was Phoenix Force's newest member. He had replaced McCarter when Yakov Katzenelenbogen retired as the counterterrorist unit's leader and McCarter stepped in to take his place. Hawkins was also the youngest warrior on the team, and still young and new enough to be in total awe of Mack Bolan.

Not that any of the Stony Man crew ever totally got over their astonishment at the Executioner's prowess, the Phoenix Force leader thought. But it did moderate over time, simply becoming a healthy respect and admiration for the man who was the very heart and soul of the Farm. If the men of Phoenix Force and Able Table were the best of the best, the man they called Striker would have to go down in history as the best of all time.

Turning to Hawkins, McCarter said, "Why don't you and Manning close your eyes and get an hour's worth? I can watch things."

A few feet behind them, Gary Manning said, "I heard that and I'm in total agreement."

"You sure, David?" Hawkins asked. "We could take turns."

"I'm not tired." McCarter chuckled softly. He pressed the binoculars to his eyes again. "Besides, you're young. Not that long past the nap stage."

Hawkins took the ribbing about his age good-naturedly as usual. "Well," he responded, "I always heard it was you old folks who needed more rest." He turned to where Manning was already stretching out in the rocks. "And the good Lord knows Gary can use all the beauty sleep he can get."

"I heard that, too," the Canadian said without opening his eyes.

Two hours later, McCarter wakened the two men. They made their last-minute preparations, checking weapons, ammo and other equipment, then crept forward.

Twenty minutes later, Hawkins had disarmed both the

electrical shock and alarm systems on the perimeter fence. Manning had snipped a hole at the bottom with his wire cutters, and the men from Stony Man Farm were inside the compound. Still on all fours, they scurried across the ground heading for a storage shed.

Manning, whose job it was to take out the sentry if he passed, pressed his face close to McCarter's ear. "Want to leave him?" he asked. "He's nowhere in sight."

The Briton thought for a moment. He didn't like killing men when he didn't have to, and the fact that the sentry was slow on his rounds made it tempting to let the man live. On the other hand, if things went well, they planned to exit the compound the same way they'd come in. That meant they'd have to deal with him on the return trip. And if things went badly, they'd be shooting far more Iranian soldiers than just this man.

The Phoenix Force leader shook his head.

Manning didn't question the decision. He leaned around the corner of the shed in the shadows and waited.

Two minutes later, the man they had watched patrol the perimeter fence came shuffling along whistling some indiscernible tune. Manning raised the barrel of his sound-suppressed Heckler & Koch MP-5A1, pulled the trigger, and the man's head quietly exploded. Hawkins helped Manning drag the body out of sight and thirty seconds after the man died the trio were on the move again.

Field reports, some CIA, others from U.S. Army Intelligence informants within the Iranian army, pointed the way toward a small house midway through the base. The men of Phoenix Force made their way quietly under the dark sky, using the shadows and buildings for cover, pausing on the rare occasions when a jeep or foot soldier was seen, then moving on. They found the barracks that housed the special forces troops exactly where the reports had said it would be. The house, just to the side, was the temporary home of Colonel Mohammed Habbibi who led the group.

McCarter pulled his men to a halt outside the house. After a quick 360-degree scan to make sure there were no curious eyes, they split up, circling the house to check for additional alarms. They met back at the spot where they'd started. All three men shook their heads. The coast was clear.

McCarter pulled a glass cutter from one pocket of his battle suit—known at the Farm as a blacksuit—and a roll of tape from another. Thirty seconds later, a silent hole had been cut in one of the windows leading into the living room. The former British SAS officer reached through, unlocked the catch, and raised the window.

The window made the creaking sound of aged wood long-closed. McCarter stopped with it midway up to listen. Hearing no sounds to indicate they'd been heard, he finished raising the pane and slid inside. Hawkins followed. McCarter stuck his head back outside and nodded at Manning, who nodded back, then took off across the yard.

The Phoenix Force leader led the way through the living room, down a short hall to the first of two bedrooms. Cracking the door, he saw it was empty. Creeping on, he looked through the open door to the rear bedroom and saw a dark-skinned woman with raven-black tresses lying on her back. On the other side of the bed lay an equally dark-skinned man, large for an Iranian. By the way he looked, McCarter would have guessed Habbibi's height and weight at around six-foot-one and two hundred pounds.

McCarter took a deep breath and thought briefly of Calvin James, the team's ace knife-handler. He wondered how he and Encizo were getting along in Mexico. Had James been with him now, he thought, as he drew the Fairbairn-Sykes dagger from its sheath, this next step would have fallen to him.

Hawkins stood in the hallway, his own sound-suppressed MP-5 covering the man on the bed as McCarter crept forward. So far so good. The man wasn't snoring but he appeared to be in deep sleep. His chest rose and fell rhythmically.

The Phoenix Force leader moved around the bed slowly, holding the black steel knife in a fencer's grip. Three more steps, he thought. That would put him directly above Habbibi. Then he would bring down the sharp point of the double-edged commando dagger into the man's throat before cutting through the veins, arteries, muscles and ligaments in his neck. With any luck, the woman next to the colonel wouldn't even wake up.

Killing Habbibi wouldn't stop the plan to take over the Strait of Hormuz. But combined with the little surprises Gary Manning should be preparing at the moment, it would slow the Iranians for weeks, if not months. At least long enough to decide on a more permanent answer to the problem.

McCarter took his final step and raised the knife over his head.

The coal-black eyes opened. Habbibi's hand shot up to grab McCarter's wrist.

Surprised, the Phoenix Force leader realized Habbibi had to have been awake for some minutes. Probably he had heard the sound of the window opening but chosen to "play possum" rather than investigate. About to bring his left hand down in a punch to the Iranian colonel's face, the Briton saw the revolver in the man's other hand. A .357 Magnum Smith & Wesson, stainless steel.

Turning his punch into a grab, the former-SAS man overshot his mark slightly, catching the revolver at the end of the cylinder rather than around the center. He felt the steel wheel trying to turn beneath his fingers as Habbibi pulled hard on the trigger. With their other hands, the two men wrestled over the knife.

Out of the corner of his eye, McCarter saw Hawkins take a step forward and raise the MP-5. But before the young warrior could pull the trigger, the woman on the bed next to them rose, blocking the shot. Her hands reached out to grab McCarter's wrist above the knife, and he felt the wheelgun's cylinder revolve a little more as he turned his concentration toward the new development.

Habbibi cursed loudly in Farsi as Hawkins tried to maneuver around the bed for a clear shot. The Iranian grimaced as he squeezed even harder on the trigger, and the cylinder moved farther. Looking down, McCarter saw the hammer was halfway back. And the man below him had the grip of an orangutan. While he was slowly turning the cylinder, his other hand was threatening to break the Briton's wrist.

The cylinder revolved another notch. McCarter cursed the weak grip his own miscalculation had forced on him; had he caught the cylinder in the center rather than at the end, he'd have been able to hold on. As it was, sooner or later, he'd slip off the weapon's frame, the hammer would cock completely, and then a .357 Magnum slug would hit his body. Another glance told him the barrel was currently aimed at his abdomen. But as they struggled, it angled up at his chest.

The woman, screaming in a high-pitched wail now, tugged impotently at the Phoenix Force leader's arm, more nuisance than threat. But McCarter's grip on the revolver slipped another millimeter, and he saw the hammer draw back almost to full cock. He sensed Hawkins directly behind him now, but the woman was still in the way. Hawkins reached forward, grabbing her by the ebony hair and yanked her off the bed.

But at the same time, McCarter lost his grip and the S&W's hammer snapped back.

The Briton let his hand follow the contour of the top strap. His fingers ripped across the sharp-edged target sights and he felt them slice open. He let them move until the web between his thumb and index finger had fallen between the hammer and frame, then curled them around the gun again.

The hammer fell, but the floating firing pin pierced the Briton's skin rather than the bullet's primer, jabbing painfully into the cartilage between McCarter's thumb and index finger.

A second later, Hawkins stepped forward, pressed the MP-5 into Habbibi's face and pulled the trigger.

McCarter stepped back as the colonel's lifeless hands fell from around both revolver and knife. He sheathed the small dagger, stuck the revolver into his belt and inspected his hand. Sore as hell, but no permanent damage. Turning his attention to the woman on the floor, he saw that she was unconscious.

"Need me to tie her up, David?" Hawkins asked. He had already pulled a length of paracord from his pocket.

The Phoenix Force leader glanced at the luminous hands of his watch, simultaneously kneeling to check the woman's condition. She was out cold but otherwise unharmed. He shook his head. "We'll be long gone by the time she wakes up," he said. He rose and, passing Hawkins, started for the bedroom door. "We're two minutes late meeting Gary as it is," he said over his shoulder.

Without further words, the two men crawled back of the window. Walking the fine line between speed and stealth, they hurried to the shed next to the perimeter fence. Manning was waiting.

"Everything go all right?" McCarter asked

Manning nodded.

McCarter saw the Canadian staring at his hand, and looked down himself to see it was still dripping blood. "Problems?" Manning asked.

"Habbibi had some objections to exiting this mortal coil," the Phoenix Force leader said. "Tell you about it on the flight back."

The men from Stony Man Farm ducked under the fence,

and jogged off into the darkness. They were halfway to the pick-up zone when the first explosion roared through the night behind them. They paused momentarily, turning to watch the flames leap into the sky.

"How many fighter planes were they planning to use, Gary?" Hawkins asked. The exact number was a detail that hadn't shown up in the intelligence reports.

"Around forty, my guess," Manning said. "I didn't have time for an exact count."

The men of Phoenix Force turned and broke into a run as Jack Grimaldi's plane sounded ahead in the sky. They stopped, watching the wheels set down in the sandy earth, then broke into a run again as the plane slowed.

"Let's go to Mexico," Hawkins said. "I hear the weather's nice there this time of year."

3

Bolan had sprinted a hundred yards while watching transport vehicles load the last of the *Marxistas*. He watched the trucks pull out. He had known from the beginning that, barring unforseen circumstances like mechanical failure, his pursuit was futile; he was too far behind. He had run after them only out of anger frustration.

So now the soldier slowed to a trot, then a jog, then a walk, finally stopping as he watched the trucks disappear in the distance. Turning, he again saw the flames and smoke rising from the cars and buses on the driveway and the summerhouse itself. He stood there motionless, watching.

A sense of despair threatened to overcome the Executioner as he pictured Fierro Blanco's wife, sons and daughter in his mind. He remembered the nervous laughter of the children as they picnicked on the blanket only an hour earlier. What was their condition now? Were they dead yet? Or were they still enduring the agony of slowly being cooked alive in an underground oven?

Had it been physically possible to run through the flaming house and descend the stairs to the basement, unlock the steel door and get them out, the Executioner would have gladly traded his own life for theirs. But it wasn't possible. His body would be aflame before he was halfway through the living room; he'd be dead before he even reached the steps. Even if he could, the Fierro Blanco family would be burned to death as they tried to escape the inferno.

Bolan clenched his fists as he stared at the fiery nightmare. The sight wasn't only appalling, it took his mind back over the years to a similar situation that hit closer to home. The Executioner's own mother, father and sister had died at the hands of another group of the world's predators—the Mafia.

Smoke drifted across the beach in the light Gulf breeze, causing Bolan's eyes to water. He had avenged his own family's deaths. And he would do no less for the men, woman and children in the basement. Looking down at the sand, he said a short prayer that the steel door wasn't too tight to prevent the smoke from entering the locked basement. Death by smoke inhalation would be faster and less painful than being baked alive. He opened his eyes as an overhead beam in the roof gave way and plummeted into the fire in an explosion of new sparks.

Somewhere in the distance, Bolan heard a boat's horn, and the deep tenor drifting across the waters of the Gulf of Mexico sounded as lonely as a train whistle in the night. His thoughts returned to the man in the ball-fringed sombrero, and suddenly his anger and frustration was replaced with a grim determination.

Nothing more could be done for the Fierro Blanco family. At least not at the moment. But the moment wouldn't last, and the Executioner renewed his vow that the *Marxista* leader would pay for the abominable crimes he had committed.

A walkie-talkie, dropped by someone during the foray, coughed irritatingly at the Executioner's feet. He reached down, lifting it, tempted to hurl it back to the ground with all his strength. But what good would that do? Would it bring Don Juan de Fierro Blanco, his wife and children, or Juanito Oliverez and his men back to life?

Another screeching buzz from the walkie-talkie broke into Bolan's thoughts. The voice was familiar, and for a split second, he wondered if the anguish in his heart had distorted his thoughts.

"Protection Team Two to Protection Team One," came over the airwaves. There was a short pause, then the same voice said, "Come in One."

Bolan looked at the instrument in his hand as the boat horn in the distance sounded once more. Oliverez? Could the federal be transmitting from the fiery basement? Of course not. Radio communication on these antiquated walkie-talkies would never penetrate the interference caused by the concrete wall, other electrical units in the area and the fire.

A smile began to creep across the soldier's face.

He turned his eyes toward the Gulf of Mexico.

A series of short, staccato blasts came from the boat's horn. Bolan saw that a fishing vessel had just broken over the horizon and was heading toward the pier in front of the house. Pressing the radio to his lips, the Executioner said, "This is One. Come in, Two."

"Is it over?" Oliverez asked.

Bolan couldn't help laughing in relief. "For the time being," he said. "I take it *el presidente* and his family are all with you?"

"Affirmative," Oliverez said as the fishing boat continued toward the shore. "The boat arrived early. I couldn't reach you by radio so I took it upon myself to change the orders."

Bolan nodded unconsciously. The boat must have arrived soon after his last communiqué with Oliverez.

"Are you coming in?"

"Yes," the captain said. "If it is safe."

"It's safe. I'll meet you at the pier."

Bolan walked through the sand, a sudden feeling of exhaustion threatening to overcome him like the despair had done earlier. He fought it off with the same resolve. He couldn't afford fatigue—not yet. The war was far from over. For the time being, Fierro Blanco and his family were safe. But that wouldn't last. The *Marxista* would try again and again. He would keep trying until he succeeded.

Or until the Executioner killed him.

Bolan reached the pier and walked out over the aged wooden planks. As the fishing vessel neared, the forms of the president, his wife, twin sons and the beautiful teenage daughter began to take shape on deck. Oliverez was standing next to them. An old man wearing a Greek fisherman's cap, and looking like something from a Hemingway novel, piloted the wheel. Bolan could see their faces now, and what he saw were alternating smiles of relief and grimaces of horror at the flames still raging onshore. All on board the vessel saw how close to death they had come. And all were witnessing firsthand just how horrible that death would have been.

The boat bumped against the wood and the soldier stepped on board to hear another Margarita Felice song playing from the tape deck. The fishing captain reversed the inboard motor and they backed out into the Gulf of Mexico once more. President Fierro Blanco stepped forward, grasping Bolan's hand in both of his. "Thank you," he said, a tear streaking down one cheek and into his beard. "My family and I owe you our lives." He paused. "Yet again."

Bolan gripped the man's hand, then released it. The Mexican president's words were strained, and the unusual accent—the result of his many years in European prep schools—was even stronger than usual under the stress.

The first lady of Mexico, her makeup streaked, her clothes a wreck, moved in between the two men. "Please," she said, sobbing softly. "I must thank this man myself." She started to speak again but at that moment Margarita Felice chose to raise her voice louder on the song's final chorus. The president's wife turned and barked sharply at her husband. "Please Juan!" she said irritably. "Turn the music down! I can't even hear myself!"

Looking back up into the Executioner's eyes, the first lady said, "Margarita Felice! Night and day, nothing else. Sometimes I believe he's in love with her!" She giggled suddenly in what was an obvious release of the tension that had built inside her.

Bolan smiled at her as she rose on tiptoe to kiss him on the cheek.

The Executioner looked back into Fierro Blanco's tearful eyes. Was this the face of a man in alliance with murderers, drug smugglers and terrorists? Was it the face of a man who could have his political enemies put to death with no second thought? Maybe. Maybe not. Bolan still had no proof of Fierro Blanco's innocence or guilt.

As the first lady stepped back from him, Bolan felt small arms encircle his legs. He looked down to see four huge brown eyes looking up at him. He smiled, and the twin boys leaned in to hug his legs.

Fierro Blanco's daughter stepped up, rose to her tiptoes like her mother had done, and kissed the soldier. "Thank you," she said, then turned away shyly.

Bolan strode across the deck to where Oliverez was grinning at him.

"I don't plan to kiss you like the others," the captain said. "I hope that doesn't disappoint you too much."

"I can live with that," Bolan said. "You'd better get on the radio and ask for some help," he said.

"I already have," Oliverez said. He glanced down at his wristwatch. "We rendezvous with a navy cruiser in fifteen minutes."

Bolan nodded. He looked back across the deck to where the Fiero Blancos were now laughing and talking. Again, he wondered about the man's character. Then, his eyes falling on the children once more, he smiled as the Gulf wind whipped across his face.

The Executioner didn't know if the Mexican president was guilty or not. But he'd find out sooner or later.

Right now, it was enough to know that the children were innocent.

THE OLD WOMAN didn't like meeting him there. She liked for the man with the beard to come to her house. She felt safe there; secure in her magic and protected by her sons.

In public, during the daylight hours, she knew her magic weakened. And her sons, Roberto and Santiago couldn't accompany her—they were wanted by the police on a number of crimes. The cops had been bought off with some of the money the bearded man supplied, but they didn't want that fact flaunted in their faces.

No, the old witch thought as she stirred her drink with the small umbrella, she would have preferred meeting at her home like they usually did. But the bearded man had grown worried of late, and far more cautious. He had come to her home on too many occasions already, he claimed, and while he usually came at night, he still feared he might be recognized. The old woman took a sip of her drink, letting the heavy dose of rum burn her lips, then her mouth, then finally her throat and stomach. So she had agreed to meet the man at the sidewalk café outside a major hotel, and she sat now at a white wrought iron table facing the street. Although they would be in public, the area was all but deserted during siesta time. The café itself had other patrons, and they could sit at separate tables and converse without appearing to be together.

Looking down the deserted street, the old woman let her eyes stare at the closed shops and sidewalk stalls without really seeing them. Three blocks away, she saw a man with a beard walking toward her. At first, she didn't recognize him. Usually impeccably dressed in suit and tie, the bearded man approaching now wore pleated khaki slacks and a striped sport shirt. On his face were black-framed sunglasses and his head was covered by a canvas sailing cap. A compact 35 mm camera case hung from his belt.

The old woman wondered briefly why the man had chosen to dress so differently, then realized it must be in order to blend into the tourist surroundings. Well, she thought, as she set her glass back down on the table in front of her, she shouldn't be surprised. The man was a master of deceit. He wouldn't have risen to his current position any other way.

The man glanced casually from side to side as he crossed the street and walked up to the café. He took a seat at the table next to the old woman but faced away from her at a forty-five degree angle. Lifting the cardboard placard that advertised the establishment's piña colada specialty, he held it up to his face to cover his lips. "Did anyone follow you?" he whispered.

Slowly, the old woman shook her head.

The man was about to speak again when the waiter appeared. Setting down the advertisement, the bearded man said, "Cuba Libre." When the waiter had disappeared inside the café once more, he pulled a rumpled newspaper from his back pocket and held it up in front of him. "The American bodyguard must die," he said in a soft voice. "And he must die very quickly. Once more, he has wrecked my plans. Earlier today, at the summerhouse."

The old woman nodded. She knew who he meant—the bodyguard currently employed by the government. "It will be done," she said.

The waiter brought the man's rum and coke, set it on the table with a paper napkin, and walked off again. "Do you have a plan?" the man asked.

The old woman cringed slightly. She did, and she supposed it might be wiser to tell the man the truth. But she feared he would forbid it, refusing to pay her if she attempted to carry out the murder in her chosen way. Her magic was strong but it fed off the strength of others, and had to be replenished periodically by human sacrifice and ritual. The strength that she and her sons derived from the ritualistic killings was in direct proportion to the strength of their victims. And the American bodyguard was strong. His strength had foiled the bearded man's plans several times, and the opportunity to harvest that power for her magic was simply more than she could afford to pass up.

The man, however, held no such belief in magic. He wouldn't understand.

"Not yet," the old woman said. "At least nothing in detail. But I can tell you this: he will be killed simply and quickly. As soon as we know enough about him to work out a plan." She wondered it the man could sense she was lying.

It didn't appear that he could. The corner of his mouth curled slightly.

"Good," he said. "The American's name is Mike Belasko."

"An unusual name."

"An unusual man."

"Which government agency does he work for?"

"The U.S. Treasury Department, I must assume. The Secret Service provides America's bodyguards. He must have come from there."

"What are his talents? His specialties?" Sometimes, the old woman knew, those specialties could be absorbed during the rituals.

The bearded man dropped his paper slightly. "Have you paid attention at all to his work here in Mexico?" he asked, slightly irritated. The question had been rhetorical, and when the woman said nothing, he added, "If you had, you would have realized that there appears to be very little about the personal protection business, espionage, battle or anything else, that is *not* one of his fortes."

A twinge of excitement crept through the old witch's loins, as if she were peering over a steep cliff at a drop thousands of feet below. She must have this man's power. Both for herself, and for her sons. "Where is this man now?" she asked, hoping that her voice did not betray her exhilaration.

"After the attack at the summerhouse, he returned to *Los Pinos*," said the bearded man. "For the most part, it has been restored since the riots. And security has been tripled." He let out a low sigh. "No matter how many federal guards are killed, there are always more to take their places. And many military troops have been assigned there." He paused as the waiter returned. When he declined another drink, the waiter dropped a ticket on the table in front of him and turned away. "I don't suggest you make your attempt at *Los Pinos*," the man said.

The old woman nodded. "How should I contact you for payment?"

"I'll contact you, as usual," the man said.

A moment later, he was gone.

The old woman sat finishing the last of her drink, wondering what she could do if the man refused to pay her after the killing. Nothing, she supposed. While she boasted great magic when her powers were fueled, the man who had just left wielded political and military power that she knew her magic couldn't overcome. But the thought didn't worry her. He wouldn't evade payment. He never had before, and she knew he would want to call on her services again in the future.

CALVIN JAMES MOVED forward slightly, adjusting the big Crossada fighting knife that was fastened in his waistband and angled across his back beneath his shirt. He pressed the phone to his ear and waited.

Pug Nelson and Encizo had gone to check out a new lead on the alleged drug tunnel leading from Mexico to the U.S. They were due any time now.

All around him, DEA agents and army personnel moved

about the office shuffling papers, manning the phones and tapping computer keyboards. James waited, the phone against his ear slightly irritating to a man geared more for action than waiting.

A moment later, the line clicked. Mack Bolan's voice came on. "Hello, Calvin. Nice to find out you're still alive."

James laughed. "Sorry. We were out of pocket for awhile."

"Did you have any luck locating the drug tunnel during your disappearing act?"

James frowned. In the heat of battle with Victorio Vega and the other bandits, he'd all but forgotten that he and Encizo's primary assignment had been to locate and eliminate the reputed underground passage through which millions of dollars of cocaine, heroin and marijuana were traveling into America. "Negative," he said. "We got tied up ridding the world of some Mexican bandits and saving a fair maiden in distress. But Rafe is already folowing a lead."

"Good," Bolan said. "I just got off the horn to Hal. Things are heating up in the bigger cities near the border. Mexican drug cartel gunners are taking each other out fast."

"And that concerns us because... ?" James asked, raising his eyebrows.

Bolan chuckled. "Because sooner or later innocent Americans are going to get caught in the cross fire." He paused, and James heard him take a deep breath. "If it gets any worse, I may want you and Encizo—maybe McCarter and the rest of the guys when they get in—to take over that end of things. Then again, if Lyons and his crew can finish up in Alaska I'll put them on it."

The Phoenix Force knife expert nodded. He needed to call Hal Brognola himself; the director of Sensitive Operations at Stony Man Farm might know if there was an ETA on the rest of Phoenix Force yet. "No problem," James said. "The guy in charge of the task force here turns out to be an old SEAL buddy, Striker. Pug Nelson—he's a good man. We'll get things rolling on the tunnel but if we get pulled off I feel comfortable letting him take the reins." Hearing running footsteps, he looked up to see the door of the office open. The hand not holding the phone unconsciously fell on the 9 mm Beretta 92 beneath his shirt.

An out-of-breath Nelson came barreling through the doorway, Encizo at his heels.

"Rafe and Nelson just got back, Striker," James said into the phone. "Looks like they've got something on the tunnel."

"Then why are you wasting time talking to me?" Bolan asked.

As the Executioner hung up, James looked up again.

"We've got a location from an informant," Encizo said.

James looked to Nelson. "Reliable?"

Nelson nodded. "I think so. But reluctant. I had to use a little gentle persuasion to convince him it was in his best interests to talk to us."

James eyes traveled back to Encizo. The little Cuban shrugged his shoulders and put on his innocent look.

James rose from behind the desk and led the way out of the task force offices, down the hall and out the building. Nelson took the wheel of the new Suburban as the black soldier slid into the shotgun seat with Encizo taking the back. Looking past the Cuban into the far rear of the big vehicle, James saw a small dark-skinned man with long black hair and a goatee. A trickle of blood dripped from one corner of his mouth, the result of the "gentle persuasion" Nelson had mentioned, no doubt. The informant was handcuffed, and a chain around his stomach secured him to a ring mounted in the middle of the floor.

James glanced at Nelson as the DEA man started the ignition. "I'm not a cop, Pug," he said as the Suburban's tires screeched away from the task force headquarters. "But isn't it illegal to lock prisoners to stationary objects?"

Nelson snorted as he twisted the wheel and entered the heavy El Paso traffic. "This son of a bitch is an informant, not a prisoner," he growled. "Besides, everything I've done since you clowns got here has either been illegal or against policy."

BOLAN STARED THROUGH the window into the courtyard as he thumbed off his cellular phone. One thing he could say about the small sleeping quarters he'd been assigned at *Los Pinos*—it had a great view. The iron steps from the balcony led down to some of the most beautifully landscaped shrubbery and flower gardens he'd ever seen. Ducks swam on the small man-made pond, and squirrels and rabbits abounded among the foliage. The first lady's two cats—one a Siamese, the other Persian—had free rein within the courtyard as well.

Disconnecting the scrambler from the phone, the Executioner shoved both devices between the mattress and boxsprings of the bed. He lay on his back, folded his arms behind his head and stared at the ceiling. James, Encizo and Nelson were on their way to check out the underground tunnel from Mexico to the U.S. Millions of dollars of drugs were reported to be traveling that route daily, and that had to stop. Once it was located and reconned, they'd have the rest of the DEA-Army task force and as many of the military troops already stationed along the border as they needed at their disposal to take control of the situation.

Able Team was in Alaska, about to finalize the destruction of Demitri's Russian Mafia and the similar drug pipelines into Canada and the U.S. Earlier in the day he had seen on CNN that a military base in southern Iran had gone up in smoke. Rumors were circulating that a small accidental nuclear explosion had taken place. That wasn't the case, he knew, and right about now David McCarter, Gary

Manning and Thomas Jackson Hawkins should be nearing Mexico to join their teammates, James and Encizo.

None of that worried him.

What did was that, once again, President Don Juan de Fierro Blanco was nowhere to be found.

Fierro Blanco and his family, accompanied by Oliverez and a new company of federal bodyguards, had returned to *Los Pinos* from the Mexican navy destroyer that had picked them up after the attack on the summerhouse. The presidential mansion was still under repair after the *Marxista* invasion a few days earlier but the offices and living quarters had been the first to be restored.

The first lady and children had gone immediately to their bedrooms upon arriving. But the president had insisted on tackling the work he knew lay waiting in his office.

When the soldier had called upon him an hour later, he had disappeared.

Where had Fierro Blanco gone? Oliverez didn't know. The president's secretary didn't know either—or at least she wasn't talking. This wasn't the first unexplained absence on the president's part. He had disappeared several times since Bolan had arrived to guard him, offering no explanation when he returned. The only person in the complex of offices who seemed to have any idea about the man was General Antonio de Razon, Fierro Blanco's chief military advisor. And the fat general would do no more than wink and avoid the Executioner's questions, assuring Bolan that the president was safe and reminding him that all men needed privacy now and then.

Bolan thought now of General Razon. The two had first met shortly after the soldier's arrival in Mexico. Bolan had accompanied Fierro Blanco and Razon on a wild boar hunt in which the beasts were killed with knives. Dangerous and adventurous sounding on the surface, the hunt had proven to be a farce with a dozen pit bulls running the boars to fatigue, then pinning them helplessly to the ground while the president and Razon inserted their knives, then basked in their false bravery. The two men, overweight and out of shape, had been in far more danger of dropping dead from heart attacks than being killed by the exhausted animals hanging from the teeth of the pit bulls. Bolan had been disgusted by the whole affair by the hypocracy of Fierro Blanco and Razon pretending they had faced death. Razon had sensed this, and there had been no love lost between him and the Executioner since.

But Bolan had noticed a pattern beginning to develop. Razon was sometimes in the company of Fierro Blanco, sometimes not. But he was *always* in the office during the president's unexplained absences; always ready with an excuse and an admonition not to worry. Razon was obviously the cover when Fierro Blanco went, which meant he knew where the president was and what he was doing.

Was Razon in league with Fierro Blanco, and was the president slipping off to meet with revolutionaries, drug kingpins or both? It was a distinct possibility. Only one thing bothered Bolan about the theory he had just come up with: Simply having Razon explain that the president was safe and advising Bolan and the others not to worry was thin. Wouldn't a man—or men in the case of both Fierro Blanco and Razon—who were smart enough to pull off the earlier deceits also be smart enough to come up with a better cover than that?

A vibration beneath the mattress shook the Executioner from his thoughts. Rolling off the bed, his eyes flicked to the door's lock to make sure it was secured. Lifting the mattress, he retrieved the cellular phone, attached the scrambler and pressed the instrument to his face. "Striker," he said.

Barbara Price, Stony Man Farm's mission controller, spoke. "Hello, Mack."

"What's up, Barb?"

"McCarter and company are about to touch down at Benito Juarez International,'' Price said. ''Where do you want to meet them?''

Bolan paused. He was on an eight-hour leave at the moment to get some sleep. It would be a perfect time to touch base with the remainder of Phoenix Force and issue his orders in person. ''What's their cover?'' he asked.

''Oil executives,'' Price said. ''Texaco. Kurtzman tapped into the company's computer files and listed them all as vice-presidents in case anybody checks.''

The soldier frowned. That meant the three warriors would more than likely be dressed in business suits. Meeting them in one of the dingy Mexico City cantinas where he'd touched base with James and Encizo earlier in the week was out of the question. But a public meeting in a place where they looked at home was equally risky—the soldier had been seen with the president at several speeches and functions and might be recognized.

Bolan glanced down at his watch. ''Tell them to take a cab to the Hilton by the airport.''

''Meet you at the bar?'' Price asked.

''Negative, Barb,'' Bolan said. ''Tell them to go to the front desk and ask for Mr. Belasko. I'll leave word with the desk clerk that I have business associates coming.''

''You've got it Striker,'' Price said. ''Do you need anything else?''

Mack Bolan was, after all, only a man and for a moment his mind drifted to the woman sitting behind the control desk at Stony Man Farm. He and Barbara Price had been involved in a sort of romance of convenience for several years, getting together on the rare occasions when their schedules permitted. They cared for each other, but they never let it get in the way of their duties. Which meant that neither had ever allowed it to blossom into a full-blown love affair. ''That's a pretty leading question, lady,'' Bolan said.

Price laughed.

"As a matter of fact, I do," the soldier added. "But it'll have to wait until I get back."

"You make sure that it does," Price said. "Stay away from the *señoritas*."

"Like I'd have time if I wanted to," Bolan said and disconnected the line.

THE HOTEL ROOM had two king-sized beds and a large round table with four chairs that stood just in front of the sliding glass door. In some ways, it reminded Bolan of his room back at *Los Pinos*. But instead of an elaborately land-scaped courtyard two stories below, the hotel room looked down on the swimming pool. As he stared through the glass past the balcony, the Executioner could see two Hispanic men, both wearing swim trunks and short-clipped beards. As the Executioner watched, sipping a Coke he had taken from the small refrigerator next to the well-stocked wet bar, one of the men strode to the end of the diving board, bounced twice, then jetted into a double forward flip. The other followed a few seconds later, adding a half-gainer to his pair of aerial somersaults.

The woman they were trying to impress lay on a plastic recliner. She had long tanned legs, reddish-blond hair and breasts that threatened to creep out of the top and sides of her bikini. But the woman appeared more interested in the *Cosmopolitan* magazine she was reading than in either of the performers.

The buzz of the telephone turned Bolan away from the window. He took a seat on the bed nearest the glass door and lifted the receiver. "Hello?" he said.

"Señor Blanski?" asked the heavily accented voice of the desk clerk the soldier remembered from checking in a few minutes earlier. "Your visitors are here inquiring about you. They are..." The man's words trailed off and Bolan heard muffled voices in the background. The clerk returned. "Mr. Emerson, Mr. Lake and Mr. Palmer."

The soldier suppressed a chuckle. McCarter's ever-present dry British sense of humor was all the proof of identity he needed. "Give them the room number and send them up," he said.

Five minutes later, Bolan heard the knock on the door. Looking through the peephole, he saw Hawkins flanked by McCarter and Manning. Opening the door, he stepped back and ushered the three Phoenix Force men into the room.

McCarter led the way past the beds to the table. "Sorry we forgot our guitars, Striker," he said. "We had the best of intentions of strumming a few tunes for you."

Bolan stopped at the refrigerator and pulled three more Cokes from the shelves. "Thanks for sparing me," he said. He carried the cans to the table and took a seat as the other men settled around the table. "How'd it go in Iran?"

McCarter shrugged. He popped the tab on his can and glanced through the glass door.

Bolan followed his eyes and saw that the two would-be suitors had given up their diving exhibition and ordered drinks at one of the tables by the pool.

"As well as could be expected," the Phoenix Force leader said. "We didn't put an end to anything. But we've undoubtedly slowed them down. At least for awhile."

"Mohammed Habbibi?" Bolan asked.

"Shaking hands with his namesake right about now, I'd suppose," McCarter said.

Bolan nodded. He glanced to the other two men at the table, then back to McCarter. "Okay, guys. Have you been in touch with James and Encizo?"

"Only through Stony Man," the Briton answered. "I gather you sent them looking for a drug tunnel and they got sidetracked rescuing a fair maiden in distress."

"That's pretty much the story. Which means the tunnel is still out there somewhere. I talked to James maybe an hour or so ago and they had a new lead. You'll be joining them. But first let me give you a rundown of the overall picture."

McCarter, Hawkins and Manning drank their Cokes and waited patiently.

"As you know, I'm officially here as Fierro Blanco's bodyguard. But at the same time I'm trying to find out if he's dirty. The Man in the White House has to decide—and decide quickly—whether or not he's going to recertify Mexico's cooperation with antidrug efforts. The wrong decision would be political suicide."

Bolan took a drink before continuing. "So far, I still don't have any proof of Fierro Blanco's honesty," he said. "Not even a decent hunch. Every time I think I've got him pegged one way or the other, something comes up to cloud the issue again." He drained the last of his Coke and tossed it into the trash can next to the dresser.

"Have you heard from Ironman and his crew?" Manning asked.

"Not directly. Barb said the deal with the Russians is about to go down. They'll be heading south as soon as it's over." He paused, glanced through the glass again, and saw that the blond sunbather was gathering her towels and tanning lotions, preparing to leave. The two Hispanic men still sat facing the hotel sipping their drinks. "I'm going to put Able Team to work along the border," the Executioner said. "Somebody's got to get a handle on the cartel killings before innocent Americans start getting hurt."

"If it wasn't for that possibility," Manning said. "I'd say let them go for it. Eliminate each other, and they do our work for us."

"James said the same thing," Bolan responded. "But the fact is, the problem exists and it's got to be solved." He rose, went to the refrigerator and pulled out another Coke.

"You flew directly from Iran?" Bolan asked as he returned to the table.

McCarter nodded. "Grimaldi's still waiting at the airport. I guessed you'd be sending us off into the wild blue yonder again and made him promise to wait."

The Executioner chuckled under his breath. Jack Grimaldi, Stony Man Farm's top pilot, was known to have a good-looking woman waiting at nearly every airport. Lifting the cellular phone from the table, Bolan handed it to the Phoenix Force leader. "Charlie Mott is on standby at the Farm. Give Barb a call and tell him to pack his plane with ammo and whatever else you think you might need." He paused and snapped open the tab of the new can in his hands. "Tell him to bring it here and take over from Grimaldi."

McCarter frowned.

"In the mean time Jack can get started north and take over Able Team's transport." The Executioner pulled a slip of paper with the address and phone numbers of the DEA-Army task force in El Paso. "Get in touch with whoever's in charge while Nelson's with James and Encizo. You should all be able to rendezvous with them by the time they've reconned the tunnel."

McCarter activated the scrambler and pressed the phone to his ear. He called James first, agreeing to take his men to the task force headquarters and await word from James and Encizo. As he tapped the buttons to Stony Man Farm, Bolan turned his eyes to the sliding glass door again. A waiter had brought more drinks to the dark-skinned men at the table who were now the swimming pool's only occupants.

An uneasy feeling crept over the Executioner as he watched the scene two stories below. Something was wrong but he couldn't pinpoint exactly what. The men resumed their conversation as the waiter left, looking from each other to the pool, to the busy street outside the hotel. And then back again. It all looked innocent enough—it wasn't as if they were staring up at the window. So why did it bother him?

Hawkins finished his Coke and sent the can flying through the air to join the one Bolan had already trashed. "So what's the deal with Ronnie Quartel and the other hostages?" he asked.

Bolan turned his attention back to the table. "The last word was that the *Legitimas* had taken credit for the abductions and were about to announce their demands. We may end up in the middle of that, too. But right now there's nothing we can do."

McCarter stopped talking into the phone and handed it across the table to Bolan. "It's Brognola," he said. "He wants to talk to you."

Bolan took the phone. "Yeah, Hal?"

"Hi, Striker," the Stony Man director said. "You got any inside on the Quartel thing?"

"If I did, you'd already have it."

"It's making international news," Brognola went on. "I'm going to try something with a couple of the blacksuits."

Bolan waited. In addition to the field operations that came out of Stony Man, the Farm sponsored extensive advanced training for select police and military personnel around the world. The men arrived at Stony Man blindfolded and left the same way, never knowing where they'd been or exactly who had trained them. But they went away roughly ten times more capable as warriors than they had been before.

"I've got two guys—one's part of Colombia's new counterterrorist squad. The other's an Oklahoma Bureau of Narcotics and Dangerous Drugs special agent—name's Martinez and he's half-Mexican, half-Black. Both are aces at undercover. I'm going to send them to Tijuana to see what they can come up with."

"I'm sure they're good," Bolan said. "But they aren't

as good as Leo.'' Leo Turrin was the Farm's own top undercover specialist.

"No, they aren't," Brognola agreed. "Nobody is. But Turrin isn't Hispanic, either." There was a short pause, then Brognola added. "Leo's going with them."

"Okay. Any word from Able Team?"

"Not since you talked to Barb. The deal ought to be going down right about now."

"Let me know as soon as you hear from Lyons. In the meantime, we're going to work." The Executioner hung up and glanced at his wristwatch. He needed to get back to *Los Pinos* soon to avoid suspicion. Turning to the men of Phoenix Force, he said, "Anything else you guys need?"

"Oh, about a year's vacation," McCarter said as he got up from the table. "Paid, of course."

"Dream on," Bolan said. He stood and walked to the door with the other men, then closed and locked it behind him. Sitting at the table, he stared through the glass again. The two men at the pool were now watching a pair of brunettes who had stretched out by the water on their stomachs and had unfastened their tops.

Suddenly, it dawned on Bolan what was wrong. The two men had not stared up at the window—on the contrary, they had *never* looked in the direction of the hotel. Their eyes had moved in every direction *except* the rooms. That couldn't be coincidence. During the length of time they'd been at the pool, they should have glanced toward the rooms at least occasionally.

They were running surveillance.

As he rose from the table, Bolan saw the waiter appear with yet another round of drinks.

Grabbing his sport coat as he raced for the door, the soldier threw it over the Beretta and Desert Eagle. He hurried down the hall, bypassing the elevators and descending the steps two at a time. He emerged from the stairwell into

the lobby, cut past a row of shops and a waiting area, and
exited the building to the pool area.

The topless brunettes both looked up and smiled at
Bolan.

But the two men were gone.

A pair of Mai Tais, the paper umbrellas twirling around
the top of the glasses in the light breeze, sat untouched on
the table.

4

Carl "Ironman" Lyons glanced to his right as he led his men across the Nugget Inn's parking lot to room thirty-four at the corner of the building. Across the street from the motel was an empty lot, the size of an acre. That was lucky.

And Able Team could use all the luck they could get in the next hour or so.

Lyons had one hand on the rubber Pachmayer grips of his .357 Magnum Colt Python as the other stuck the key into the door. Demitri and his fellow Russian gorillas had departed the café in the opposite direction and wouldn't have had time to beat them to the Nugget Inn. But they could have stationed other men there while Able Team met with the Russians.

And attempted rip-off was in the Alaskan wind. Lyons could smell it.

The door swung open, and Lyons used his free hand to reach in and switch on the light. He stepped inside, covering the left side of the room as Blancanales—his 9 mm Beretta 92 leading the way—moved in and to the right. Schwarz walked between them, going immediately past the open door toward the closet and the bathroom. The other men stood their ground until Able Team's electronics whiz had made a quick check under the bed, looked up and nodded. "It's clear, Ironman," he said.

Lyons closed and locked the door behind him, then turned toward the room. The bed was roughly three feet from the left wall. Across from the foot of the bed, beneath the room's lone window, which faced the street, was the dresser. To the right, against the wall, was a round wooden table and chairs.

The Able Team leader turned to his fellow soldiers. "Okay," he said. "We don't have much time, and we need to do some rearranging." He glanced from Schwarz to Blancanales, then to the dresser. "Swap that thing with the table."

A quizzical look came over the faces of the two soldiers but they had followed Lyons too long to ask why. The Russians could arrive any moment and this was no time for questions. They moved the table to the window and dragged the heavy dresser against the wall to the right of the room.

"We'll need weapons stashed at different spots," Lyons said when they'd finished. "I don't see them getting the drop on us but I didn't get these wrinkles around my eyes by taking chances." He paused and frowned, then said, "But keep a gun showing. They won't buy us going into this unarmed, either." Moving to the closet, he shifted two large duffle bags to the side, then unzipped a black canvas bag and pulled out his Atchisson Assault 12 shotgun. He rolled across the bed and laid it out of sight against the wall. Turning back, the Able Team leader saw that Schwarz and Blancanales had also pulled weapons from the bag. Schwarz opened the deep bottom drawer of the dresser and dropped in one of the team's 50-round 9 mm Calico submachine guns.

The sound of footsteps outside on the sidewalk snapped all three men's heads toward the door. The steps walked past the room and the warriors returned to their tasks.

Blancanales, nicknamed "Pol" for Politician, opened the small door of the night stand and set another of the Calicos on top of the Gideon Bible, then shoved a Beretta 93-R—identical to the one Mack Bolan always carried—just under the bedspread. Both men kept their Beretta 92s in their belts, as Lyons did his Python. The .357 Magnum pistol was stashed in the front of his belt, and as backup he added a Colt Gold Cup .45 with a sound suppressor screwed onto the barrel. The quiet weapon went into the waistband of his jeans at the spine.

Schwarz and Blancanales dug through the bags and came up with backup weapons as well. The electronics ace chose a second Beretta 92, with Blancanales opting for an .44 Special S&W 696 revolver.

"Everybody see where everything went?" Lyons asked.

Both men nodded.

Lyons wasn't the kind of man to hand out compliments lightly but inside he smiled with pride. Each man had their individual preferences when it came to firearms and other weapons. But there wasn't a fighting instrument known to man, primitive or modern, that they both weren't capable of using with deadly efficiency.

Schwarz and Blancanales were damn good men. And he was proud to lead them.

Turning to Schwarz, the Able Team leader said, "Gadgets, take another of the Calicos, go in the bathroom and turn on the shower. Stay there and be ready." His gaze shifted to Blancanales. "Pol, you'll answer the door. Then I want you at the dresser. You can sit on top of it if you want. I'll have Demitri set the dope on the bed. Then one of us will go to the closet as if we're going for the money."

As Schwarz disappeared behind the bathroom door, more footsteps clattered outside. The click of a lock opening in the door next to them sounded, and a moment later the faint sounds of a television in the room next door drifted through the wall.

Blancanales looked at Lyons, frowned, and hooked a thumb over his shoulder. "These walls are like paper," he whispered. "The 9 mm slugs are going to go right through them. I'd hate to kill some little old lady."

"That's why we've repositioned," Lyons said. He glanced behind him. "We've got the parking lot back there—the direction you'll be shooting. Schwarz will be in the bathroom facing the table where the Russians will be. Behind them is the empty lot across the street." His eyes moved to the wall behind Blancanales again. "That's the only high-risk direction—my angle of fire. I've filled the Atchisson with birdshot. Not ideal, but at close range like this it should do the job." He saw his fellow soldier glance at the Colt Python in his belt. Nothing went through walls and other substances like a .357 bullet. "Switched to .38s," he said, answering the unasked question. "Low-velocity wadcutters. The same with the .45."

Blancanales whistled and shook his head. "Not much in the way of stopping power, Ironman," he said. "And the .45 worries me. Are you sure the low-velocity rounds have enough power to work the slide? I'd say you're taking some big chances."

"I'm never sure of anything, Pol," the Able Team leader said. "And taking chances is in my job description." He propped both pillows against the headboard, then glanced at the Atchisson against the wall. A quick roll would put him in reach of the 12-gauge with the mattress and boxsprings as cover.

The sound of running water drifted from the bathroom as Blancanales took a seat on top of the waist-high dresser and cracked open the drawer that hid the Calico. Then, in one swift movement, he jerked it open farther and reached inside. The 50-round full-auto submachine gun came out and up, pointed toward the door. Satisfied, he returned the weapon to hiding.

Lyons and Blancanales waited—always the hardest part of any mission, they both knew. They listened to several more sets of feet shuffle past on the sidewalk to the parking lot, then finally the loud clomps of Russian brogans worn by heavy men pounded to a stop outside the room. A moment later, knuckles rapped on the door.

Blancanales rose, hurried to the door and looked through the peephole. He turned to Lyons and nodded. The Able Team leader nodded back.

Blancanales opened the door.

The Russian stood in front of the opening, his broad shoulders blocking the light from the street behind him. Blancanales stepped back and ushered him in. He was followed by two of his men carrying suitcases. Blancanales closed the door.

Lyons swung his legs off the side of the bed and sat up. "Just set them here," he said, looking down at the mattress.

The two burly Russians complied, spreading the suitcases across the bed.

"Where are the rest of your friends?" Lyons asked.

"We agreed, you and I, to bring only two men with us. I have complied with that agreement."

The Able Team leader stared at him. He wasn't buying a bit of it. The other three men were somewhere close. Just outside the room. Maybe in the parking lot. But somewhere.

"I might ask you where your other man is," Demitri said. "But I can hear the shower." The former-KGB man flashed Lyons his carnivorous smile again. "Clever. I have used that one myself many times."

The Able Team leader stared into Demitri's eyes, not sure how to take the last statement. The Russian could have meant that he knew Schwarz was in the bathroom out of sight as a precaution. Or it might mean he suspected Able Team was planning its own rip-off. The only thing he was certain of was that the mobster knew no one was really washing his armpits right now.

"Have a seat while I test the stuff," Lyons said, waving toward the table.

Demitri turned to the table, then shot a quick glance at

the wall to his right where Blancanales now sat. Lyons thought he saw a moment of doubt flash into the former-KGB man's eyes. It was gone as quickly as it had come but it left the Able Team leader wondering what had prompted it.

Lyons frowned inwardly. Demitri had told them back at the café that he'd stayed at the Nugget before. That meant he was familiar with the layout of the rooms. Was he just used to having the furniture arranged differently? Or was there something else?

The Russian and his two cronies sat around the table as Lyons opened the suitcase nearest him. He found the inside packed with large Ziplock freezer bags. The white powder could be seen clearly through the plastic. In his peripheral vision, he thought he saw the Russians around the table exchange looks of concern. He couldn't be sure.

Reaching into his shirt pocket, the Able Team leader pulled out a field test kit and held it up. He looked up and smiled. "Nice thing about working for the Treasury Department," he said, forcing a smile. "You get to know the boys over at DEA and they give you presents like these."

The Russians either didn't understand or didn't think it was funny.

Lyons selected one of the freezer bags at random, broke the seal on the test kit and mixed a small amount of the powder with the solution. The results were positive.

The room remained silent save for the noise from the shower as Lyons proceeded to test arbitrary bags from each of the suitcases.

All of the bags Lyons tested proved positive and he was closing the last suitcase when Demitri suddenly said, "I have stayed at this motel many times before. In all of the rooms, the table is against that wall where the dresser is in your room."

"And your point is?" Lyons asked.

He got his answer a split second later when the mobster's hand went for the Tokarev pistol in his belt.

The Able Team leader rolled off the bed toward the wall, coming up in a kneeling position facing the room. The Atchisson Assault 12 swung up and over the mattress. The Russian fired, the round whizzing past his ear and into the wall behind him. Before Lyons could pull the shotgun's trigger two things happened at once.

The mob boss dived for cover below the foot of the bed.

And the blunt end of a police battering ram poked through the wall from the room next to them. The ram traveled through the opening, struck Blancanales in the back of the head and knocked him off the dresser.

Everything around Lyons seemed to slow. He watched the Russians rise from their chairs and reach for the weapons beneath their coats. To the Able Team leader, they looked as if they were in slow-motion instant replay. He had experienced the psychological phenomenon before, however, and knew they were moving quickly.

Just not as quickly as he was.

As he thrust the shotgun's stock against his shoulder and pulled the trigger, Lyons saw the bathroom door swing open. The Atchisson roared in his hands and the Russian sitting closest to the bed caught the birdshot squarely in the face. The load may have been light but it was heavy enough, and the man's eyes disappeared in a mass of red froth.

To his side, Lyons heard the staccato rattle of 9 mm slugs. Out of the corner of his eye he saw that the bathroom door was now open. Schwarz couldn't be seen but the Russian gunner falling face first toward the table was proof that the team's electronics ace and his 9 mm Calico, were alive and well.

The mob boss rose from the floor for a shot. Lyons swung the shotgun slightly to the side and lined up the barrel on his nose. But a microsecond before he pulled the trigger, the big Russian dived to the floor again. The load of birdshot flew over his head. The Russian disappeared below the foot of the bed once more.

Lyons started to direct Schwarz's fire toward the mob boss but Schwarz was engaged with the third Russian who had risen from the table.

The battering ram had disappeared from the cavity in the wall and now the barrel of an AK-47 nosed through the hole. Lyons cursed silently, wishing he had never replaced the loads in the shotgun or his pistols. But there had been no way of knowing that the room next to them would be occupied by the Russians—it could just as easily have been the allegorical little old lady Blancanales had speculated about.

Lyons swung the Atchisson toward the wall and pulled the trigger, emptying the magazine of birdshot. He doubted that any of the Russians in the next room had suffered greatly but it was enough to drive the rifle back out of sight. Dropping the Atchisson on the bed, the Able Team leader withdrew the Python. The pistol would penetrate the wall at least a little better than the birdshot. He was about to fire through the hole when a hand holding a Tokarev suddenly rose over the foot of the bed, firing blindly.

Lyons dived over the bed, trying to keep low to stay out of Schwarz's line of fire. He felt 9 mm billets zipping past his head as he came to rest on the floor next to the nightstand. Sticking the Python under the bed, he fired his own blind return shots in the Russian's direction. The Python's hammer finally fell on an empty chamber and he threw open the nightstand door, reaching for the Calico hidden there.

A burst of gunfire from the hole in the wall drove back his hand. Drawing the sound-suppressed Colt Gold Cup from the back of his jeans, he thumbed off the safety and aimed at the wall. Four of the low-velocity rounds popped from the semiauto pistol before their feebleness caused the weapon to jam. The Able Team leader then emptied the rest of the magazine through the hole.

The third Russian fell to the floor in front of the table as Lyons dropped the Colt and dived for the Calico once more. This time he was successful and the 50-round 9 mm pistol came out of the nightstand and into play. "Gadgets!" he yelled into the bathroom. "Concentrate on the wall!"

Next to him, Schwarz stepped out of the bathroom and began cutting zig zag patterns through the wall behind the dresser. White dust and chunks of wallboard flew through the air like a snowstorm.

Lyons had just gotten the Calico pointed in the right direction when the mob boss screamed and rose above the mattress, the Tokarev gripped in both hands. Blood dripped from one cheek where one of Lyons's shots must have nicked him.

The Calico's rounds didn't nick. They bored through the Russian's belly and upper torso one after the other, causing him to drop his gun and fall facedown on the bed.

Lyons turned his weapon toward the wall and joined Schwarz. As the 50-round hexagonal-drum mags atop the Calicos wore down, other holes in the wallboard began to appear. Finally releasing the trigger and holding up a hand, the Able Team leader directed Schwarz to cease firing as well. He realized he was stepping over Blancanales's prostate form on the floor as he rushed to the perforated wall, and a wave of concern washed over him as he realized his fellow soldier hadn't moved since the battering ram struck him in the back of the head. He had been unconscious throughout the entire firefight.

Had he taken a stray round? Was he dead? There had been no time to take notice during the gunfight, and there still wasn't. The answer would have to wait until they were sure the threat from the next room had ended.

But Lyons's concern about the Russians in the neighboring motel room proved unfounded. Looking through one of the holes, he saw all three men on the floor awash with blood. Not enough remained of any of them to sustain life. But like he'd already said once that day, he hadn't lived as long as he had by taking chances.

"Go double-check them, Gadgets."

"Pol..." Schwarz started to say.

"I'll take care of him," the Able Team leader snapped. "Go."

Schwarz didn't need to go out the door and into the adjoining room. He simply reached out, tore one of the holes in the wall a little bigger and stepped between the wooden studs.

Lyons quickly circled the room, making sure no life remained in the mob boss or the other Russians who had been at the table. As quickly as he could, he returned to Blancanales on the floor.

Blancanales lay on his face, a huge bump already forming on the back of his head. No blood could be seen on his back. Gently, Lyons rolled him over.

The pain that came from the floor pressing against the swelling caused Blancanales's eyes to shoot open. For a moment, they stayed unfocused, which brought a frown of concern to the Able Team leader's face. Reaching into his pocket, he pulled out a Mini-Mag flashlight and directed the beam into Blancanales's face. As he watched, the pupils cleared.

Lyons breathed a sigh of relief. He was no doctor but it didn't look like a concussion to him. He reached down and grasped his fellow warrior's wrist, then turned his eyes to his watch, checking the pulse.

"I guess I overslept again," Blancanales suddenly said.

Lyons set the man's arm back down. The pulse was fast but that was to be expected. "Don't move," he said. "How do you feel?"

"Like somebody hit me in the back of the head with a battering ram."

Lyons wasn't sure if he actually knew that was what had happened or was simply making a comparison.

"You know who I am?"

"I'm okay. Quit worrying."

"Do you know who I am?" Lyons repeated testily.

"Well, you're not St. Peter, which means I'm not dead. And you sure aren't Sandra Bullock, so I'm not dreaming. You're as ugly as a bulldog so you must be our fearless leader, Ironman. Got any more trick questions?"

Lyons held up his hand. "How many fingers am I holding up?" he asked.

"Four."

Lyons eyebrows dropped in concern.

"And a thumb, Ironman," Blancanales added. He sounded as irritated now as Lyons had a moment before. "Will you please get out of the way and let me get up?"

Schwarz reentered the room in time to hear the last exchange. "The guys next door are all on their way to the Great Gulag," he said. "What's wrong with you, Pol? Sleeping on the job again?"

"Yeah, yeah, yeah," Blancanales said as he rose. He rubbed the back of his head lightly and grimaced. "I've got one hell of a headache, that's all."

"Some people will do anything to get out of work," Schwarz said.

Lyons turned to the electronics ace. "Demitri was wired," he said. "he made the comment about the dresser so the guys in the next room would know."

Schwarz nodded. "I figured as much." He glanced at the carnage of the wall behind him. "They had receivers and earplugs. It's hard to tell now but it looks like a section of the wallboard had already been removed on their side. And they'd taken out one of the studs to make it easier to get through."

"The dresser slowed them," Lyons said. "Nothing but dumb luck that we moved it there."

Lyons was already gathering the weapons and dumping them into the bags. "I could use some help, guys," he said. "It's about time to leave. That is, unless either one of you wants to hang around and explain all this to the cops."

A few minutes later the sounds of sirens filled the air.

But by then, the men of Able Team were already en route to the airport where Jack Grimaldi would be waiting to take them to Mexico.

THE BLADES OF THE AH-64A Apache attack helicopter whirled overhead as David McCarter looked through the glass at the ground below. They had just passed over the state line between New Mexico and Arizona and were a half-mile into the U.S. side of the Mexican border.

McCarter glanced to his side where the young army pilot—Sgt. Dawson, his name tag read—sat behind the controls of the chopper. After he, Manning and Hawkins had met with Bolan in Mexico City, Charlie Mott had arrived from Stony Man with fresh weapons, ammo and other gear, relieving Grimaldi to head for Alaska and Able Team. Mott had flown them to the DEA-Military task force headquarters in El Paso where they had made phone contact with James, Encizo and Pug Nelson.

Nelson, it seemed, had come up with an informant who knew the whereabouts of the drug tunnel linking Mexico and the U.S. The four men were on their way to the Arizona site in one of the DEA vehicles.

McCarter continued to watch the rugged southwestern terrain below as he reached forward, unclipping the microphone from the control panel. Thumbing the red button on the side of the mike with his thumb, he spoke into the transmitter. "Phoenix One to Two. Come in, Two."

The crackling of airwave interference was his only answer.

The former British SAS officer dropped the mike to his lap and waited. The American President's budget cuts to the military had, among other things, left many helicopters with antiquated radio units subject to dead zones. Knowing he would have to try again in a few minutes, he settled back in his seat and closed his eyes.

According to Nelson's snitch—a Mexican national named Lopez who was a former employee of the Saltillo cartel—the American end of the tunnel lay east of Douglas, Arizona. It was well hidden and secured, and Lopez had made the underground trek several times with loads of both cocaine and Mexican brown heroin. He was guiding them to the site now.

If he was telling the truth, McCarter thought as a small air pocket dropped the helicopter a few feet and caused him to open his eyes again. And Nelson thought he was. Lopez had been the first arrest in the gangland killings that were taking place in southwestern U.S. cities between the cartels. He had been convicted in the States twice before and was looking at a life sentence if he didn't cooperate.

McCarter tried the radio but still got no response. Pulling the cellular phone from the breast pocket of his desert camouflage BDU shirt, he activated the scrambler and tapped in James's number. A moment later, the black soldier's voice came on. "Phoenix Two." In the background, the Briton could hear the hum of a fast-running car engine.

"'ello, mate," McCarter said, exaggerating his Cockney accent. "And 'ow's everything on the ground?"

"We're in the process of finding out."

"You've located the site?"

"Not yet. We're on our way. Pug's man knows where it is." There was a brief pause, then, "He also knows there's a shipment scheduled in about two hours."

"You've formulated a plan?" the Briton asked.

"Not yet. Been waiting on you guys."

James had been in charge when it was just him and Encizo, but now that Phoenix Force was one unit again, that responsibility returned to McCarter. After a brief pause, he spoke into the phone again. "Do you have other troops with you?"

"Just the three of us reconning. But there's task force personnel standing by. We've access to as many as we need."

"Give me a minute to think," McCarter said. He thumbed off the phone.

Behind him, T. J. Hawkins said, "We need to locate and block both ends of the tunnel, David."

McCarter turned in his seat in time to see Gary Manning nod. "There's always the chance that the bad guys will get word that trouble's waiting on the other side. If they do, then they can just turn and go home."

Resting an arm over the back of the seat, the Phoenix Force leader said, "What are you...?"

"James and the others need U.S. troops on their side of the border," Hawkins said. "We've got to locate the Mexican entry point and follow the drug runners in, blocking it off in case they turn back. We'll need support from the Mexican army."

McCarter fought the urge to smile. Hawkins was good when it came to fighting. But as the youngest member of Phoenix Force, by very definition he had the least experience. The Briton was about to explain why the young warrior's plan wouldn't work when Hawkins corrected himself.

"Wait a minute," Hawkins said. "Let me retract that statement. We don't know who, if anybody, in the Mexican army we can trust." He paused. "How about Striker sending up some federal guards?"

McCarter shook his head. "No time to get them there."

Suddenly the phone rang suddenly and McCarter answered.

"Thought I'd better call you back," James said. "We're getting close to the site and I'm going to turn this thing off once we're on foot. Lopez says they post guards and I don't want it ringing."

"Ask your man where the Mexican end of the tunnel is."

"Hang on."

McCarter heard James and another man's Mexican-accented voice in the background. A moment later, James came back on. "Have you crossed the San Bernardino yet?"

McCarter looked down and saw the river a mile or so in the distance. "Just approaching," he said.

"Follow it south to where it crosses the border," James told him. "Then look for the first creek splitting off to the west. About a mile and half later you'll see the ruins of an old hacienda. About another half-mile west, you'll come to some hills." James cleared his throat. "With me so far?"

McCarter repeated the directions back. He glanced at Dawson. The chopper pilot nodded.

"Right," James said. "If you spot a little village, you've gone too far. Anyway, there's an abandoned silver mine in the hills. The shaft is the entrance."

"Doesn't sound too hard to find."

"No," James said. "But it may not be too easy to get into. Lopez says they've got armed guards at that end, too." There was another pause. Then he added, "You aren't going in by yourselves, are you David?"

"I don't see any other way."

"Be careful."

"Always," the Phoenix Force leader said. He hung up.

Dawson guided the Apache over the river and cut south. They spotted the winding creek before they had even crossed the border, veered west again and flew over the crumbling hacienda. Manning had unbuckled his seat belt and leaned forward between McCarter and Dawson. "There they are," the Canadian said, pointing at something beyond the Apache's glass. The hills were rugged and rough like the rest of the terrain. McCarter raised a pair of binoculars to his eyes and looked below. The entrance to the mine shaft wasn't visible from the air which didn't surprise him. It would take ground recon to locate it.

"It doesn't make sense," Manning said. McCarter lowered the binoculars, then glanced to his side and saw the barrel-chested man deep in thought. "They've got to get the dope into the tunnel somehow, and with the size of the deliveries we've been hearing about that means trucks or at least horses or burros. That kind of activity at an abandoned mine out in the open like this one should have drawn some attention."

McCarter didn't have an answer for his fellow warrior. Manning was right—they were several miles from any village, and a caravan or even a lone transport truck was taking a hell of a chance being spotted in the open spaces below. But Nelson had said that his informant—Lopez—had made several trips through the tunnel. He'd have the answer.

Tapping the numbers back into his cellular phone, the Phoenix Force leader let it ring but got no answer. James had said he was turning off the unit when they set out on foot. They must already be on the ground. He tried the radio for good measure but it still didn't work.

The helicopter flew over the hills. McCarter brought the binoculars back to his eyes when he saw the valley below. Strategically hidden by nature, it was flat and long enough to easily land a small- to medium-sized aircraft.

Good. He didn't need Lopez after all—he had his answer. The drugs were flown in on one or more planes that disappeared suddenly between the hills. Less than half a mile from the border, the dope could then be transported through the tunnel on foot.

McCarter lowered the binoculars to his lap. Lopez had told James that a shipment was scheduled to arrive within the next two hours. The best method of attack would be for the men of Phoenix Force to arrive ahead of time, locate and take out the guards Lopez had mentioned, then wait.

When the smugglers flew in, they would watch them un-
load, then follow them into the tunnel at a safe distance.
But the guards might well have seen the American chopper
fly over. And if they had, it might or might not be a problem. Considering the current border problems, the men
probably wouldn't attribute much importance to the sight-
ing—unless they saw it again.

They would have to land somewhere out of sight of the
hills and make their way to the mine unseen.

McCarter turned to Dawson. "Go in toward the village,"
he ordered.

The pilot changed course slightly, flying toward the border village in the distance. As soon as he saw a narrow
blacktop road leading into town, McCarter said, "Drop and
follow the road."

Dawson raised an eyebrow but did as he'd been
instructed.

Roughly two miles from the village, McCarter spotted
an aging Ford pickup puttering slowly along the road. The
bed had been fitted with a tall wooden rack, and what appeared to be bottled water shifted and shook in the holes
as the truck bumped over the road.

The Phoenix Force leader smiled silently. It wouldn't be
fast. But it would be great cover.

"Speed up and land about a quarter mile on."

"Which side of the road?"

"Neither," said McCarter. "Set us down *on* the road,
right in the middle."

This time Dawson looked at McCarter with an expression of amazement. But the chopper pilot was a man of
few words and was used to taking orders from his superiors.
He did as he was told.

The blue Ford came ambling down the blacktop a few
seconds after they had landed. McCarter dropped to the
pavement, ducked under the chopper blades and walked to
meet the pickup.

An old man with a ragged straw hat sat behind the wheel of the Ford. McCarter, dressed in camouflage and wearing his Browning Hi-Power, held up a hand.

The old man must have been accustomed to obeying men in uniform. He brought the pickup to a halt.

The Phoenix Force leader walked forward to the open driver's seat window. His command of the Spanish language was limited. But he figured for the simple transaction he had in mind, he could get by. *"Buenos días,"* he said.

The old man wore a faded plaid shirt that had lost its sleeves at the shoulder seams years before. A half-chewed toothpick extended from his mouth, and it stuck to his bottom lip as his mouth fell open. *"Buenos diás,"* he returned. He looked surprised, afraid and curious.

"I'm afraid we're going to have to take your truck," McCarter said in Spanish.

Now the split expression turned to complete fear. "Please, Sir," the old man answered. "This truck is my living. I beg of you—"

McCarter shook his head. "I don't intend to steal it," he said. "I want to buy it."

The old man closed his eyes and shook his head. "Please," he said again. "I don't wish to sell it. I must have it to deliver my water. I can't afford to buy another truck for what this one is worth."

The Phoenix Force leader looked at the dilapidated Ford. It had a dented and unpainted body, bald tires and an engine that sounded as if it had the croup. He guessed it was an early '70s model, and doubted it was worth five hundred dollars. "Don't be so sure," he said. He reached into his pocket and pulled out a roll of cash.

The old man's eyes widened in awe. McCarter suspected he had never seen so much before. Removing the rubber band from the stack, he began counting. When he reached five thousand dollars, he handed the money through the window.

"Sir," the old man said, "The truck is so old—"

"Come now," McCarter said, smiling.

"But it isn't worth—"

"It is to me," McCarter said. "Now take the money before I force more of it on you."

The subtle humor seemed to confuse the old man.

"My time is valuable, too," McCarter said. "Now, please, take this and get out of my new truck." He pressed the money closer to the Mexican's face.

Still astonished, the old man's hands shook as he reverently accepted the money.

McCarter opened the door and helped him out. Together, they walked back to the helicopter.

Manning and Hawkins had figured out what was going on and were unloading their equipment. McCarter helped the old man into the chopper and secured the seat belt around his skinny waist.

Dawson was equally confused. "What am I supposed to do with him?" he asked McCarter.

"Do you speak Spanish?"

The pilot nodded.

"Good. Take him home."

5

Roberto Rodriguez tapped his hands on the steering wheel of the Mercedes-Benz. He kept his eyes glued on the front porch of the house across from where he had parked. A man in the blue uniform of the Latin America Parcel Service had just mounted the steps with a small package. As Roberto watched, he rang the doorbell of the home, waited not longer than three seconds, then set the package on the porch and started back toward his truck. Roberto watched him scribble briefly on the clipboard in his hand as he walked. Reaching the driver's side, he tossed the clipboard into the truck and pulled himself up behind the wheel. The vehicle had been left running, and a second later it pulled away from the curb.

Roberto threw the Mercedes into first gear, wishing he and his brother had brought their faster rebuilt '57 Chevy. But the five-seven, as they called it, would have looked out of place in this fashionable residential area of Mexico City, so he had chosen to steal the Mercedes instead. He turned to his brother as they fell in behind the delivery truck, noting Santiago's typically blank face. Most of Santiago's acquaintances considered his quiet nature and lack of expression as evidence of deep thought. Roberto knew better. Santiago thought very little, he knew, and when the man did, his thoughts were limited to four subjects: eating, drinking, fornicating and killing. No, he wasn't a deep thinker or a great conversationalist. That was because he

wasn't exceptionally smart. But he was a good listener—
he followed orders well. Like when they had staked out the
hotel room the big American thought he had secured so
secretly. Santiago hadn't questioned him when Roberto ordered his brother to put on a diving performance at the
pool; he had just done it without knowing why. Roberto,
on the other hand, had known it would look to anyone
watching as if the two men were trying to impress the blond
woman sunbathing.

Roberto indicated the truck ahead with a forefinger.
"You see," he said. "Taking the truck will be simple. The
more the driver delivers, the more his boss pays him so
he's in a hurry and doesn't pay attention. He doesn't deliver
drugs or handle money, so he has no reason to be
suspicious."

Santiago stared straight ahead, not even bothering to nod
his head or grunt that he had heard. But Roberto knew he
had.

The truck turned a corner and pulled into the circular
drive in front of another house. Roberto stopped three
houses away and turned to his brother once more. "You
must hurry, Santiago," he said. "As we have seen, this
man doesn't wait long for someone to answer."

Without speaking, Santiago reached over the backseat
and pulled a long object wrapped in a blanket into the front.

"No, Santy!" Roberto snapped, shaking his head in disgust. "Leave the machetes here. We don't want blood all
over the truck!" He reached over the backseat and pulled
a short aluminum Louisville slugger from the floor. "Take
the bat. Kill him if you must but don't leave any blood."

Santiago remained silent as he unwrapped the machetes
and tossed them back over the seat. He threw the blanket
around the Louisville slugger, and got out of the car. But
he had taken only a few steps when the LAPS man returned
to his truck with the clipboard.

Roberto sighed. "Get back in the car, Santy," he said

through the window. He watched the deliveryman glance their way as he boarded the truck once more.

Santiago got back in the Mercedes as the truck exited the opposite end of the circular drive and took off. Roberto gave it a block's head start before pulling way from the curb.

"Santy," he said. "We must carry out the plan on the very next stop. The driver is unconcerned now but he has noticed us. If we aren't successful this time, he will become suspicious." He turned to his brother. "Do you understand?"

This time, he got a barely perceptible nod.

"Perhaps we should trade places, Santy," Roberto said. "You're a much better driver than I am." When dealing with his brother, Roberto had found it never wise to insult him.

"As you like," Santiago said. For him, that many words was a full-length sermon.

The truck stopped once more two blocks ahead. Roberto took advantage of the fact to pull over and trade places with his brother. With Santiago now behind the wheel, they waited for the delivery man to start again, then followed. From the distance they were at, Roberto couldn't be certain but he thought he saw the man glance their way again.

"He is suspicious now," Roberto said. "We can't afford to park behind him again. Stay a block or so back. When you see him slow and begin to park, take the next turn and circle the block."

The LAPS truck left the neighborhood and cruised across a thoroughfare into another equally fashionable area. The Mercedes followed two blocks behind. Three turns later, the truck slowed in front of a house.

Santiago took the next right hand turn at slow speed, then floored the accelerator as soon as he was out of the truck's vision. Roberto, as usual, marveled at his brother's seeming contradictions. No, Santiago wasn't the most intelligent person walking the streets, but he had a remarkable animal cunning about him. When it came to his areas of interest, he could be a regular Einstein. When Roberto watched his brother set up a mark and finally make a kill, it was like watching a maestro at work.

The Mercede's tires squealed through a left-hand turn, then another as it circled the block. Without having to be told, Santiago slowed again just before the final turn that would bring them back to the street where the delivery truck was parked. The man in the blue uniform had gotten an answer at the door this time—a stroke of luck for them—and was still holding the package in his hands while a woman with curlers in her hair signed the clipboard in the open doorway.

Santiago slowed further as they neared the truck. Roberto had the passenger's door open and slid out, running a few steps forward to catch his balance as Santiago rolled down the block. As soon as he had his bearings, he dropped to his belly on the pavement and looked beneath the truck.

The woman was handing back the clipboard to the deliveryman and taking the package.

Roberto pulled himself to his feet and scrambled aboard the truck. Through the opening on the driver's side he saw the deliveryman beginning to turn back just as he squeezed between the seats to the cargo area. Finding himself surrounded by packages of every shape and size, he drew the curtain that separated the storage area from the cab and quickly looked around.

One of the things he saw brought a smile to his face: another stroke of luck. An extra blue LAPS shirt and pants hung from hooks on the wall.

The smile faded as Roberto realized suddenly he had forgotten the baseball bat. He cursed under his breath. The job could still be done, just not as swiftly or easily. His eyes shot around the cargo area for a makeshift bludgeon but he found nothing suitable. Drawing a large folding knife from his pocket, he gripped it in his fist but left the blade closed.

The driver was whistling as he returned to the truck. Roberto heard him climb on board. A second later, the curtain was thrown back and a hand reached in for the next package to be delivered.

The driver's mouth fell open in surprise as Roberto reached out and grabbed his extended wrist, jerking him off balance and into the rear of the vehicle. With his other hand, he brought the hilt of the closed folding knife down hard against the man's temple. The deliveryman's eyes closed as he tumbled to the floor of the cargo area, a bruise already spreading across the side of his face.

It took Roberto less than two minutes to change into the deliveryman's uniform. He pulled the truck away from the curb, and found Santiago waiting six blocks down the street. Santiago followed him to the parking lot of a supermarket, where he abandoned the Mercedes, climbed on board the truck and changed into the extra uniform.

Roberto had found a stack of LAPS address labels in the console next to the steering wheel and he pulled a ballpoint pen from the pocket of his uniform. As Santiago, now clad in identical blue, took a seat next to him, the witch-woman's oldest son clicked the end of the pen with his thumb and glanced down at the label. In the box marked Sender he neatly printed U.S. Department of Treasury. Where it read To, he wrote Mike Belasko.

Handing the label to his brother, Roberto Rodriguez threw the truck into gear and pulled away from the parking lot.

GENERAL AVIA PORTILLA, leader of the *Partido Revolucionario Marxista* walked slowly through the camp. In the last few days, his numbers had been cut by half. And of those who had survived the assault on *Los Pinos* and then the strike on the president's summerhouse in the north of Mexico, many now lay wounded across the grounds.

A mixture of sadness and pride filled Portilla as he thought of the brave revolutionaries who had died for the cause. Many he had known personally, others by sight. But as he strolled through the grounds, stopping now and then to hold a hand or say a brief word of encouragement to one of the wounded, even the faces he had never before seen brought a tear to his eye.

A large man, tall and brawny with short black hair lay on his back as Portilla approached. Blood had soaked through the outer bandages encircling both his chest and head, and none of the *Marxista* medical personnel had yet had time to change them. As Portilla neared, the big man stared up into his face and a faint smile curled the man's upper lip. He held out a blood-covered hand. "General," he whispered in a hoarse voice.

Before Portilla could take the hand, the man's body went suddenly ridged. His dark eyes widened in pain and surprise. Then his body went limp, his eyes glossed over and his hand fell to the ground.

A white-hot fury overtook Portilla as he looked down at the man who only seconds before had been alive. He was reminded of the man who had shot him. The American. Mike Belasko. A man Portilla swore he would kill, or die trying.

"General!" a voice called out behind Portilla. He turned to see his second-in-command, Colonel Francisco Paz, scurrying from the headquarters toward him. Paz carried his swagger stick, as always, and the irritating little affectation slapped against his thigh with every stride he took. In his other hand was a small spiral notebook.

Paz came to a halt and saluted, the notebook still in his hand. Then, looking down at it, he said, "General, we've had a call."

"From?"

Paz shook his head. "He wouldn't say. He was one of yours. He gave the number twenty-three."

Like many successful leaders, Portilla still kept his own personal informants who insisted on being known to no one else. They were assigned numbers for times when they were forced to deal with someone else. Like now. Portilla nodded his understanding and waited for Paz to continue.

"Number twenty-three wishes you to contact him," Paz said.

Portilla turned away and sighed. All of his informants would call within the next few hours asking questions about the incidents at *Los Pinos* and worrying that their identities had been compromised. They would have nothing to offer. "Did he leave a number?" he asked Paz, knowing the man wouldn't have done so.

"He said the usual number. He said you would have it."

"All right," Portilla said as he began to walk away. "I'll handle it later."

"He said it was important."

"It always is," Portilla said and kept walking.

"But General," Paz said, and something in his tone made Portilla stop and turn. "He said he had located *el presidente's* American bodyguard. At an insecure site away from *Los Pinos*."

Portilla broke into a jog, hurrying back across the grounds to his office. He picked up the phone, tapped in the number and waited for it to be answered.

"Hotel Diaz," a voice said. "May I help you?"

"Number twenty-three," Portilla said.

There was a short pause, then the voice lowered. "He's here, General," the voice finally said. "The American bodyguard. In room 223."

Portilla's fingers tightened around the receiver. "When did he check in?"

"This morning, I assume. Before I came on duty. He's registered under another name—a Mr. Michael Blanski. I would have suspected nothing except that he came rushing down the stairs earlier and ran out to the pool. That jogged my memory and I recognized him.''

''Why?'' Portilla demanded. ''Why did he run to the pool?''

''I don't know. But I recognized him and watched him. He seemed to be looking for someone or something there. He walked to a table where two men had been earlier, then came back inside.''

''Who were the two men?''

''I don't know.''

''Guests of the hotel?''

''Perhaps yes,'' said the desk clerk, ''perhaps no. No one checked them to see if they were registered. I didn't check them in, of that I am certain.''

Portilla paused. Why would the American have secured a hotel room when he was staying at *Los Pinos*? Because he must be up to something he didn't want the president knowing about. But what? ''Anything else?''

''Yes,'' said the clerk. ''He had visitors earlier. Also gringos, although one spoke with an English accent if I'm not mistaken. They went up to his room.''

''What did they look like?''

''Soldiers,'' said the clerk. ''Soldiers not in uniform but soldiers.''

''Has the American checked out yet?''

''No, and checkout time has come and gone. I assume he is keeping the room for at least one more night.''

Portilla let a smile creep over his face. ''You have done well,'' he said. ''Your loyalty to the cause will be rewarded.''

''Thank you,'' the clerk said. ''I'm a poor man and will gladly accept but it is enough to know I have served the—''

Portilla hung up in mid-sentence. Like most informants, twenty-three was a sniveling self-serving little snitch who would sell out to the highest bidder, and the *Marxista* leader had no desire to let the man's truckling words dampen the excitement that had come over him. Hurrying to the doorway, he saw Paz walking across the grounds. "Colonel!" he cried out. "Bring me your ten best men!"

"My ten best men are dead," Paz said.

"Then bring the ten best men you have, fool!" Portilla screamed. He turned back to his desk and sat in the chair to wait.

Portilla grinned ear to ear. Mike Belasko was at the Hotel Diaz. He thought no one knew, and therefore he wouldn't expect an attack, which meant the American bodyguard would die. And when Mike Belasko was gone, killing Don Juan de Fierro Blanco, president of Mexico, would be simple.

BOLAN CHECKED THE CRACK between the door and the frame and found the hair-thin piece of paper he had left there still in place. Sliding the card-key down through the lock, he waited for the green light to flash on, then pushed into the hotel room. It was as he had left it.

After a quick security check of the bathroom, closet, and beds, the soldier walked to the sliding glass door and looked down at the pool. Deserted. The drinks the two bearded men had left on the table had been taken away.

Bolan took a seat in one of the chairs at the table. He didn't expect the two men to return. Whatever they had been up to, their departure meant one of two things: They'd learned what they needed or they knew they'd been spotted. The full drinks left on the table led the soldier to suspect the former. In either case, they wouldn't return to the pool.

But they might return to the hotel under a different guise, Bolan knew. They might be watching right then, which initially inclined him toward meeting Able Team somewhere else. Even though he was sending Lyons, Schwarz and Blancanales to take care of the cartel murders along the border, it could all be connected, and he didn't want

the men of Able Team being identified later by someone
who saw them at the hotel. Besides, he had a short job for
them before they left Mexico City.

But there was always a chance he would spot the two
bearded men again. And if he did, they might be able to
throw some light onto the presidential assassination attempts, Fierro Blanco's honesty or dishonesty, or one of
the other many facets of this mission, which was growing
increasingly more complex as it went on. That was an opportunity he couldn't afford to ignore if it presented itself.

So he had contacted Able Team while they were still in
the air with Grimaldi and made other arrangements to in-
sure they weren't identified.

The knock on the door jolted Bolan from his thoughts.
Rising from the chair, he walked across the room and stared
through the peephole. A once-tall but now stooped gray-
haired man stood in the corridor leaning on a cane. He wore
white tennis slacks, a matching shirt and a panama hat.
Around his neck was a cheap instant camera, and an electric
blue fanny pack made of cheap plastic encircled his waist.

The soldier opened the door and stepped back.

The old man hobbled into the room and suddenly lost
several decades of age. He straightened to a full six-foot-
two in height, tossed the cane onto one of the beds and
ripped the hat and gray wig off his head to reveal short
blond hair. As he turned to face Bolan, the Executioner saw
the ice-blue eyes of Carl Lyons behind the makeup
wrinkles.

"Check the fridge then have a seat, Ironman," Bolan
said. He had heard other footsteps at the end of the hall as
the door closed and stayed there, waiting.

Lyons opened the small refrigerator, dug through the
contents and came up with a Dos Equis beer. He took it to
the table with him as another knock sounded.

This time, two people stood in the hallway. Another old
man, dressed in typical tourist fare as Lyons had been, and

an elderly woman in stretch slacks and a floral-print top. Her hair was in a bun and covered by a scarf. Bolan smiled. She had exceptionally large shoulders for a woman. He held open the door as Gadgets Schwarz and Politician Blancanales entered the room.

"Looks like you drew the short straw, Pol," the Executioner said.

Blancanales pulled the wig and scarf from his head and tossed them next to Lyons's wig and cane. "Nah, Striker, I *like* this kind of stuff," he said. "I've got a whole secret cross-dressing life you don't know about."

"Well, you make a pretty ugly woman, old friend."

"Careful," Blancanales said, holding up his handbag. "I'll hit you with my purse."

The two men found beers and took seats. Bolan grabbed a Coke and joined them. "I take it things worked out in Alaska?"

Lyons nodded. "Demitri and his gang are finished."

"But there's a thousand more Demitris ready to step in and take his place," Blancanales said.

"There always are," Schwarz said. "No matter what we do, they just keep coming."

"What we do," Bolan said, "is keep killing them."

The others all nodded.

"I want you guys to start in Los Angeles, Houston and Dallas," Bolan said, getting to the point. "Pick any of the cities where the cartel violence has broken out. Get some leads, follow them to the shooters and put an end to it."

Lyons nodded. "So why'd you call us all the way down here?" the ex-LAPD officer said. "You could have told us that over the phone." The former police detective took a swig of his beer.

"The LAPD has always been known for its tact and manners," Blancanales said with a straight face.

Lyons shot him a dirty look. "That hurts. Especially from a man wearing a dress."

Bolan chuckled. Lyons was a fine leader of men and Blancanales and Schwarz were fine men. But Blancanales was a born wisecracker, and Lyons hadn't come by the nickname "Ironman" because of his sense of humor. "Okay," the Executioner said. "Carl's got a legitimate question. First, I wanted to give you the rundown personally, give you an overall picture of the situation as it's developing." He then did so, explaining in detail the assassination attempts on Fierro Blanco, the drug-smuggling tunnel Phoenix Force had taken off to find, the *Marxistas* and the man with the ball-fringed hat, ending with the capture of movie star Ronnie Quartel. Included among the facts were his suspicions, intuitions and guesses.

"We heard about Quartel on the news in Alaska," Lyons said. "Tough luck. Although the guy makes a lousy cop when he plays them, if you ask me."

"You said you wanted to give us the rundown first, Striker," Schwarz said. "That implies there's a second reason you called us here instead of sending us directly into the cartel wars."

Bolan nodded. "I've got a quick surveillance job that needs handling before you leave town," he said. "I can't do it by myself—it'll take all of us." He cleared his throat and turned to Lyons. "What I need you to do, Ironman, is pick up—"

Before he could finish, the glass in the sliding door suddenly exploded.

A split second later, a hand grenade struck the table in front of the men, skidded onto the floor and rolled to a halt next to Bolan.

WITH DAVID MCCARTER behind the wheel, the ancient Ford pickup jolted down the blacktop road on what was left of its shock absorbers. Gary Manning sat against the door, his eyes glued to the sky, with Thomas Jackson Hawkins jammed between the two.

"Any sign of air traffic, Gary?" McCarter asked as they neared the hills.

Manning shook his head. "You'll be the first to know if there is," he said.

The ex-SAS commando pressed the accelerator to the floor again but it did little good. The Ford was a forty-five-mile-an-hour vehicle, top speed. He glanced at his wrist-watch. They still had close to an hour before the plane was scheduled to arrive. They could see the hills less than a mile in the distance but in addition to getting there, they still had to hide the truck, find the entrance to the old silver mine and get set up before the drug smugglers arrived.

Pulling the cellular phone from his shirt pocket, McCarter handed it to the Hawkins. "See if James has turned his phone back on, T.J.," he said. "Find out if they've secured the other end."

Hawkins tapped in the number, then switched the device to speakerphone so Manning and McCarter could listen. James answered on the first ring.

"What's your situation, Cal?"

"We've taken control on this side," James came back. "Got about two-hundred troops as backup hidden a couple of miles away."

"Just you and Encizo and...what's that other guy's name?" Hawkins asked.

"Nelson," James said. "Yeah. We're hiding out waiting for you to push them through. As soon as we hear from you that they've arrived, we'll call in the cavalry."

"What about the guards they had stationed over there?" Hawkins asked.

James cleared his throat. "I told the reinforcements to bring body bags," he said.

The Ford came to a curve in the blacktop and left the road for a sandy trail. "We're at the site," McCarter said, leaning over to speak into the phone. "Call you when they arrive. Then see you on the other side."

"I don't like the sound of that, David," James said. "See you on the other side?"

"The other side of the *tunnel*," McCarter chuckled. "Over and out."

Hawkins took the phone and stuffed it back into McCarter's pocket for him.

The Phoenix Force warrior had driven only a hundred yards on the sandy trail when he slowed the Ford to a stop. "There's no place to hide this thing," he said, surveying the flat terrain around the hills. "They'll see it from the plane. Even if they don't figure it out, they'll wonder about it and be on double alert. We can't give them that edge."

"We don't have time to take if far away and hoof it back," Manning said, looking at his wristwatch.

"No," McCarter agreed. "But I've got an idea." Cutting a U-turn, he bounced the pickup back to the blacktop, crossed the road and parked it on the other side.

McCarter, Manning and Hawkins jumped out. They grabbed their weapons and other equipment. "Find the spare tire, T.J.," McCarter ordered. Squatting next to the right front tire, he drew the Fairbairn-Sykes commando dagger from the sheath sewn to his shirt and jabbed the point into the rubber next to the rim. A low hiss escaped the tire as it flattened.

Hawkins appeared with the spare, set it on the blacktop next to the pickup and began rumbling through the bed of the truck. McCarter stabbed the new tire, then tossed it slightly to the side. Hawkins found the jack and dropped it on the ground to complete the illusion.

McCarter stepped back. It looked right. Anybody seeing the pickup—from the ground or the air—would see a disabled vehicle. If they inspected closer, it would appear that the truck had suffered a flat, the spare had been flat as well and the driver had abandoned the vehicle to get help. He rose and slid his arms into his backpack. Lifting the

M-16 by the sling, he said, "Let's go," and broke into a run.

The men of Phoenix Force covered the mile to the hills in a little over six minutes, slowing to a walk as they reached the first rise. "We don't know where the mine entrance is," McCarter said. "So I suppose out best course of action is to go directly to the valley and look for tracks. They shouldn't be that hard to find if this tunnel is in constant use." He led the way over several hills until they came to the valley they had seen from the air. Descending quickly, they headed for the end of the landing strip.

If he had entertained any doubts as to his theory about planes landing clandestinely with their drug shipments before, they were erased from McCarter's mind now. The tracks of airplane tires were clear in the sandy earth over which they trod. Near the end of the landing strip, the Phoenix Force leader spotted a footpath leading up into the hills. He had just started toward it when Hawkins grabbed his arm. "Listen!" the young warrior whispered.

McCarter and Manning both stopped. A few seconds later, they heard the whine of airplane engines far in the distance. "Double-time," McCarter ordered. He sprinted up the path. "You've got good ears, T.J.," he said over his shoulder.

"Hasn't had time to have too many rounds fired off in them yet," Manning grunted behind him.

The Briton led the way up the path until they came to a grove of short scraggly oaks. Turning, he waited for the other two men to catch up. The path led around the side of a hill, and they could be out of sight in a few seconds. It was time to slow their pace. And somebody needed to watch and see how many men would be coming.

"Gary, you and I will go around the corner," McCarter said, pointing the barrel of his M-16 at the hill. "T.J., find yourself a hiding place. Do a head count and pick up any other information that's useful. We'll wait for you."

"Can you see as well as you hear?" Manning grinned at Hawkins.

"Like a hawk," Hawkins said straight-faced.

Manning groaned in mock disgust and turned to Mc-Carter. "Jokes like that make me miss Katz."

McCarter laughed, did an about-face and started around the hill. Yakov Katzenelenbogen, the former Phoenix Force leader, had finally retired from active combat to take a job as an adviser at Stony Man Farm. McCarter had stepped into his role as leader, with Hawkins coming on board to fill the gap.

Two minutes later, the Phoenix Force leader heard the plane landing in the valley below. But five minutes after that, the sounds repeated.

McCarter frowned. Two planes? It must be a bloody big shipment they were bringing.

Shortly after the second plane had landed, Hawkins came hurrying around the side of the hill. The young warrior still had a set of binoculars clutched in his hands. He reached behind his head, unzipped the top opening of his backpack and dropped them into it as he spoke. "They brought two planes," he whispered.

"We heard," Manning said.

"That's the good news," Hawkins went on. "The bad news is, they're big planes. I quit counting at fifty men. All of them have AK-47s and side arms. They were transferring the dope from the planes to backpacks when I left."

McCarter nodded. The smugglers' preparations would take some time so there was no immediate emergency. He glanced at the sky, noting that they had maybe a half-hour of daylight left. It would be better to find the entrance to the tunnel and get set up before darkness fell. He dropped his eyes back to Hawkins. "Lag behind us a little, T.J. Keep an eye on the blokes from the front but don't take any chances of being seen." Turning to Manning, he said, "We'll go on. Lopez said there would be guards. And if

James and Encizo had to take out men on their side, they're bound to be at this end, too. Let's go.''

McCarter and Manning followed the path through the hills. The going wasn't easy, even for men in their top physical condition, and the Briton wondered why the cartel men had chosen it. The answer was obvious, and no different than the age-old dispute between management and labor. The men who had made the decision to use the hidden landing strip and tunnel wouldn't actually be the ones who had to haul the heavy loads to the mine entrance. To the top dogs of the cartel, at least, the extra effort of their laborers was justified by the security it provided.

That train of thought led McCarter to another—could he have made a mistake? Could they be following the wrong path, with the drug mules even now preparing to take another course behind them? The Phoenix Force leader shrugged aside the thought. If that were the case, there was nothing he could do about it now. But he didn't think they were on the wrong trail. It was well traveled, with fresh footprints, cigarette butts and other signs of human existence scattered around. But there was another, more important reason the former SAS man knew they were on the right track.

His gut instinct told him so.

The sun continued to fall as the Phoenix Force leader and his explosives expert moved on. Occasionally, they heard quiet sounds of movement behind them, telling them that Hawkins was following. The young warrior's movement was different than theirs, however. While McCarter and Manning plodded at a steady pace, Hawkins would be quiet for awhile, then the sounds of hurried scrambling would float up the trail. Hawkins was following orders, waiting and watching, then hurrying on before the men behind him got close enough to spot him.

The two men of Phoenix Force had started up a winding path to the hilltop when they suddenly stopped. McCarter closed his eyes, listening. What sounded like faint voices drifted down the trail from somewhere ahead, and as he listened, he thought he heard soft laughter. He turned, looking out in the direction of the blacktop road and breathed a sigh of relief. They were deep enough in the hills that the road, the pickup they had left there and their approach would have been unseen. Turning to Manning, he saw the big Canadian nod that he had come to the same conclusion. Without a word, they slowed their pace but moved on.

The voices became louder as they rose up the trail. Both men let their M-16s fall to the end of the slings. Slowly and quietly, Manning unzipped on his backpack. In the failing light, McCarter saw him pull out a Colt Woodsman Match Target .22 Long Rifle fitted with a long tubular sound suppressor. The former-SAS man chuckled. The long-out-of-production semiauto was still one of the most accurate target pistols, and the big Canadian had toted it ever since McCarter had known him.

The Phoenix Force leader wished for a moment that he had brought a sound-suppressed weapon himself. Silently, McCarter unsheathed the Fairbairn-Sykes knife.

Ahead, the Briton saw a brief flicker of light. A moment later, the odor of cigarette smoke drifted his way. He looked up at the rocks to his side, saw a narrow ledge, then nodded that way to Manning. The Canadian understood. Jamming the pistol into his belt, Manning reached with both hands and hauled himself onto the ledge.

McCarter walked on, making no effort to be quiet now. He held the Fairbairn-Sykes dagger at his side, concealed against his leg in an ice-pick grip. His foot kicked a loose rock across the pathway. The rock rolled off the trail and down the short embankment opposite.

The voiced ahead suddenly quieted.

A moment later, a voice called out, "Sanchez?"

McCarter didn't answer. He moved forward, watching Manning crawl along the ledge just above him. The big

Canadian was keeping up as best he could, but crawling was slower than walking, so McCarter decelerated his pace. A few seconds later, a man holding an AK-47 across his body stepped out from behind cover and stood spread-legged in the middle of the trail. He had started to call out again when a soft coughing sound came from just above McCarter's right shoulder.

The man fell to the ground.

McCarter ran forward as the second man stepped into view. Another sputter came from the ledge and the tunnel guard jerked but didn't go down. He twisted the assault rifle in his hands toward McCarter as another suppressed round sounded and he jerked again.

The Phoenix Force leader twirled the commando dagger in his hand, grasping its cold round grip and raising it over his shoulder. His arm flew forward as yet another quiet .22 round came from his side.

The bullet and knife struck the second tunnel guard almost at the same time. The Fairbairn-Sykes disappeared into the man's chest. McCarter didn't know where the .22 slugs had gone, or whether it had finally been the knife or bullets that killed the guard. Nor did he care. The man toppled to the trail on top of his partner.

Manning dropped back to the trail and joined McCarter as the Briton knelt over the bodies. "That's the trouble with .22s," he whispered. "You can make them quiet but you give up stopping power."

McCarter nodded. The first man had taken his lone round between the eyes. That had done the trick. But the second man had been moving when Manning shot, and the Canadian had been forced to aim for the larger chest target.

Dusk had fallen and night was coming by the time McCarter and Manning had dragged the bodies off the trail and dropped them into the shallow gorge below. It wasn't an ideal hiding place but it was the best they could do in the time they had. The Briton had to hope that nightfall would be complete by the time the men from the plane arrived at the site.

The two men had just rounded an outcropping in the rocks when they saw the entrance to the deserted silver mine. Rotting boards that had once been nailed over the opening had been torn away and discarded to the sides. The sandy dirt in front of the dark hole, like the trail itself, was packed hard by thousands of footsteps. McCarter's eyes skirted the area. The shallow gorge fell to the left of the path. The flat wall of rocks to the right made climbing into hiding impossible. Hurrying to the gorge, the Briton pulled an ASP laser flashlight from his pocket and thumbed the button on the end.

The bright light shone only for a moment. But it was enough. The gorge dropped fifteen feet through scraggly bushes. The Phoenix Force leader turned to Manning. "It's the only chance," he said. "Go, I'll wait for T.J."

Manning nodded, took a deep breath and jumped over the side. Dry twigs snapped as he plummeted through the vegetation and then a dull thud sounded as he hit bottom. McCarter flashed the ASP quickly once more and saw the Canadian give him the thumbs-up sign.

Thomas Jackson Hawkins came sprinting into view a moment later. McCarter made sure the young warrior saw him, then leapt over the cliff himself. He moved away from the spot where he'd landed just in time to prevent Hawkins from dropping onto his head.

"They're less than thirty seconds behind me," the young warrior breathed. "They're wondering what happened to the guards they had posted."

"The general consensus?" McCarter whispered.

Hawkins grinned in the faint light. "Got a split jury. Half of them think it's tequila and marijuana. The others are betting on women."

Footsteps sounded on the trail twenty feet above them. Close to the tunnel and convinced that the guards were derelict in their duties, the men were grumbling loudly about the weight of their loads. The three men from Stony Man Farm pressed their backs against the rocky side of the gorge, staying out of the beams of the flashlights that danced above the trail and occasionally spilled over the side and down into the shallow gorge.

The noises came and went. When the voices and footsteps had disappeared into the tunnel, Hawkins turned to McCarter. "They're gone, Chief," he said. "Are you ready to move out?"

McCarter didn't answer him. He pulled the cellular phone from his pocket, called James and miraculously got through, considering the interference of the hills. "They've gone into the tunnel," he told his fellow warrior.

The connection was bad, sounding more like a two-way radio almost out of range than a cellular phone. But McCarter made out James's words. "Understood, David," the Phoenix Force knife expert said. "We're ready. Don't take any chances."

McCarter hung up and replaced the phone. He turned to T. J. Hawkins, finally answering him. "Yes, I'm ready to move out," he said. "There's just one thing I didn't think of."

"What's that?"

McCarter's eyes moved up the fifteen-foot embankment to their side. "How do we get back up?"

carried by tight lines, the men were sprinting, following the headlights both Toshi Tanaka and Ardi Story
Vinh Peun bumped into _____ across the floor, a shot at the
large, shadowy cut of the figure of the flashlights that
rained across the a.d. _____ finally spilled a off the side,
ate down the _____

Bolan flew out of his chair and dived for the grenade, his
fingers clamping the handle and deactivating it once more.
He wondered briefly how long it had been held before being thrown through the glass door, but it really didn't matter. He had gotten to it in time, and like the old saying
went, they weren't playing horseshoes. Coming *close* to
killing him, Lyons, Schwarz and Blancanales didn't count.

As he rolled to a sitting position in the middle of the
floor, the grenade held up like an outfielder who has just
made a leaping catch to rob the batter of a home run, a
fusillade of rifle fire followed through the broken glass.

The men of Able Team didn't have to be told what to
do. Lyons drew his always-present .357 Magnum Colt Python and moved to the side of the door as Bolan rose.
Schwarz and Blancanales had ducked the gunfire and both
had drawn their 9 mm Beretta 92 pistols.

The big .44 Magnum Desert Eagle leapt into the Executioner's other hand as if on its own accord. Rifle rounds
continued to sail through the broken glass. He moved to
the edge of the sliding glass door opposite Lyons and
looked back into the room, seeing several rounds strike the
ceiling and leave holes in the plasterboard. From the angle
of trajectory, the assault had to be coming from the pool
area. He remembered looking down at the deserted chairs
and recliners only moments before.

"Hold your fire a second," Bolan shouted over the

chaos. Then bringing his hand back behind his ear, he lobbed the grenade over the balcony rail.

A splash sounded. A second later, a dull rumble came from below and water sprayed into the air like a geyser.

Bolan stepped onto the balcony as the water fell through the air. His feet crunched broken glass, and his body brushed sharp shards still clinging to the door frame and sent them shattering to the concrete floor. He ducked as he neared the balcony rail, the Eagle gripped ahead of him.

A good twenty yards away, five men stood around the swimming pool firing AK-47s up at the room. Bolan dropped his sights on the rifleman next to the diving board. The Desert Eagle roared in his hand and the head above the AK-47 seemed to split into two parts. The rifle clattered to the concrete and the man who had held it toppled into the pool. Crimson blood mixed with the blue water.

Bolan heard a roar next to him almost as loud as the Desert Eagle, and saw a man on the other side of the pool sprawl onto his face. The Executioner didn't have to turn to recognize the sound of Lyons's Python. The revolver was considered outdated to many soldiers in this day of high-capacity semiauto pistols but the ex-cop was living proof it could still get the job done. And the Able Team leader could restoke his wheel gun with speed loaders faster than the average gunman could change magazines.

Behind him, Bolan heard Blancanales and Schwarz trying to crowd onto the small balcony. "Stay where you are!" he shouted over his shoulder. "Watch the front door!" He swung the Desert Eagle toward a rifleman who had rested his weapon on the short wall between the pool and the hotel. The Executioner pulled the trigger once more and another big .44 Magnum round struck the man squarely in the chest. The 240-grain hollowpoint slug blew a hole the size of a quarter through the front of the man's shirt but grew to softball proportions by the time it exited his back, drawing blood, tissue and fragments of spine in its wake.

Behind him in the room, the Executioner heard the sound of the door being kicked in as the rear attack he had sensed would follow commenced. He heard a short burst of automatic fire answered by 9 mm explosions from Schwarz and Blancanales's Berettas.

Hearing another pair of Lyons's .357-caliber roars to his side, the Executioner saw a chubby man with a mustache fall into the pool. He turned toward the last man at the pool as the rifleman decided that prudence was the better part of valor. Turning toward a gate in the wall around the pool, the man dropped his AK-47 and sprinted away.

Bolan took a brief second to think. He wanted badly to know who the attackers were. Were they sent as a result of the recon the two men posing as divers had conducted earlier in the day? Were they *Marxistas* under the direction of the man in the ball-fringed hat? Or were they from some other group? He needed to know.

But he wouldn't find out from the man sprinting toward the gate. Before he could get to the ground, the man would escape.

Somewhat reluctantly, Bolan raised the Desert Eagle and fired. Another 240-grain semijacketed hollowpoint slug entered the running man's torso just under one arm and exited under the other. Without breaking stride, the runner smashed into the iron gate and rebounded to his back on the concrete.

Two bodies lay on the floor inside the hotel room, Bolan saw as he turned. Lyons had entered the fight in the room while the Executioner took care of the man trying to flee the pool, and the Python coughed in the Able Team leader's hand once more as he came into Bolan's vision. A head, two arms and a rifle that had just fired around the corner from the hallway exploded in a rainstorm of red.

Blancanales, who had taken cover behind the overturned

table, looked to Bolan and held up one finger, then pointed to the hall. Bolan took it to mean that at least one man remained outside the room.

Sirens sounded through the open glass, signaling that the police were on the way. The Executioner had no desire to explain his presence at the Hotel Diaz to President Fierro Blanco, which meant they had to shut down the threat and get out of there. Fast.

Schwarz was behind the bed, his Beretta resting on the mattress and aimed at the doorway. He, Blancanales and Lyons were all within whispering distance. "Wait until I give the signal, then fire high, over my head for cover," the Executioner whispered. "I'm going out."

An expression of concern came over the faces of all three Able Team warriors. But they had known Mack Bolan too long to argue. They nodded.

Bolan ejected the partially spent magazine from the butt of the Desert Eagle and inserted a fresh load. He walked slowly forward, the hole in the end of the big .44-caliber barrel aimed at the center of the doorway, ready. Ten feet from the hall, he raised his free hand over his head, then brought it down and dived forward.

The Executioner heard the fire from his rear as he shoulder-rolled through the opening and into the hall. Out of the corner of his eye he saw a lone man aiming a rifle his way. As the rounds from Able Team punctured the wall on the other side of the hall, the trigger finger of the man with the rifle jerked involuntarily.

A burst of 7.62 slugs sailed over the Executioner's head. Bolan rolled to a halt, twisted at the waist and angled the Desert Eagle upward. A lone round caught the rifleman just under the chin and snapped his head back as if he'd been caught by an uppercut from Evander Holyfield. But there was a big difference between a heavyweight's punch and this Magnum uppercut. As the man fell to the canvas, only half his head remained.

The Executioner walked back into the room as the sirens wailed louder below. Five men dead at the pool, three in the room and one in the hallway. Nine bodies altogether. That wouldn't be easy to explain.

He was about to order Able Team to load up and move out when he heard the faint sound outside on the balcony. Looking up quickly, he saw the man with the rapelling line drop onto the porch and fumble for his rifle.

The man's approach had been too little too late, and inept. The .44 Magnum round that blew him over the balcony rail seemed like an anticlimax to the battle that had just taken place.

Below, the wail of a siren announced the first car had arrived. Bolan took off down the hall with the men of Able Team behind him.

DAVID MCCARTER'S COMMENT as to how they would get out of the gorge had been meant as a joke. But it proved to contain at least an element of truth. Although only fifteen feet deep, the ground on which the men of Phoenix Force stood was a surface of crossed vines and leaves. It was bouncy enough to prevent their getting a good shove off the ground to jump but didn't have sufficient spring to help them upward. After a couple of vain leaps on the part of the former-SAS man, Manning squatted against the wall of rock.

McCarter climbed onto the big Canadian's shoulders, balanced precariously as Manning stood to his feet, then leapt up and pulled himself back onto the trail. He reached down, helping Hawkins up off Manning, then the two of them reached down for the explosives man. Manning's upstretched hand was a good three feet below reach.

"Guess we'll have to leave you, Gary," Hawkins grinned.

"Got a deck of cards?" Manning asked with a straight face.

McCarter unclipped the nylon sling from his M-16, adjusted it to full length and dropped it. Then both men pulled the Canadian back up to the trail.

"Keep your voices low," McCarter warned. "Sound will carry in there. And be very careful with the flashlights—no lasers—just the red photons and then only when you have to." He reached into a pocket, produced a tiny diamond-shaped plastic object, and pushed the button on the side with his thumb. A red beam shot out a few feet but, unlike yellow lights that gradually fade away, it seemed to halt abruptly. Killing the light, he said, "T.J., you and I will go on." He glanced at Manning's backpack. "Gary, do that thing you do so well."

"You've got it," Manning said and unzipped his pack.

McCarter led the way into the tunnel, ducking under aged wooden beams and following the sparse moonlight that drifted in from outside until it had played out. He could hear Hawkins's quiet breathing and footsteps just behind him. Ahead, the sounds made by the drug smugglers were louder; those men saw no reason to conceal their sounds.

Good, McCarter thought. He didn't want to risk even the red Photon lights unless there was an emergency. That meant they would have only the voices and footsteps to lead them. Even if they could get close enough to trail the drug men's own flashlights, it was doubtful that the tunnel would be a straight line—there would be times when they would find themselves behind twists and turns in the darkness. And McCarter didn't want to accidentally lead his men down a side route within the deserted silver mine.

The Phoenix Force leader kept one hand against the side of the tunnel, letting his finger run lightly along the rocky wall. He quickened his pace slightly, trying to maintain as much speed as possible without sacrificing silence. After a few minutes, he thought he heard the faint steps of Manning trying to catch up. He couldn't be sure, which was encouraging. If he couldn't be certain there was someone coming up behind him when he knew Manning would be doing just that, it was unlikely that the men ahead would hear them.

Feeling the wall begin to curve, McCarter followed its contour. He felt his steps angling downward as they left the silver mine and entered the newer part of the tunnel extended by the drug men. Suddenly, the dancing beams of flashlights appeared a hundred yards in the distance. He led Hawkins quietly on. By his estimation, the tunnel had to be at least a mile to a mile and a half in length to reach the border. Add to that however long it extended into the U.S. His guess was it wouldn't be much—the cartel smugglers wouldn't have wanted to dig any farther than necessary.

McCarter considered dropping back and trying to contact James on the cellular phone but discarded the idea. There was always the risk that the drug smugglers would hear his voice. And the phone wasn't likely to work underground anyway. Besides, James knew they were coming.

The men of Phoenix Force moved on. The men they pursued rounded another curve ahead and their lights disappeared again. McCarter was forced to slow in the pitch blackness of the underground. The voices ahead began to diminish. He stopped, holding out an arm to halt Hawkins as well. Behind him, he could hear the sounds of Manning's footsteps more clearly now. They waited until the Canadian caught up.

Tapping the button on the tiny Photon flashlight, McCarter briefly illuminated Manning with the red glow. He moved in next to the man and killed the light again. "You set?" he asked.

"Yeah," Manning whispered back. "I was worried that the electronic pulse wouldn't bend around the turns. So I set relays along the way. That's what took so long."

"Okay. If it looks like they plan to retreat, hit the button.

Use your own discretion," McCarter said, then turned and started down the shaft again.

Another turn brought them up to the flashlights again. Five minutes later, McCarter thought he saw light ahead of the men but after being so long underground he couldn't be sure his eyes weren't playing tricks on him. Similar to dying men in the desert spotting mirages of water, sustained darkness could sometimes fool the eye into thinking it saw light.

But a few minutes later, the flashlights ahead began to switch off. Now the moonlight drifted into the tunnel, silhouetting the drug mules ahead. McCarter slowed his pace. "Get ready," he said. "We need at least one of them left alive for questioning, and James knows that. He'll issue a warning before shooting."

"They won't pay any attention to it."

"Probably not. But there's always the chance."

No sooner had the words escaped his lips than Calvin James's voice echoed into the tunnel. "Freeze!" the unseen Phoenix Force warrior yelled. "Federal agents!"

For a moment, the men ahead obeyed, stopping in their tracks.

Then all hell broke loose at the end of the tunnel.

The first rounds were directed out of the tunnel at the unseen voice. But some of the return fire from the task force blew into the shaft. Several men dropped where they stood. Others moved back into the tunnel, while a few sprinted out, hoping to take cover out of sight.

McCarter, Hawkins and Manning stayed well back. Only a few of the bullets flying into the tunnel made their way to them, and those that did, had expended their energy as they ricocheted along the walls.

The battle at the mouth of the tunnel raged for a few minutes, then a sudden burst of gunfire seemed to occur directly in front of the exit. A moment later, the drug runners who had stayed in the tunnel suddenly spun in their tracks and ran toward the Phoenix Force warriors.

"Time to let them know we're here," McCarter said. He aimed his M-16 down the shaft and held down the trigger. Hawkins and Manning did the same.

Automatic fire filled the tunnel. Empty brass casings flew from the rifles' ejection ports, illuminated by the glow of the muzzle blasts. A few of the men running toward them fell to the ground. The others ground to a halt and fired ahead of them, their rounds whizzing past the men of Phoenix Force and deeper into the tunnel. McCarter heard a groan from one of his men, and then the sound of a body falling next to him. "Move back! Take cover!" he shouted over the gunfire. He dropped his rifle to the end of the sling and reached down, grabbing the man next to him and hauling him back down the tunnel.

The men of Phoenix Force retreated around the first curve. McCarter pulled the red photon light from his pocket and shone it on Thomas Jackson Hawkins. The young warrior looked more embarrassed than hurt. "Knocked my feet out from under me, I guess," he said. His shoulder and chest glowed red in the light.

"Gary, keep them busy!" the Phoenix Force leader ordered.

Manning moved up to the edge of the rock and began firing sporadic bursts down the shaft. McCarter examined Hawkins's wound. It was nasty and bleeding but no bones had been hit or nerve centers shattered. "Can you move your arm?" McCarter asked.

Hawkins tried. "Barely," he said.

McCarter slid the sling of the man's rifle over his head and added it to his own shoulders. "Switch to your pistol," he said. Jerking a bandanna from his pack, he pressed it against the wound and said, "Hold it there. Hard."

Manning continued to fire down the tunnel. "They've stopped halfway between us and the end," he said. "I may be scaring the hell out of them, but they're too many. Their return fire keeps forcing me back before I can get an aimed shot.''

McCarter looked into the darkness from which they'd come. As outnumbered as they were, there was a chance that the drug smugglers would get past them and back into Mexico. If that happened, both the men and drugs would disappear and cross the border somewhere else.

They couldn't afford to let that happen.

''Close them off, Gary.''

McCarter stepped up and took Manning's place, firing down the tunnel. He ran his magazine dry but rather than take the time to reload he switched to Hawkins's M-16. He could see Manning in the light coming from the almost constant muzzle-flashes, and watched as the big Canadian pulled the remote-control device from his pack and punched a series of buttons.

Roughly a mile and a half behind them, a rumble sounded. The hill shook gently around the tunnel as if they were on the edge of an earthquake.

''How much C-4 did you use?'' McCarter asked, letting up on the trigger.

''Enough,'' Manning said. He moved in at McCarter's side and fired his own burst down the shaft. ''The entrance to the mine might as well never have been there.''

A laugh that sounded more like a growl came from Hawkins in the darkness. ''Well then,'' he said in his slow Texan drawl. ''I guess you might say the bad guys are literally between a rock and a hard place, then.''

McCarter fired another burst down the tunnel. ''You might say that, mate,'' the Phoenix Force leader said. ''But so are we.''

CALVIN JAMES PULLED a black bandanna from the front pocket of his BDU shirt and wiped the sweat from his forehead. The temperature in the desert along the Mexican border usually dropped after the sun went down. Tonight, it seemed to have gotten hotter instead. He started to jam the bandanna back into his pocket, then realized it was the third time he had pulled it out in the past five minutes. Resting the M-16 in his hand against the large boulder in front of him, he rolled the rag into a sweat band and wrapped it around his forehead.

As he tied the knot at the back of his head, James stared through the darkness. Ten feet away, he could see Pug Nelson behind another boulder. The former U.S. Navy SEAL-turned-DEA agent wore Administration-issue cammies and carried his own assault weapon—the 9 mm Colt carbine version of the M-16.

James lifted his rifle again and slid his arm into the sling. The weapon fell from his shoulder, barrel forward, in assault mode. He settled in to continue the wait for the men who would soon be bringing heroin or cocaine or both through the tunnel from Mexico.

For James, like most warriors, the waiting was the hardest part of any mission. Waiting gave someone too much time to think. Thinking in itself wasn't bad, of course. But eventually he ran out of legitimate things to think about and his mind began to second-guess all earlier decisions. So the wise warrior-planner did his best to keep his mind occupied with other things.

The Phoenix Force warrior stared down through the moonlight at the black tunnel exit in front of him. Whoever had planned the tunnel had done well, surveying the terrain on this side of the border and instructing the diggers to bring it up into another hill on the U.S. side. The opening was partially hidden by large boulders, dry shrubs and even a few scraggly dwarf trees that grew through the sandy dirt and rocks. Unless someone knew exactly where it was, and looked specifically for it, it couldn't be seen. From the air, especially, it would be invisible.

James glanced down at the luminous hands of his wristwatch. He had spoken to McCarter a half-hour earlier, right after the drug mules had entered the tunnel. The enemy was on the way. Battle was coming.

Calvin James unbuckled the leather case of the night vision scope hanging around his neck and pulled out the instrument. He had called in the two-hundred backup troops, and a quick survey of the rugged land around him showed glimpses of the men. There were far too many of them to all find hiding places in the rocks. But that made no difference anymore. He, Encizo and Nelson had taken out the guards as soon as they'd arrived. Even if they had missed some cartel man on this side, he wouldn't have any better contact with the mules in the tunnel than Phoenix Force had between their two parties. Cellular phones and radio were blocked by the rock and sand.

Aiming the night-vision scope directly at the mouth of the tunnel, James saw the black hole. He raised the instrument slightly. Rafael Encizo sat on the ledge just above the dark exit, looking down. For perhaps the thousandth time James wondered if he's been wise to allow his friend and fellow warrior to take that position. True, it offered a vantage point from which Encizo could shoot directly down at any of the smugglers who came out of the tunnel and took cover behind the surrounding boulders. But it also placed him dangerously close to the line of fire from the DEA-Army task force troopers. James shook his head uncertainly in the darkness. Had it been McCarter, Manning and Hawkins with him there in the hills, Encizo's position wouldn't have concerned him. The men of Phoenix Force all shot at the distinguished master level, but even more important than that, they didn't panic under fire. In fact, a recent test run by John "Cowboy" Kissinger, Stony Man Farm's armorer, had involved equipping each team member with a portable heart-rate monitor to be worn in battle. The monitor—a small computer, much like those that bicyclists used—had recorded the men's heart rate throughout the battle. None had risen over five percent, and Encizo's had actually gone down, as if being shot at somehow relaxed him.

But the men around James now weren't Phoenix Force warriors. They weren't even elite soldiers. Could they be trusted to keep their cool, or would Encizo fall victim to the erroneously named "friendly fire?"

Seconds became minutes, and then the minutes became another half-hour. Finally, the silence was broken and James heard voices again. But this time the sounds came from inside the tunnel. As he and the others waited, the voices grew louder. Finally, when he saw the first shadowy head stick out into the moonlight, Calvin James rose. The fingers of his right hand curled around the M-16's pistol grip while his left drew an eight-cell flashlight from the carrier on his web belt. Activating the flashlight's beam, he shone it into the drug smuggler's face.

"Freeze!" James shouted at the top of his lungs. "Federal agents!"

For a moment, the Phoenix Force warrior thought the drug mules might actually comply. Then the crack of 7.62 caliber rifle rounds broke through the night and the entrance to the tunnel lit up with muzzle-flashes.

James kept the flashlight angled down at the tunnel as he aimed his rifle one-handed into the beam. He pulled the trigger, and the M-16 danced in his hands. The man shooting the AK-47 became his partner in the dance, jerking in cadence to each successive round that struck him as if he and James were engaged in some macabre ballet of death.

Other men had stepped out of the mouth of the cave, and they now sighted on James's muzzle-flash. The return fire forced the Phoenix Force warrior back behind the cover of the boulder as rounds from Nelson and the other task force men began to explode in the night. The hills of the southern Arizona desert lit up.

James moved back to the edge of the boulder and saw

that several of the men had exited the mouth of the cave and taken cover behind rocks in front of it. He glanced over their heads and saw Encizo moving quietly along the ledge above them, trying to get into position to take them out.

The task force troopers continued to fire, occasional rounds flying high and striking the rocks near Encizo. James cursed under his breath. The Cuban could take a wild round from one of his own at any moment. But to watch him moving smoothly along the rocks, he didn't even appear to know he was in danger.

James leaned around the boulder and fired a full-auto burst at the rocks in front of the men, more to keep them back than with any hope of hitting them. He watched a round strike the rocks behind Encizo, two feet away from the Cuban's head. Dust and sand blew from the ricochet but Encizo crept on.

James's temper flared, and he fought the urge to shout a reprimand into the mike in front of his face. But a warning to the other task force members to watch their fire might also alert the drug runners to the man creeping into post above their heads. Instead, he continued to pull the trigger of the M-16 as he watched Encizo move. He knew what his fellow warrior was up to. Encizo had to get into a position from which he could quickly dispatch all of the men in the rocks below. As soon as he began firing, the drug mules would know there was someone above and behind them. They would turn and return fire, and Encizo would be fully exposed. He had to take them all out in one long burst, and he would have only seconds to do it.

James grimaced at his partner's predicament. But there was nothing he, Nelson or the other men of the task force could do to help him. The drug mules were still behind the boulders and out of sight

It could have been only seconds but to James it seemed like hours before Encizo finally halted on the ridge above the tunnel opening. As if in slow motion, the Cuban raised the stock of the M-16 to his shoulder and tipped the barrel downward. A second later, flame burst from the assault rifle as Encizo held down the trigger and swept the barrel back and forth at the rocks below. When the magazine ran dry, the desert suddenly fell into silence.

All of the men outside the tunnel lay dead on the desert floor. But there were others inside—James could hear their muffled voices. How many, he didn't know. But as he listened, he suddenly heard gunfire erupt again—this time, from somewhere deep inside the tunnel. There was a pause, then more explosions, stifled by the rock, drifted out of the mouth of the tunnel.

James knew what had happened. McCarter, Manning and Hawkins had followed the drug mules through the underground pathway. When the men still inside decided to retreat, they had opened fire. The drug runners had answered back. He had barely worked out the chain of events in his mind when another sudden explosion—this one dull and different and far away—came rumbling through the night. The earth vibrated around him for a second or two, then stopped.

James nodded to himself in the darkness. Manning. The explosives expert would have set a device at the other end of the tunnel, just in case the drug runners tried to escape that way. The problem was that closing off the Mexican exit also trapped James's three fellow warriors underground as well.

Shoving a fresh magazine into the M-16, Calvin James rose from behind the boulder and made his way down through the rocks toward the dark opening before him. "Nelson!" he whispered urgently into the microphone in front of his lips. "Pick two dozen men to go inside with us. Tell the others to move forward and cover the entrance."

Reaching the opening to the tunnel, James took up a position just to the side and pressed his back against the rocks. The fact that McCarter, Manning and Hawkins were underground had prevented the use of their radios and cellular phones until now. But with the Phoenix Force men close he might be able to raise them.

As the boots of the men Nelson had picked came clomping and sliding down the embankment to join him, James pulled out his cellular phone and punched in several numbers. The line rang but no one answered. Killing the instrument, he turned it on again. This time he held out the phone in front of the tunnel entrance. The rock was blocking the airwaves. He didn't know exactly where his fellow warriors were inside the tunnel, but if it was a fairly straight shot they might pick up his transmission. He never found out.

As he tapped the last digit into the face of the phone, the instrument exploded in his hand. Jerking his arm back behind the rock as more rounds sailed out from inside the tunnel, he looked down at his fingers. They felt as if a hundred wasps had attacked his palm but he saw no blood. The bullet had struck the phone, not his hand, and no permanent damage had been done.

A moment later, Nelson and the twenty-four men he had chosen stood around James. "We're going in," the Phoenix Force warrior said.

"Why?" asked one of the men, a private. He looked frightened. "They can't go anywhere. We heard the explosion. They'll have to come out sooner or later on their own."

"We can't wait until later," James said irritably. "I've got friends trapped inside."

"That's no reason to—"

James was fighting the urge to slap the coward when Nelson did it for him. "Get your stinking cowardly ass out of my sight!" the former SEAL shouted into the man's reddening face. Shoving the private toward the hillside, he turned to James. "You want him replaced?"

James shook his head. "We've got enough," he said. "But I want to say one thing first." He addressed the remaining soldiers. "There's a good chance that one, or more, or *all* of us are going to die in the next few minutes. Anybody else want out?"

No one answered.

James turned and led the way to the edge of the tunnel entrance. He couldn't help but smile. The men he was about to lead into battle weren't highly trained elite warriors like Phoenix Force or Able Team but they were brave men just the same. They were willing to fight, and even die, if that's what it took.

Bolan glanced through the balcony door of his sleeping quarters at *Los Pinos*. Beyond the courtyard, the sun was dropping beneath the horizon. Shifting in his chair, he turned his attention back to the chart on the table. Earlier in the day he had drawn it from memory, and now he studied it once again. Did it mean anything? He didn't know.

The chart plotted, as best he could remember, the dates and exact times of President Don Juan de Fierro Blanco's unexplained disappearances from Bolan and the other members of his protection unit. The soldier had begun to see a rough pattern in the president's truancy. Seeing it on paper reinforced that pattern in his mind. And while the pattern didn't guarantee that the man would vanish from sight again this night, it certainly indicated that he might.

Since Bolan's arrival, the Mexican president had vanished for a few hours without explanation every other day Like clockwork. That pattern had been broken by their forced evacuation of the presidential residence after the riot. But it had resumed immediately upon their return. In fact, before the family was even resettled after their time at the summerhouse, Fierro Blanco was gone again.

Sometimes the president disappeared during the daylight hours. Other times at night. In any case, if the chart meant anything, he was due to fade from sight without explanation again soon. He'd been around all morning and afternoon.

Again, the Executioner glanced through the window as

the shadows of night fell over Mexico City. He heard a cat
hiss loudly, and stood, crossing to look down the iron steps
leading to the courtyard to see the first lady's felines about
to engage in combat. As he watched, the Siamese took a
swipe with his claws that barely missed the Persian.

Bolan returned to the table and picked up the chart. If
Fierro Blanco stuck to the pattern, and was about to disappear again, it would have to be soon. The day was almost
over. Where did the man go and what did he do? And with
so many attempts being made on his life, why did he not
take Bolan or other guards? The answer to the last question
was easy in a general way, difficult in specifics. Obviously,
the president was doing something of which he didn't want
the soldier to be aware and he considered it important
enough to risk his life to get it done. But exactly what it
was remained a mystery.

Walking to the bed with the paper in his hand, Bolan
sat. He studied the chart again. There was another aspect
to the president's disappearances it didn't reflect, and pulling a pen from his shirt pocket he wrote *Antonio de Razon,
general* next to the chart.

A loud knock sounded at his door. The soldier rose from
the bed, stuffed the chart underneath the pillow, then
walked to the door and swung it open. A man wearing a
white jacket—a member of the *Los Pinos* kitchen staff he
had seen several times—stood in the hallway holding a
tray. White linen covered the top, and on it sat a wine bottle
and one stemmed crystal glass.

"*El Presidente* requested that I bring this to you personally," he beamed. "He asks me to tell you that he can
never repay you for all you have done. But this is a small
token—symbolic of the deep gratitude he feels in his
heart." The man took a deep breath, happy that his mem-
orized words were out of the way. "Do you have a cork-
screw, Señor Belasko?"

Bolan shook his head.

The man fished one out of his white jacket and set it on the tray next to the glass.

Bolan reached into his pocket and pulled out a five-dollar bill.

The eyes of the man in the white jacket sparkled momentarily then dulled. "No," he said. "Thank you but I can't accept it. You're a guest of *Los Pinos*." He turned on his heel and walked away.

Bolan shut the door. He set the tray on the nightstand next to the bed, pulled the chart back out and sat on the bedspread. He glanced at the label on the bottle—an expensive Beaujolais. One glass wouldn't hurt.

Popping the cork, the soldier poured a small amount of the dry red wine into the glass and took a sip as he continued to study the chart. Five minutes later, he drained the last of the wine from the glass, set it on the table and lay back on the bed.

Bolan closed his eyes. Razon was a frequent visitor to *Los Pinos*, as befitted any nation's top military advisor. But the fat general had *always* been there just before and during Fierro Blanco's mysterious absences. That hardly seemed a likely coincidence. It was Razon who was always ready with his oily smile for Bolan, who told him not to worry, the president was all right. What, exactly, did that mean? Again, Bolan didn't know. It might mean that Fierro Blanco was conferring with members of the terrorist groups, drug cartels or other mobsters. It might mean he was setting up the murders of more opposition candidates and journalists as he had been accused of doing in the past. Or it might mean something else—something Bolan had no way of guessing. But whatever it was, General Antonio de Razon was in on it. Of that, the Executioner had no doubt.

Bolan opened his eyes. Razon had returned to the mansion an hour ago. He was in conference with the president right now. Everything pointed toward Fierro Blanco pulling his Houdini act again, and soon.

The cellular phone on the table next to the bed vibrated suddenly. Bolan lifted it, checked to make sure the connection between the phone and scrambling device was secure, then answered. "Yeah, Carl?"

"Subject just left the back gate in a green late-model sedan," Able Team's leader said. "He's alone—driving himself."

The soldier felt his eyebrows lower. "You're sure it's him?" he asked.

"No mistake, Striker. He's wearing a hat and sunglasses—looked like a wig beneath the hat. Not much of a disguise, if you ask me. The car has tinted windows. I guess he thinks they'll keep him hidden...wherever he's going."

"Okay," Bolan said. "Are Gadgets and Pol set to pick him up?"

Lyons cleared his throat. "They're on the side streets. I'm about two blocks behind. We'll switch around enough that he doesn't get a make on any of us." There was a pause. "Are you coming?"

"In a few minutes," the soldier answered. "I want to give Razon enough time to think his buddy is way beyond my reach."

"Understood," Lyons said. "We'll switch to radio contact once you're in your vehicle. I've got you a two-year-old Chevy, light blue. It's parked a block and a half east. I stuck the walkie-talkie under the front seat."

"Got it," Bolan said. He hung up. After the problems he'd had with so many of the federal bodyguards, it was nice to be working with the best again. He had instructed Lyons to rent four nondescript vehicles earlier in the day and provide radio contact to go with the cellular phones. It had been done almost before the Executioner ordered it. If he'd made the same request of the guards, they'd still arguing over the color of the cars.

Bolan rolled off the bed and glanced at his watch. He'd give Fierro Blanco another ten minutes head start to relieve

Razon of any suspicions, then take off. If the president reached his destination before that, the men of Able Team would have him in sight.

Sliding into a pair of black Levi's jeans and a matching T-shirt, the Executioner strapped the Desert Eagle onto his side and slipped his arm into the Beretta's shoulder holster. Extra magazines for the Beretta and the Applegate-Fairbairn knife all hung in leather under his opposite arm, doing their best but not quite balancing out the heavy 9 mm pistol. He slid a six-pack magazine carrier onto his belt with extra loads for the .44 magnum, and then covered the arsenal with a lightweight black sport jacket.

A moment later he was in the hall and locking the door behind him.

Bolan walked quietly toward the elevators, hearing footsteps around the corner. He had just pressed the down button when Razon's bulk lumbered around the corner. As always, the general wore his dress uniform and seemingly every medal known to man. The overhead lights glistened brightly off the gold and silver on his chest, and Bolan wondered dryly if even his heavy 240-grain .44 magnum rounds could penetrate all that steel. He nodded to the general.

Razon nodded back but didn't speak.

"*El presidente* is in need of nothing, I assume?" the soldier asked as they waited for the elevator.

Razon hesitated, then said, "He's resting. I don't believe he will require your services for the rest of the evening."

Bolan chuckled good-naturedly as the elevator door opened. "Good," he said. "I think I'll go for a walk, maybe have a beer." He stepped back and let Razon onto the elevator first, then got on and pushed the button for the ground floor. He stared straight ahead, listening to the music piped into the car—another in what appeared to be a never-ending line of Margarita Felice songs. As he listened, he watched the general in his peripheral vision. The man believed Bolan had bought his story about the president.

On the ground floor, the two men went their separate ways. The Executioner left the mansion, waved at the gate guards as he exited and turned onto the sidewalk. He quickened his pace when he spotted the Chevy. A minute later, he was starting the engine and pulling the walkie-talkie from under the seat.

"Stony Man One to Able One," Bolan said into the radio.

"Able One here," Carl Lyons came back.

"What's your 10-20, Ironman?" the Executioner asked as he pulled the Chevy away from the curb.

"Just followed our man onto Insurgentes Centro. I've had to drop back so he wouldn't spot me. Pol is tailing him while he's on the expressway, with Gadgets somewhere in between."

"It'll take me a good fifteen minutes to get there."

"Not if you drive the way I've seen you," Blancanales's voice came over the air.

"You've got visual on him, Pol?" Bolan asked as he turned the corner and headed for the expressway.

"That's affirmative," Blancanales said. "He's keeping about five under the speed limit. I don't know why. I can't see any cops giving their president a ticket."

"That's not it," Bolan said. "Wherever he's going he doesn't want to be spotted."

"Okay," Blancanales said. Bolan could hear the rush of wind in the background as Able Team's psychological warfare expert sped down the highway. "He's slowing. It looks like he's going to take the exit at Paseo de la Reforma. Gadgets, do you want to take over for me?"

"I'm flooring it now," Schwarz said over the airwaves.

Bolan smiled. As an LAPD detective, Carl Lyons had had plenty of practice tailing subjects, and he had passed on his expertise to his fellow Able Team warriors. Blancanales, who had stayed directly behind Fierro Blanco, would pass the Reforma exit so as not to draw suspicion. Schwarz would move forward to take his place with Lyons behind him. Blancanales could take the next exit, then cut back and rejoin the surveillance team by taking radio cues from the other two men of Able Team. Vehicular rotations of this sort would continue at any other points where Fierro Blanco might spot a tail, and by the time Blancanales's turn to follow came again he wasn't likely to be remembered.

The Executioner continued to drive through the streets of Mexico City, hurrying as fast as he could toward the expressway. He was in a similar situation as Fierro Blanco himself—a speeding ticket was no big deal but he couldn't afford the time it would take. Since his arrival in Mexico he had been trying to find out if President Don Juan de Fierro Blanco was honest or dishonest. His efforts had not only been thwarted at every turn, each attempt had seemed to open a whole new can of worms making the answer increasingly cloudy.

But now he was at least going to find out where Fierro Blanco went during his disappearances. Would that knowledge answer his primary question? Or like his searches of the presidential office and residence, would it only confuse the issue further?

Bolan hit the expressway and floored the accelerator, cutting in and out of the evening traffic. "Stony Man One to Able Team," he said into the walkie-talkie. "What's your 10-20 now, guys?"

"He's cut under the expressway," Schwarz said. "It looks like he's getting ready to get back on and head back the way he came."

"He's trying to spot a tail then," Lyons said. "Gadgets, make a right and drive out of his sight. I'll pull up and take over."

Bolan slowed. If Fierro Blanco was heading back that way the best thing he could do was take the next exit, cross to the opposite ramp and pick up the man when he came by.

Bolan hit the brakes and slowed as he followed a Mercedes down the exit ramp. "Keep him close, Ironman. But not too close. I'm going to find a place to park and wait near the access ramp. Let me know if he turns off again. If he doesn't, warn me. I'll get on, let him pass me and you can fall back again."

"Understood," the former LAPD cop said.

The Executioner left the expressway, made a left-hand turn under the overpass and saw a gas station a hundred yards from the access ramp on the other side. There was only one car at the pumps, and it drove away as Bolan entered the lot. Slowing, he cut a U-turn back toward the expressway, threw the transmission into park and left the motor running. In the rearview mirror he saw a tall dark-skinned man come out of the office building holding a red oil rag. The man shouted something indiscernible at the Chevy.

Bolan ignored him.

The man stood where he was for a few seconds, then started toward the parked car.

As he neared, the soldier saw that he wore oil-stained khaki trousers and a matching shirt. His long gray hair was tied back in a ponytail, and his face reflected Indian blood. "If you're not a customer you're trespassing," the man said in an angry voice as he reached the driver's window.

Bolan tapped the button to roll down the glass. "I'm waiting for a friend," he said. "I won't be long, and I'll stay out of the way of your customers."

"No, you will leave immediately!"

Bolan glanced to the expressway. It would be a matter of minutes before Fierro Blanco returned to this point, and there was no other place to park where he could watch the expressway. He reached into his pocket and pulled out a roll of bills. Peeling off a twenty, he stuck it out the window. "Here's my parking fee," he said.

The tall service station attendant slapped away the Executioner's hand. "I don't want your money, gringo!" he shouted. "If you don't leave immediately I will call the cops."

The Executioner stuck the money back into his pocket and let out a low sigh. He doubted that the police would arrive before he left again, but he couldn't be sure. And he couldn't afford any delay. "Would it help if I paid you more?" he asked the man, knowing the answer.

"You gringo pigs are all alike," the attendant said. "You think you can buy anything you want in this country—even the people."

"That's what I was afraid you'd say," Bolan said. He reached across the Chevy and unlocked the passenger's door. Then drawing the Desert Eagle from his hip, he aimed it through the window at the surly man. "Get in," he said. "We need to have a little talk about your attitude."

The man's eyes widened in surprise. "I'm sorry," he said quickly. "You aren't in the way. Please stay." He started to turn away from the car.

"I told you to get in."

The man froze. He looked away from the car as he spoke, "Don't worry, señor," he said. "I won't call the authorities." He started to walk off again.

"Want a bullet in the center of your spine?"

The man froze again, and turned slowly.

"I told you to get in." Bolan indicated the passenger's side with the Desert Eagle.

The attendant walked around the car and opened the door with a trembling hand.

"I'm very sorry," he said. "I didn't mean to—"

"Just sit where you are, keep your hands in plain sight and your mouth shut," the Executioner said.

No sooner had the frightened man settled in than the

walkie-talkie crackled with static. "Able One to Stony Man One," Lyons said. "Fierr—"

The soldier thumbed the transmit button to cut off the Able Team leader's words. "No names," he said into the walkie- talkie. "I've got company."

"Understood," Lyons came back. "Subject just passed the last exit before you. Still heading your way."

"Affirmative," Bolan said. "Take the course of action we discussed earlier." He turned to the man at his side. "Get out," he said.

The man sat frozen in his seat.

"Get out. Go back inside. I'm leaving."

"You won't shoot me?" the attendant asked in a quivering voice.

"I might if you don't get out like I told you to."

The attendant shot out of the Chevy almost as fast as one of Bolan's .44 Magnum rounds.

The soldier holstered the Desert Eagle and pulled out of the lot, up the ramp and onto the expressway. He kept his speed well below the limit, waiting for Fierro Blanco's car to pass. The president's green sedan appeared a few moments later as it passed the Chapultec exit. Gradually, Bolan bore down on the accelerator, increasing his speed. "I've got a visual on him, Ironman," he said into the radio. "Drop back."

"Understood," Lyons said. "Gadgets, you and Pol move up. Who was your visitor, Striker?"

"It's not worth explaining right now," Bolan said. "Just a guy who didn't know when to back off." In the rearview mirror he saw Fierro Blanco's vehicle gaining on him. When the car was fifty yards behind, he increased his speed to match that of the Mexican president.

The Executioner followed in front until he saw the president's turn signal begin flashing. "He's getting off at Oro," he told the men of Able Team. "I'll have to go on. One of you pick him up."

"I've got him," Blancanales said.

Bolan waited until Fierro Blanco had exited the expressway behind him, then floored the accelerator and hurried to the next exit. The Chevy's tires screeched around the turns as he made his way back to the other side of the highway again. "Location, Pol?" he asked over the airwaves.

"Take Oro to Medillin and turn right," Blancanales said.

Bolan followed the directions. Just as he made the turn, Blancanales came back on. "He's turning right again on Hamburo, Striker."

"Got it." The Executioner gunned the Chevy's engine, hurrying down the street until he came to Hamburo. He had followed it past Florencia and Genova when Blancanales said, "Turning left on Niza and slowing."

Bolan drove on. Just before he reached Niza, Blancanales said, "He's pulling into what looks like a motel—nope, wait—turning out again. This guy is really worried about a tail, Striker."

Bolan turned at Niza and slowed to a crawl along the street. Ahead, he could see Schwarz's and Lyons's vehicles and knew Blancanales and Fierro Blanco must be close. Pol confirmed it by saying, "Okay, he's turning into another hotel. This time he's parking. Getting out." He paused. "I'd stay back if I were you, guys. He's staying this time and there's no sense taking chances."

The Executioner took his advice, pulling over to the curb in front of an open air produce market. Several minutes of radio silence went by, then Blancanales came back on. "*El presidente's* gone inside. Want me to follow?"

Bolan hesitated, then said, "Only if you can do it without him spotting you, and that doesn't sound like it's going to be easy the way he's watching for a tail."

"I'd hate to lose him after all this."

"So would I. But he's seen your car several times now.

And he may have looked through the window and seen your face."

"I can take care of that," Blancanales said. "Gadgets, do you want to pull up closer while I'm away from the vehicle?"

Schwarz agreed. "Don't see any reason not to."

Bolan sat back to wait, wondering what he was about to find out and where it would lead.

GETTING A HEAD COUNT in the dark tunnel was impossible. Especially since everytime he stuck his own head around the corner, someone tried to shoot it off. But as best David McCarter could estimate, between twenty-five and thirty men were still trapped in the tunnel between the two Phoenix Force factions.

McCarter shone the red photon light on Thomas Jackson Hawkins. The young warrior had lost some of the coloring from his face. Even with direct pressure constantly on the wound it seeped a steady flow. Hawkins needed medical attention, not immediately, but soon. And if this Mexican standoff—any humor which might have been found in the pun was lost on McCarter under the circumstances—went on too much longer Hawkins would bleed to death. "Are you doing all right, T.J.?" the Phoenix Force warrior asked.

He smiled weakly in the red glow of the photon. "I probably won't donate blood to the Red Cross for a while."

McCarter nodded. "We'll get this thing over and get you fixed up."

Hawkins's smile became an ironic grin in the red light. "Don't worry about me, David," the young man said. He glanced toward the bend in the tunnel separating the Phoenix Force men from the drug smugglers. "They'll probably kill us all long before I have a chance to bleed out."

McCarter chuckled and killed the light, casting the tunnel into darkness once more. He knew exactly what Hawkins meant; the young warrior's statement had been made only half in jest. Though they probably didn't know it yet the drug mules around the bend, fifty yards away, outnumbered the Phoenix Force roughly ten to one. But the drug runners men did know about the American troops at the other end of the tunnel. Common sense dictated that in this particular case, they would choose to face the devil they didn't know rather than the devil they did.

McCarter took a deep breath and readjusted his rifle sling where it dug into his shoulder. The drug mules wouldn't be escaping the tunnel on the Mexican side, either—Manning's C-4 had insured that. But they didn't know that the exit was closed. And before they found out that a retreat was futile, he, Manning and Hawkins would have to face them.

McCarter knelt and peered quickly around the bend again. But before his eyes could focus on the silhouetted men, a flashlight beam struck him squarely in the eyes. He pulled back his head a half-second before the burst of gunfire could take off his head. But the sudden light had caused his pupils to contract, and he cursed himself silently for the foolish move. For all effective purposes, he was now blind. It would take time before his night vision returned.

Time during which the drug mules might well decide to storm their way and take their chances of tracking back through the tunnel.

Manning, McCarter knew, had seen him peer around the corner and knew what had happened. "Gary," the Phoenix Force leader whispered. "Take the bloody watch for awhile."

Manning didn't respond. But McCarter knew he had heard him. The creak of leather and swish of ballistic nylon drifted to his ears as Manning moved into position.

McCarter pulled the cellular phone from his shirt. Unless he missed his guess, James and Encizo would be getting ready to lead a group of men into the tunnel. The black Phoenix Force warrior needed to be aware of his, Manning's and Hawkins's predicament. He didn't know if the phone would work through the rocks. It wasn't likely, but it was the only chance they had of contact.

The phone rang all right, but no one answered it. McCarter wondered why.

The Phoenix Force leader felt a wave of despair threaten him as he folded the phone and stuffed it back into his pocket. Would the end come here after all these years? After all the close calls Phoenix Force had faced and survived? Normally, considering the cover of the bend in the rock, three well-trained men could have held off thirty with autofire. At least until their ammo ran out. But if James burst into the tunnel with his own squad, they would force back the drug mules regardless of what gunfire he and the other two Phoenix Force warriors could present. James needed to know that. And he needed to know it now, before he became the catalyst for his own fellow warriors' demise.

The phone was ringing which meant the connection could be made. So why wasn't James answering?

Bright lights still danced across McCarter's vision. He hit the photon and swung it onto Manning, then turned it off again. He could make out movement and shadows but nothing distinct yet. He took a deep breath. "Gary, T.J.," he whispered. "No matter what happens, I need both of you to stay behind me. Understand?"

A shadowy blob he thought was Manning nodded its head.

"Still can't see?" Hawkins asked from the floor.

"No. But when they come, I'm going to shoot at anything that moves. So stay back." McCarter took a deep breath. "They are coming, you know."

"We know," Manning said.

"Get your weapons and extra magazines ready," McCarter whispered in the darkness. "Then lock and load, mates. Lock and load."

A SUDDEN THOUGHT struck Calvin James. He stopped just to the side of the tunnel entrance and held up a hand so the men behind him would follow suit. In the heat of battle, with everything happening at once, there was one aspect of what was about to commence that he hadn't considered.

An aspect that could prove fatal to his fellow Phoenix Force warriors if he didn't handle it correctly.

McCarter, Manning and Hawkins were somewhere behind the drug mules, trapped in the tunnel after the explosion. James didn't know how many of the mules were left, but there was sure to be far more than his three fellow Phoenix Force warriors. If he pushed the enemy too hard they'd turn and run that way. The men from Stony Man Farm wouldn't stand a chance.

Clearing his throat, James stuck his head next to the tunnel. "You!" he shouted. "In the tunnel! This is your last chance to surrender and come out alive!"

No one answered. But down the long shaft he could hear muffled voices that told him he'd been heard.

James took a deep breath. He had never put much stock in bluffing—at least not when the bluff couldn't be backed up. Those were always the times, it had been his experience, that the opponent called the bluff. The enemy, if they were at all sharp, seemed to sense the deception. But at the moment, Calvin James saw no other choice.

"Listen to me!" he shouted around the edge into the dark. "We've got two hundred men out here waiting for you to surrender! There's another two hundred and fifty behind you in the tunnel!" He paused to let it sink in. "There's no escape. There's no way out. The only decision you have to make is whether you want to live or die!"

James waited. There was more mumbling in the tunnel. "Get ready," he said over his shoulder. "Something's about to happen."

"Yeah," Nelson said. "Something's about to happen. But have you got any idea what?"

Calvin James flipped the safety off his M-16. "No," he said. "But there's only one thing I'm praying for."

ROSARIO "POLITICIAN" BLANCANALES knew that Fierro Blanco might have noticed his rented Plymouth sometime during the tail. So he pulled it around to the back of the hotel as the Mexican president entered the lobby. He also knew the man might have looked through the window as he passed the Plymouth, and even gotten a glance at him.

Blancanales killed the engine, pulled the keys out of the ignition and dropped them into his pocket. But a glance was all the president would have gotten, which meant he would have keyed in on Blancanales' most distinguishing characteristic—his prematurely white hair. Well, the Able Team warrior thought as he reached into the backseat for the duffle bag he had thrown into the vehicle for just such an eventuality, that was remedied easily enough.

Blancanales pulled the bag over the seat and dropped it on the passenger's side. Digging through the contents, he pulled out a dark-brown shoulder-length wig and slipped it onto his head. Looking into the rearview mirror, he could see the white nylon backing peeking out along the scalp. That, too, could be taken care of, and a Dallas Cowboys baseball cap quickly did so.

Blancanales dug deeper into the bag and came up with a small plastic case. Flipping open the lid, he pulled out a mustache and applied a quick coating of adhesive. He used the mirror again to make sure it was straight, then stripped off the light bush jacket he'd been wearing and traded it for a Dallas Cowboys warm-up jacket. He smiled into the mirror. Mama Blancanales might recognize him, but Mexican President Don Juan de Fierro Blanco wasn't likely to.

Exiting the Plymouth, Blancanales hurried around the side of the building and into the office. Fierro Blanco stood at the front desk, his back to the door.

"Yes, Señor Alvarez," the desk clerk was saying as he

entered. "You are expected. Please add your signature to the registration card."

Blancanales walked casually to a rack holding tourist brochures. The wig, hat and sunglasses Fierro Blanco wore were as bad as Lyons had told Bolan. He looked exactly like what he was—a man trying to disguise himself. But they did hide his features. Anyone, like the desk clerk, who had only seen pictures of the Mexican president would not recognize him. It would be assumed he was simply a common man, possibly cheating on his wife at a hotel with another woman. But that was all the cover Fierro Blanco needed to meet with drug-cartel kingpins or assassins or whomever he chose, Blancanales realized. He picked out one of the brochures and held it up as if he was reading. In fact, the ruse was perfect. It gave a false credence to any furtive actions the president was seen undertaking.

The desk clerk looked up at Blancanales and said, "One moment, please."

Blancanales nodded, replaced the brochure and picked out another. A moment later, Fierro Blanco picked up his key and turned.

The Able Team warrior replaced the brochure and started forward. Don Juan de Fierro Blanco passed him without a second look and Blancanales took his place at the desk. "Just a single," he said in Spanish as Fierro Blanco exited the lobby again. The clerk picked up the registration card to which el presidente had added his signature before Blancanales could see the room number or the name of whoever had rented the room earlier. He dropped another registration form in its place.

Blancanales leaned over to pick up the pen and his long hair fell into his face. Waving it back behind his ears, he started to write. Bolan and his fellow Able Team members might or might not be in position to see which room Fierro Blanco entered. He couldn't count on it. But he couldn't afford to catch the president's attention either. So his timing had to be good.

The Able Team warrior wrote John Henry Johnson in the box for his name, then suddenly set down the pen and patted his jacket pockets. Taps to both front and rear trouser pockets followed, then he looked up into the eyes of the desk clerk and said, "Damn, I left my credit cards in the car. Be right back." Spinning swiftly on his heel, he left the lobby.

Fierro Blanco was ascending a staircase outside the motel as the glass door swung shut behind Blancanales. The Able Team psychological warfare and undercover expert walked beneath the stairs, mumbling unintelligibly to himself. The president appeared to pay no attention.

Blancanales walked toward his car, fishing in his pocket for the keys. With the president behind him now, he wouldn't be able to see which room the man entered. He slapped the keys still against his thigh as he walked, trying to listen to the footsteps on the concrete walk behind and over his head. They were faint, and he sensed them stopping more than he actually heard them.

Letting the key ring fall from his hand, Blancanales took another step, then turned swiftly around. He looked up beneath the bill of the baseball cap as he bent over to retrieve the keys and saw Fierro Blanco had stopped in front of a door. The long hair of his wig had fallen into his face again, and pausing to tuck it behind his ears gave Blancanales the excuse he needed to delay another couple of seconds. As he snatched the keys off the asphalt, the president stuck his own key into the lock. But before he could reach for the knob, the door opened on its own.

Blancanales turned again and returned to the Plymouth, pulled the walkie-talkie from under the seat and thumbed the transmit button. "Able Three to all units," he said. "I know where he is."

There was a moment's pause, then Bolan's voice said, "Where are you?"

"Back of the parking lot. I can still see his door." He paused, then said, "It's weird. He signed the registration card but somebody had already rented the room. The door was opened for him."

"You get a look at who it was?"

"Negative, Striker. Just saw a blur of an arm."

"Did you register?"

"Didn't have time."

The airwaves were quiet for several seconds, and Blancanales knew Bolan was trying to decide which course of action was called for next. He knew what *he'd* do. But before he could suggest it, the man known as the Executioner did.

"Go back inside and try to get the room next to his," Bolan said. "Gadgets, have you got your magic bag with you?"

"Always."

"Get it ready," Bolan ordered. "Ironman, move up where you can watch the door to the room. We'll all meet Pol at the back of the parking lot at his car."

"Okay," Lyons said. "I'm on the way."

The air waves went dead as Blancanales exited the Plymouth again. He glanced overhead as he passed Fierro Blanco's room and saw the number—224.

Reentering the lobby, Blancanales pulled a billfold from his back pocket and smiled sheepishly at the desk clerk. "I'd forget my head if it wasn't tied on," he said in Spanish.

The desk clerk had evidently heard the saying too many times to think it was funny.

Blancanales finished filling out the registration form as the desk clerk ran the credit card that matched the name. "Can I get a room on this side of the building?" he asked the man. "Upstairs? I like the view over back onto Niza. Reminds me of an area of San Antonio where I grew up."

The desk clerk turned to a board with keys hanging from it. "I have only one room left on that side," he said. "It's downstairs."

Blancanales shrugged. "Guess I'll take what I can get," he said.

It wasn't as bad as he'd thought it might be, however. As the desk clerk slid the key across the counter, he looked at the number—124.

For what he suspected Bolan had in mind, it would work. A little differently, of course, but it would work. Pocketing the key, he turned and left the lobby.

Bolan, Lyons, and Schwarz were all waiting for him when he returned to the Plymouth. "The adjoining rooms are occupied," he said. "But we're directly underneath."

Bolan glanced at Schwarz, who had a black nylon bag slung over his shoulder.

Schwarz pursed his lips and nodded. "No problem."

The four men from Stony Man Farm started across the parking lot. Out of the corner of his eye, Blancanales saw Schwarz eyeing his disguise. "Why Pol," Schwarz said, "have you done something new with your hair?"

"And I was afraid you wouldn't notice."

Lyons turned to Bolan as they walked. "You see what I have to put up with?" he asked. "Day in, day out. It's like working with two of the Three Stooges."

"Nyuck, nyuck, nyuck," Blancanales said.

A moment later, the four men from Stony Man Farm had entered room 124. Bolan took a seat on the bed. Schwarz dropped his bag onto the bedspread next to him and unzipped it. The electronics wizard began pulling out equipment. "Turn on the TV, Pol," he said. "It'll help mask the noise."

Blancanales complied, and a commercial for a Mexico City car dealership came on.

Schwarz pulled the chair from the desk, took a look at the bed frowning, then said more to himself than the others, "The room above should be laid out pretty much the same..." Lifting a small cordless drill and a small black box, he climbed onto the chair.

"What's the black thing?" Blancanales asked.

Schwarz smiled down at him. "My latest invention," he said. "I could bore you with the details—"

"Spare us," Blancanales said quickly.

"Okay then," Schwarz whispered. "Basically, it's a muffler. We don't want *el presidente* wondering what all the buzzing on the floor is now, do we?" He connected the two devices, inserted a small bit into the drill, and aimed it overhead.

Far at the end of the tunnel, David McCarter could just make out Calvin James's voice as the knife expert ordered the drug mules to surrender. James's words—to the effect that 250 men stood behind them in the tunnel—brought a silent chuckle from the Phoenix Force leader's chest. James had grown up a tough kid in Chicago's South Side. Along with other talents now imperative to the team, he had learned the art of deception early.

But the laughter faded as quickly as it had come. The bright lights caused by the flashlight beam in his eyes a few minutes earlier still danced across his vision. And regardless of whether or not the mules believed James's story, he figured the odds against them actually surrendering were about a million to one. James's words did, however, serve another very useful purpose, and McCarter suspected they had been carefully chosen for that reason as well as to instigate the surrender of the drug runner.

He, Manning and Hawkins now knew that their teammate at the other end of the tunnel fully understood their predicament. Which meant that James wouldn't push the mules back into the tunnel any harder or faster than he had to. Which meant the three Phoenix Force warriors trapped inside might still stand some chance of survival.

"Get ready," the former-SAS officer whispered to Manning and Hawkins. The bright lights still plaguing his vision, he pulled back the bolt on his M-16. Checking with his finger to make sure a round was chambered, he readied himself for battle.

The muffled voices he had heard arguing in the tunnel suddenly stopped. Then the sounds of dozens upon dozens of feet pounding the dirt echoed from around the bend.

McCarter heard Manning whisper, "You won't believe this David! Those idiots bought it, and they're charging forward!"

Hawkins blurted out a relieved laugh, and from the direction it came from McCarter could tell that the young warrior had risen to join them. "Guess they figured they'd rather face two hundred men on open ground than two-hundred and fifty in here," he said.

McCarter moved to the bend, cursing himself again for taking the flashlight beam in the eyes. "You two still make sure you're behind me," he warned. "There's bound to be a few who change their minds once the shooting starts, and I don't want to put any .223 slugs in either of your backs by mistake."

"That idea has no appeal to me either," Hawkins responded.

A second later the first of the drug mules hit the mouth of the tunnel. McCarter squinted into the dancing lights and shadows that his eyes sent to his brain as a combination of .223 and 7.62 gunfire split the night. He turned quickly to the side, knowing that even at that distance, the muzzle-flashes would impede the return of his night vision. The sharp cracks of the rifles echoed down the narrow shaft as if he were standing right next to the battle. "What's happening, Gary?" he asked Manning.

"Hard to tell," Manning said. "But it looks like James had men just to the side of the exit. The first wave of mules fell like they'd gone through a threshing machine. The others have pulled back."

"How many are left?"

"I'd say half, maybe. Let me try to count while their

attention is still that way.'' A few seconds went by, then he said, ''Fourteen, fifteen men left, best I can tell.''

McCarter's fingers squeezed the pistol grip of his rifle. ''Some of them will come this way,'' he said.

''I know,'' Manning answered. ''How're your eyes?''

''Not good. I can make out shapes. That's about it.''

''Just flip it on rock 'n' roll and aim at center mass,'' Hawkins said. ''We'll all carpet the place with wall-to-wall, floor-to-ceiling lead.''

McCarter nodded silently. ''How are you?''

''I'm okay,'' Hawkins said. ''Give me my rifle back. I can shoot it.''

''You need that other arm to keep pressure on the wound.''

Hawkins let out a breath of air. ''David, if we don't use all available manpower, this wound won't make much difference. Besides, it won't be for long. The whole thing will be over in a matter of seconds, and we'll either have won or lost. I can tend to the bullet hole again then. Or else I'll be dead.'' He paused. ''Either way, I won't bleed to death.''

The Phoenix Force leader found himself chuckling. He didn't resist when a hand came through the shadows and pulled the extra M-16 from his shoulder. ''Just keep the pressure on until the firing starts,'' he said.

''I will,'' Hawkins said. ''I'm not trying to bleed to death, you know.''

They didn't have long to wait. The men remaining just inside the tunnel made another halfhearted escape attempt in that direction. But they were far more cautious this time, and only two men fell to the rounds of the task force. The voices mumbled and argued again, and then those still standing split into two groups.

The first began laying down distraction fire through the tunnel exit.

The second turned and started cautiously back toward

the Phoenix Force men peering around the bend of the tunnel.

"They're coming, David," Manning said. "You'd better move in front of us. Stay close to the bend."

McCarter felt his way along the stony wall of the tunnel until he found the spot where it bent toward the exit. He stuck his head briefly around, and could see a faint white glow of moonlight at the end. But the men walking toward them were still indistinct. They looked like one big floating blob that just gradually got bigger. "How many, Gary?"

"Eight," Manning whispered.

"We can do it," McCarter said. "Wait until they're within twenty yards and open fire. Hawk and I'll use your rounds as our cue."

"You got it," Manning said. "Hey, David?"

"What?"

"That new suit you bought. Seville Row? The one you took to Madrid a few weeks ago?"

"The one I lost? What about it?"

"You didn't lose it. I needed something decent for my date with that flamenco dancer."

McCarter kept his laughter low. "Why didn't you just give it back afterward?"

"Because I lost it."

"Do I want to know how?" McCarter laughed quietly.

"Maybe," Manning said. "But I'm afraid it'll have to wait."

A moment later, McCarter heard the roar of an M-16 just behind him and to his rear. And a second after that he had leaned around the bend and was firing his own weapon into the shadowy mass coming toward him.

As Hawkins had predicted, an almost solid wall of lead flew down the tunnel. McCarter, his M-16 on full-auto, began firing at what he hoped was chest level of the mass. Trigger back, he swept his rifle back and forth from one side of the tunnel to the other. His ears rang as the explosions bounced off the narrow walls of the underground passageway. Hot empty brass flew through the air, one casing hitting the rock to his side and rebounding to burn the Phoenix Force leader's cheek. For a moment he thought he had taken a round to the face, but he continued to hold back the trigger, and by the time the magazine had run dry his brain had registered the reality of what had happened.

In a movement practiced thousands of time over the years, in both training and actual battle, the Phoenix Force leader ejected the empty mag from the rifle's carriage. At the same time his opposite hand ripped a new magazine from the carrier attached to his assault suspenders and shoved it into the receiver. Less than a second after his last round, he was firing again.

The shape moving toward them had at first slowed, then divided into shadowy pieces as some of the drug mules fell to the surprise gunfire and others pivoted back toward the exit. McCarter continued to hold back the trigger as his ears rang with the blasts all around him. The muzzle flashes of his own, his teammates and the drug mules' rifles drove away his partially returned night vision and his sight became a constant yellow glow again.

Then, suddenly, the gunfire around him halted. A few rounds at the other end of the tunnel popped off, and then they too ceased. McCarter continued to fire until his rifle ran dry. He was reaching for yet another magazine when he suddenly felt a hand on his own.

Words from a voice which sounded far away tried to invade his brain. He wondered if it came from one of the mules or his own men. Slowly the ringing in his ears began to diminish.

"It's me, David!" Manning's voice shouted an inch from his ear. "It's over!"

McCarter's fingers loosened around his rifle. He closed his eyelids over the burning white illumination in front of his eyes. "Take over for a few minutes, Gary," he shouted back. "I'm blind."

The Phoenix Force leader dropped to a squat as he heard footsteps coming down the tunnel. He felt a hand grab his rifle barrel, then Manning said, "It's Calvin and Rafe, David! Don't fire!"

McCarter nodded and lowered the rifle barrel, letting it rest on the ground in front of him. The footsteps came closer, then more voices—still indistinct in his reverberating ears—began to speak.

The Phoenix Force leader rose to his feet, reaching out to the tunnel wall for reference. Both his hearing and sight began to return. He heard an unfamiliar voice shout, "Get me a medic in here fast!" Then James's voice said, "I'm a medic! Get me a kit!"

Feeling a presence next to him, McCarter heard Manning's voice again. "It's T.J., David," the Canadian said. "He took another round. He's passed out."

"How bad?" the Briton asked.

"I don't know yet," Manning answered. "Calvin is checking him."

"Take me to him."

Manning led McCarter by the arm to where he heard several voices whispering. He knelt and reached out, his hand coming into contact with the downed Phoenix Force warrior. "How bad is he, Calvin?" he asked, knowing James would be close by.

He heard James's voice but the man was speaking to someone else. "Get to the end of the tunnel where your radio will work," James ordered. "Get a chopper in here and alert the closest hospital that we've got a wounded man. Get me a stretcher and tell the chopper pilot to bring blood—A-positive." There was a moment's silence, then James's voice roared, "Now, dammit!"

Running footsteps pounded down the tunnel.

James knelt next to McCarter. "He's not good, David," he said. "He's unconscious."

The ex-SAS man nodded silently in the darkness. "Stay with him. Anybody else hurt?" He was beginning to be able to make out shadows once more.

"A couple of guys outside took rounds. Nothing serious. The medics are looking after them."

The Phoenix Force leader nodded again. "Manning?" he said.

"Yeah, David?"

"Any of the mules make it through alive?"

McCarter heard his teammate cough. "One guy down the tunnel," he said. "There's a medic with him now."

McCarter rose. He heard the sounds and saw the blurry arms and hands that transferred Hawkins onto the stretcher. "Take me to the man, Gary. Then start gathering the dope. Leave it inside and blow this end like you did the other. I don't want this thing reopened after we leave."

"What about the bodies?" Manning asked as he took McCarter's arm and began escorting him down the tunnel.

The Phoenix Force leader thought of Hawkins, by now probably being transferred to the helicopter. "Leave them inside, too," he said. "It's a better burial than they deserve."

"Here he is," Manning said.

McCarter looked down in front of his feet and saw the obscure shape of a man on the ground. He knelt next to him like he had with Hawkins. "Can you hear me?" he asked.

He got no answer.

A voice which must have belonged to the medic finally spoke. "He's faking it, sir. He's not hit that bad, if he's hit at all. I can't even find any blood."

A sudden surge of anger swept across the Phoenix Force leader as his mind flickered back to Hawkins. He could barely make out the face below him, but it was all the target he needed. Raising an open hand over his head, he brought it down against the face and a loud crack echoed down the tunnel. Drawing the Browning Hi-Power from his hip, he shoved muzzle into the smuggler's face and said, "You've got exactly one second to start talking. Two seconds from now, you get a 9 mm hollowpoint round through your slimy, good-for-nothing, drug-dealing, child-killing head. Now, can you hear that?"

"Yes!" the man beneath him screamed. "Don't shoot!"

McCarter's thumb flipped the manual safety off the Browning and the click sounded almost as loud as the slap a moment earlier.

"No, please!" the man screamed. His voice rose two octaves into a disgusting feminine whine. "Don't kill me!"

"When is the next shipment due to arrive?" McCarter demanded. He had enough sight back to make out the tears streaming down the mule's face.

"Later tonight," the man whimpered, and his irritating snivel combined with thoughts of Hawkins tempted the Phoenix Force leader to pull the trigger.

"What time?" he demanded. He heard his own voice become a feral growl. "What time tonight, you mewling little bastard!"

"Midnight!" the man shrieked. He began to cry openly, and volunteered the next words without being coaxed. "But not here! It will go to one of the other tunnels!"

The words hit McCarter like a lightning bolt between the eyes. He rose, staring down at the man trembling on the ground. Holstering the Browning, he said, "Get him out of my bloody sight."

As uniformed arms reached down and jerked the drug mule to his feet, David McCarter turned away. He was able to follow using his own hazy vision now and made his way toward the tunnel exit without help.

Reaching the opening, the Phoenix Force leader stepped out into the moonlight. He had heard the mule's words.

The next shipment was coming to *one of the other tunnels.*

David McCarter suddenly felt tired. But not too tired to realize that the operative word was *one*. They had operated so far on the rumor of one drug tunnel. Now it appeared there were many.

With a deep breath, the Phoenix Force leader left the tunnel and started across the sand.

BOLAN SAT AT THE FOOT of the bed, watching Schwarz carefully drill though the ceiling. They were lucky, he thought. In most American cities, building ordinances mandated that hotels and motels have what was called two-hour fire-breaks between walls and ceilings of adjoining rooms. That was usually done with concrete, and had that been the case in this Mexico City establishment, there would have been no way to drill through the ceiling without Fierro Blanco—and whoever had opened the door for him—noticing.

As it was, Schwarz's muffled device penetrated the wooden ceiling-floor easily. Pulling it quickly out of the hole, he looked down at the other two men and held a finger to his lips.

The Executioner understood. With the hole in the ceiling, any noise could easily drift upward and give them away.

Pointing to Blancanales, Schwarz got his attention, then indicated to the bed.

Blancanales walked over, lifted a small plastic box and handed it to his partner.

Schwarz opened the box and removed a tube of super glue and a small brass device. Reaching overhead, he shoved the object into the hole and caulked the edges with the glue. "Okay," he whispered. "That one's done."

Bolan looked up to see what appeared to be an everyday door peephole now mounted in the ceiling.

Schwarz climbed off the chair and began digging through

his bag again. "The drill suppressor I can take credit for," he said, "but the lens was sort of a joint effort between Kurtzman and me. Had to resort to his computers to get a grasp on the thing."

"And it is...?" Lyons asked. He had taken a seat on the other side of the equipment on the bed.

Schwarz glanced up and grinned. "You want the technical specs, or the idiot-version like I'd have to give Pol?"

"Humor me," Lyons said stone-faced.

"Okay," the electronics expert answered as he pulled another small black plastic box out of the bag. "It's like a wide- angle camera lens. But smaller. Things will be a little distorted but we should be able to see ninety percent of the room above us." He climbed up on the chair, then added. "It's installed right in front of the bed. I've angled it up toward the mirror," he pointed at the mirror directly across the bed in their own room, "so we can see anybody who might be sitting there, too."

"What genius," Lyons said. A trace of sarcasm had crossed Ironman's face.

"Gadgets, you're my hero," Blancanales said.

"Well, that's all fine and nice," Schwarz said as he aimed the drill at the ceiling again. "But I'm about to drill another hole. So if you two think you could hold down the third-rate comedy routine until I've plugged it, too, things will probably work out a lot better."

The sound-suppressed drill began twisting up through the ceiling once more.

Bolan watched Schwarz work, his mind reviewing all the events that had transpired since he'd first arrived in Mexico on his dual mission. So far, he had successfully achieved the first part of the assignment in that he had kept President Don Juan de Fierro Blanco alive in spite of the numerous attempts on his life. But he'd had a lot more trouble with the second part of the mission. So far, he had made no progress at all in determining whether or not the president was an honest man who had been set up to look like the power behind the narcotics trade, political assassinations and revolutionary activity currently so prevalent in Mexico or whether he was indeed the culprit pulling the strings. Bolan's searches of the man's offices had proved nothing either way. Many things led him to believe that Fierro Blanco was dirty, but other events suggested he wasn't. The assassination attempts—at least on the surface—implied that the Mexican president was an honest politician and that the *Partido Revolucionario Marxista* and other terrorist groups wanted him dead. But in light of the vast number of attempts, the simple fact that none had succeeded was in itself suspicious. Had they been setups to cloak Fierro Blanco's real involvement? If so, the man was playing a very dangerous game that could easily go wrong. Yet it was a possibility the Executioner couldn't entirely rule out.

The drill bit disappeared through the ceiling again and Schwarz held his fingers to his lips once more. He began installing another device.

Honest or dishonest—which was Don Juan de Fierro Blanco? Bolan still didn't know. But what caused him to lean toward the "dirty" theory most were the president's unexplained absences from *Los Pinos*. Considering all the attempts on his life, why would the man choose to leave the Executioner's protection? The immediate answer was simple—Fierro Blanco wanted to do things secretly.

Bolan shook his head. His thinking had come full circle and returned to where it had started. It was going nowhere further at least until Schwarz finished with the ceiling.

Schwarz snapped the cap back on the Super Glue and dropped it into his shirt pocket. "It's sealed," he said, then looked at Blancanales and snapped his fingers. Blancanales handed a small set of headphones upward.

The electronics wizard plugged the headphones into the receiver he had just installed and looked back down. "Who wants first watch?" he asked.

"Go ahead," Bolan said.

Putting the headphones on, Schwarz twisted so he could look up into the peephole. He watched and listened silently for a few moments. Finally, his head shook in disbelief and he said, "Unbelievable." He turned back toward the bed. "Striker, this is something you'd better witness for yourself. I'm not sure I can adequately describe it."

Bolan rose as Schwarz climbed down and handed him the headphones. Adjusting them over his ears, Bolan stepped onto the chair and pressed his eye to the peephole.

And within the first two seconds he had the answer to why the Mexican president was willing to risk his life every other day away from his bodyguards.

In the mirror over the desk in the upstairs room, Bolan could see the woman half sitting, half reclining on the bed. She was quite literally a knockout. Long hair, so blond it was almost white fell past her naked shoulders, contrasting dramatically with her deeply tanned skin. Her half-closed deep brown eyes stared off into space.

Beneath the sheet, her hips moved gently and rhythmically as soft moans, picked up by the receiver and relayed to the headphones, met the Executioner's ears. The sheet had fallen to her waist to reveal perfect silicone-injected breasts.

Sticking out of the other end of the sheet was a large, flabby, hairy male posterior. Fierro Blanco's head and shoulders were out of sight beneath the sheet, but Bolan could see them moving back and forth with the same rhythm as the woman's gyrating hips.

The soldier looked back at the woman's face, distorted in passion. He frowned. Had he seen her somewhere before? He couldn't be sure.

"What are they doing?" Blancanales asked.

"Well," Schwarz said. "They aren't playing marbles."

Bolan removed the headphones and stepped off the chair.

Handing them to Blancanales, he said, "See for yourself."
He moved back to the bed as Blancanales took his place.

Bolan shook his head in disgust. He had hoped to catch
Fierro Blanco meeting with a terrorist connection, his political assassins or at least someone who would provide him
with concrete proof that the president was either an honest
man or Mexico's version of Adolf Hitler. But again, he had
learned nothing. The woman might be who he met every
other day, and then again she might not be.

The Executioner's fists clenched in frustration. He was
back to square one. Worse than that, the mere fact that
Fierro Blanco and the women were engaging in sexual ac-
tivities didn't preclude the fact that she might also be a
political contact. It wouldn't be the first time beautiful
women traded sex for information from powerful men.

Looking up, Bolan saw Blancanales frown and nod his
head. "Very interesting," he said. "Ironman, see what you
make of it." He handed the headphones down to Lyons.

A moment later Carl Lyons stood on the chair. What he
said wasn't meant for virgin ears.

Schwarz turned to the Executioner. "Ready to pack up
and go home?" he asked.

"I wish we could. It's not a pretty sight."

"*She* is," Blancanales said.

"I'm glad you feel that way," Bolan said. He stood and
walked to the shade covering the window, then turned
again. "Because somebody has to keep watching. Sex may
only be part of their reason for meeting and we've got to
find out."

"You mean we've got to watch *him?*" Schwarz asked.

"Them," Bolan nodded. "Watch and listen."

Lyons was climbing off the chair. He handed the headphones back to Blancanales.

"Hey, you had them last," Blancanales protested. "You
do it."

Lyons shook his head. "I hardly ever pull rank on you guys," he said. "But this is an exception."

Blancanales looked hopefully at Schwarz, who grinned and shook his head. "I've got to start gathering my gear," he said. "She is nice. Just concentrate on her, Pol."

Blowing air through his lips in disgust, Blancanales climbed back on the chair.

"What are they doing now?" Schwarz asked as he replaced the drill in its case.

"Believe me Gadgets," Blancanales said. "You don't want to know. It's not for the weak at heart."

"The listening is the important part," Bolan said. "Are they talking at all?"

"I don't think talking is actually what you'd call it," Blancanales said. "I don't think talking would even be possible at the moment—at least for her." He shook his head in amazement. "Somebody want to tell me how an ugly old geezer like that gets a woman like her into bed?"

Schwarz laughed. "It's like you having to peek through the peephole instead of Ironman. Rank has its privileges."

Blancanales snorted in disgust. "Well, consider my resignation tendered immediately after this mission," he said. "Considering what *el presidente's* doing, and what I'm having to do, I think I'll run for office."

The rest of the men in the room started to laugh.

"Just keep watching and listening," Bolan said. "It can't go on forever."

"The listening is almost as painful as the seeing," Blancanales said. "But you're right about it not going on forever. In fact, if you could see what I'm seeing right now you'd know it can't go on much longer."

Schwarz finished packing his gear and Blancanales looked down hopefully. Schwarz pretended not to see him. The three men sat silently, waiting as Blancanales made various faces of distaste.

A minute or so later, Blancanales said, "Okay, it's over. The talking has begun."

Bolan leaned forward. "What are they saying?"

"Okay, we're getting the standard drivel about whether or not he's told the first lady he's leaving her yet...nope, not yet, he's stalling around, surprise, surprise. Oh, this is great. Now he's giving her the presidential version of why he can't tell his wife yet..." Blancanales paused, then smiled, then laughed out loud. A moment later, he said, "I knew it! He can't divorce his wife while he's still in office...but he will as soon as his term's over...wait a minute...he's throwing the sheet back and getting off the bed...my God, I didn't want to see this...and he's walking over to the dresser. Picking up a box. Yeah, sure, should have seen this coming too...it's the payoff."

"Huh?" Schwarz asked.

"The payoff, you idiot," Blancanales said. "He bought her a gift...a necklace...she's putting it on." He looked down at Schwarz again. "Want to see it?" he asked hopefully. "She really is beautiful."

"He really isn't," Schwarz said. "And to see her, I'd have to see him too. No, you go on, Pol. You're doing a great job."

Blancanales raised his hand in an obscene gesture and Schwarz laughed.

"We don't need a play-by-play unless the subject changes," Bolan said and the room fell into silence again.

Finally, Blancanales said, "Okay. Looks like another dangerous liaison comes to an end. They're up and getting dressed. She's happy about the necklace but she's still pouting about the fact that he won't get a divorce yet. She either really loves him or she's one hell of an actress." He looked down at Bolan. "I don't think she's anything more than what she appears to be, Striker—a woman on the side."

Bolan stood. He had been afraid of that. He walked to

the door, grabbed the knob and turned back momentarily. "Okay guys," he said. "Thanks for your help."

"Oh no," Blancanales said. "Thank you. Thank you so very much for such a fun evening, Striker. Next time, I'd prefer just getting shot at if you don't mind."

As disappointed as he might be that he had learned nothing of value, Bolan still couldn't help but laugh. "Glad you liked the show, Pol. Now, you guys go put an end to the gang killings back home. We'll meet up somewhere along the way or after this thing is over."

The men of Able Team nodded.

Bolan stepped outside the room, glancing overhead to make sure the door to room 224 was still closed before going farther. Satisfied that Fierro Blanco couldn't see him, he broke into a jog across the parking lot, wondering briefly who the woman might be. Had she looked vaguely familiar or was that just wishful thinking on his part? He had wanted almost desperately to finally get some answers tonight.

Bolan reached the Chevy and opened the door. It didn't really matter who she was. Like Blancanales, he was convinced she was nothing more than the president's mistress. All he had learned was that the president of Mexico cheated on his wife. He could be no more certain of Fierro Blanco's integrity in other areas than he had been when he'd first arrived in Mexico.

Bolan started the engine, threw the Chevy into gear and drove away. He switched on the radio but a Margarita Felice song was airing and he turned it off again. That was the only music that was played at *Los Pinos*, and he chuckled briefly to himself at Fierro Blanco's adolescent fascination with the famous singer and actress.

He was halfway back to the presidential mansion when he saw the billboard advertising tequila on the side of the road. A beautiful blond woman, her hair almost white and her skin as tanned as a chestnut, smiled down at him, her perfect teeth gleaming in the light. A tequila bottle rested strategically between her breasts, the tops of which were threatening to pop out of the silky beige low-cut nightgown.

The soldier drove on. No, he hadn't found out the answers to what he'd wanted to know this night. But he had learned the answer to another question that had been on his mind, however unimportant, for days.

He now knew why Margarita Felice music played constantly wherever President Don Juan de Fierro Blanco went.

9

For what seemed like the hundredth time, Scott Hix tried to lean back, stretching his cramped legs and back muscles. He, like the other men and women who had been kidnapped by the *Cuididano para Democracia Mexicana Legitima* had been chained in the same position for two days now. But there were differences in the way they were being treated. Big differences.

Hix gave up his attempt at comfort, knowing he'd involuntarily try again in a few minutes even though he knew it wouldn't work. He stared down the two rows of hostages to where Ronnie Quartel sat—when he was with the rest of them. Since the first time he had been taken out to make the ransom call, Quartel had been treated better than the rest of them. He was gone again now, presumably making another call. When he was in the room, he still sat in chains but there the resemblance ended. Quartel was never struck, spoken to harshly, or treated with anything but respect. Occasionally Jesus Hidalgo, the leader of the *Legitimas*, came into the room to speak to him. At those times the two men conversed in hushed voices, and it even appeared that Hidalgo was consulting with Quartel.

Hix's eyes left Quartel's vacant space and drifted up and down the captives. Some appeared to be sleeping, others stared wild-eyed into space. A few, particularly the blond Hollywood starlets Quartel had brought to Hix's party outside of Tijuana, tried to whisper among themselves. But they rarely got more than a few words out before being stopped by one of the guards. Sometimes stern words were their only punishment. Other times, a slap stopped the talking. Usually, it depended upon whether the guards came from what Hix had originally referred to as the "clean group" or the "dirties." He had since learned, by piecing together bits of overheard conversation and other clues, that his guess that they were two groups who had recently banded together was accurate. Hidalgo's *Legitimas* were short on manpower, and the revolutionary leader had cut a deal with a band of common bandits led by Pablo Huertes. The different men came from different classes. They had different goals and different morals. It was little wonder that Hix had sensed conflict between them almost from the beginning.

Hix tried to stretch again and his mind returned to the different ways the captives were being treated. While Quartel was given deference, the women of the group—both those from Hollywood and the Tijuana prostitutes—were pretty much ignored. The bandidos, however, openly lusted after them, and only the fact that Hidalgo was wise enough to keep at least one of his own men in the room at all times kept those men in check. Even that couldn't prevent the occasional tweak of a breast or a hand running up and down an extended leg. All of the hostages were taken individually to the bathroom twice a day, and that duty was one especially fought over by the bandits. Hix suspected they watched the women perform their humiliating chores, and his blood pressure rose when he thought of Normandi West being subjected to such degradation.

Leaning forward again, Hix tried to look down the line of seated prisoners next to him. He could barely make West near the end. She sat with her back against the wall, her eyes open. Patches of dirt clung to her face, and her hair was showing signs of two days without a shampoo. But like all truly natural beauties, the dirt and grime somehow brought out a different radiance. Perhaps it was the fact that even in these circumstances, she refused to give up her dignity. She was magnificent, and Hix had thought so almost from the moment he had laid eyes on her at his party. Bringing her along had been almost an afterthought of Quartel's, she had told him, and she suspected it was only because the movie star had been unable to seduce her on the set and wanted another chance. She had teased Hix that the blond starlets had been brought for his amusement. So why was he wasting his time with her? Why didn't he go take advantage of them?

Because he had indulged in enough women like that to last him a lifetime, Scott Hix had told West without hesitation. He was looking for something real. And he was having more fun talking to her. Hix had literally been shocked at how easily the honest words had left his mouth.

They had talked until daybreak then retired to separate bedrooms with plans to meet later in the day for lunch. But before that could happen, Hidalgo, Huertes and their mixed band of revolutionaries had burst into the house and taken them captive.

Hix grimaced. It tortured his already screaming muscles even further to stay in that position and look at West, and finally he was forced to give up. He sat back into the least-uncomfortable post he had found during the last two days but she stayed on his mind. She was being treated much the same as the other women, being ignored by the *Legitimas* and occasionally pawed irritatingly by the others. Hix ground his teeth at the thought of the filthy bastards touching her. He had kept track of each man who had tried, and he renewed his vow to kill each and every one of them as soon as the opportunity presented itself.

If the opportunity presented itself, he was forced to realize as his muscles cramped again. Which brought him to the third way the hostages were being treated—the Scott Hix way. He was in a class all his own.

Hidalgo had made no secret of the fact that he knew Hix was a former military intelligence officer and close-quarters combat expert. So while the other guards in the room watched all the prisoners, he always had one assigned specifically to him and him alone. Right then it was a fat bandit who stood near the door eating some kind of pastry and drinking from a bottle of mescal tequila. The man's watery eyes flickered back and forth from Hix to the food and drink as he neared the worm at the bottom of the bottle.

Hix watched the man watch him. Even in his drunken state, the fat man clearly saw every move the American made, which meant that even though Hix had an ace up his sleeve he couldn't get to it to play it.

Back at his house, after he and West had finally separated and he'd returned to his bedroom, he had just sat on the bed and removed the Seecamp .32 caliber semiauto from his pocket when the *Legitimas* burst through his door. Finding the small pistol, they had searched no further and the Applegate-Fairbairn fighting knife had stayed in his other pocket. Hix always carried the knife—a gift from its designer, Colonel Rex Applegate himself—in his right front pocket, the sheathed six-inch blade extending through a hole cut in the bottom. He had transferred it to deeper cover inside his underwear at a bathroom break along the ride, and still had it hidden beneath his shirt.

Scott Hix shook his head. For what good it was doing him at the moment. He couldn't reach it to cut the tape, and it was too big to pick the locks on the handcuffs. Even if those things could have been accomplished, he couldn't do it with the pastry-eating tequilamonger constantly watching him. And even if all those things somehow took care of themselves, he had been locked in this cramped position so long that he'd be moving at half-speed once he was free.

The door next to the fat guard suddenly opened and Jesus Hidalgo led Quartel back into the room. Quartel was all smiles and laughter. Hidalgo stopped for a moment to speak to the guard but Quartel walked on. He took his usual seat and clasped the handcuffs around his own wrists. Hix frowned. There was no sense in trying to escape or cause trouble when it wasn't in their own best interests. But Quartel was getting along a little too well with the captors. It was almost like they'd become friends.

Hidalgo glanced from the guard to Hix, then back to the guard. "He's behaving himself?" he asked in Spanish.

The guard stuffed the last of the pastry into his mouth and smacked his lips while he answered. "How can he not?" he said, indicating Hix's restraints.

The *Legitima* leader turned and dropped to one knee next to Hix. He checked the chains and cuffs, then the duct tape that still bound the American's wrists and ankles. Satisfied, he closed his eyes tightly for a moment, then opened them again. "Señor Hix," he said quietly. "Please believe me when I tell you I don't enjoy this. I'm sorry we must keep you taped as well as chained."

"If you're so sorry why don't you take one or the other off?" Hix said. "My wrists are bleeding from the tape. You've got the cuffs chained down so much farther to the floor than anybody else. I can't even stretch and my back and legs are on fire. Hell, you could take all of it off and I still wouldn't be able to move for a week because I'm so stiff."

Hidalgo shook his head. "You're not restrained like the others because you aren't like the others," he said. "You're a former military intelligence officer and an expert fighter." He drew in a deep breath. "In short, you're dangerous." He paused again, then said, "Even now, your import-and-export business is probably just a CIA cover."

Hix couldn't keep from laughing in the man's face. "That's what I love about you terrorists," he said. "You think everybody works for the CIA."

Hidalgo's eyes narrowed. "I don't appreciate being laughed at," he said.

"I don't appreciate being kidnapped."

"We aren't terrorists," Hidalgo said. "We are freedom fighters."

"Whose freedom are you fighting for?" Hix asked, looking down at his restraints. "It doesn't appear to be mine."

Hidalgo stared at him for another moment, then stood. "In time," he said, "if all goes well and you cause no trouble, we may be able to remove the tape." Without waiting for a reply, he turned and walked down the line to where Quartel sat. He knelt again, conversing briefly with the movie star. Hix saw Quartel glance his way several times while he spoke. A moment later, Hidalgo left the room again.

As soon as he was gone, one of the bandit guards stationed against the opposite wall knelt next to the blonde named Errin and began speaking to her in a soft voice. Gradually, his hand moved to her knee, then up her leg to her crotch. The petrified woman didn't move.

"Hey!" Hix called out.

The *Legitima* guard at the end of the room looked at Hix.

Hix nodded across the room and the *Legitima* turned that way.

The bandit's hand shot back from the woman's legs. He stood again and resumed his place against the wall.

Minutes passed, then the man who had molested the blond starlet pushed away from the wall and moved across the room. Stopping in front of Hix, he bent at the waist. "When this is over," he said, his foul breath threatening to knock the American cold, "I plan to do two things."

"Let me guess," Hix said. "Take a bath and brush your teeth? No, I doubt if it's that."

The bandit's long stringy mustache curled as he grinned. "First," he said, "I will have your woman."

"I don't have a woman."

"Perhaps. But there is one you would like to have." The man's eyes moved down the line to where West sat, then returned to Hix. "Then, after you have watched me do it, I'll let you watch me kill her. Before I kill you."

Hix stared at the man. He would have given up everything he owned at that moment if he'd been able to reach the Applegate-Fairbairn dagger in his jeans and plunge the double-edged blade through the man's throat.

Hix closed his eyes. The situation looked hopeless at the moment. But that would change. Soon, he'd see an opportunity to escape and save the others. In the meantime, his challenge was threefold. First, he needed to come up with a plan. Second, he needed to do something about the charley horses and spasms that were torturing his muscles and that would prevent him from moving with the crucial speed and agility once he was able to put that plan into motion. Starting with his toes, he began squeezing the muscles, ignoring the pain. He did ten reps of contractions, then moved to his ankles and calves, then up his body.

Slowly, some of the feeling began to return.

Hix paused for a moment when he reached his thighs. They were going to be extremely painful, and he needed to prepare himself mentally. As he got ready, he thought about the third and most important thing he had to do right then.

Not lose hope. And that might very well be the hardest part of his three-pronged plan.

The former American intelligence officer looked down the row of captives to where Normandi West sat. As he did, she looked his way. A faint smile crossed her lips. Hix smiled back.

With a deep breath, Hix began flexing and relaxing his thigh muscles. Each repetition of the isometric exercise brought flames to his legs and he fought to keep from screaming.

But each painful breath he took, combined with the mental image of the woman who had just smiled at him—the woman with whom he suspected he was actually in love—also kept his hope alive.

DAVID MCCARTER had been looking forward to getting the whole team back together. Phoenix Force trained and fought as a unit, and while they could function superbly either as individual warriors or split into pairs or trios, they were at their best when together.

But it didn't look as if McCarter was going to get what he wanted. At least not for a while.

Rafael Encizo, Gary Manning, Calvin James and a man McCarter suspected must be Pug Nelson surrounded him as the Phoenix Force leader watched the helicopter bearing Thomas Jackson Hawkins rise into the sky. The chopper tilted toward Tucson and the hospital that had been put on alert.

"You're the sawbones, Calvin," McCarter heard Manning say. "Just how bad is he?"

James shook his head. Deep worry lines were etched across the former SEAL's handsome face. "I don't know," he said. "I can't tell. He'd lost a lot of blood already. And that second round didn't help any, either."

"Where'd he take it?" Encizo asked.

"Through the leg," James said. "It missed the bones and arteries. But I couldn't tell how bad it is for sure."

McCarter surveyed the area outside the tunnel. Eight trucks had driven to the scene after James, Encizo and the task force troops had already secreted themselves prior to the arrival of the mules. These had been the pickup vehicles that would drive the heroin to distribution sites. The drivers had been easily overtaken but the trucks were left where they were so nothing looked out of place.

McCarter turned his attention back to the men and clapped his hands together. "All right," he said. "We're all worried about T.J. but there's nothing else we can do for him right now. So let's just hope and pray and concentrate on what we can do." He looked at James. "Where's the whiner I talked to in the tunnel?"

The medic who had looked after the injured drug mule shoved him forward. The man was now on his feet. "He wasn't even hit, sir," the soldier said. "The pansy-ass just played possum." He had a Texan drawl that reminded McCarter of Hawkins. The Phoenix Force leader didn't need that right now, not at all.

"Thanks, soldier," he said. "Return to your men."

The man saluted and took off.

The Briton reached out, grabbed the collar of the mule's shirt, and dragged him across the sand to one of the boulders. The men of Phoenix Force and Pug Nelson followed.

McCarter bent the mule over the rock backwards almost folding him in half. "Pug, you're a federal law enforcement officer," he said over his shoulder. "And I'm about to break every one of this dreg's Constitutional rights…along with several of his bones if he doesn't talk. If this will cause you any problems, I suggest you join the other men."

Nelson's guttural laugh was almost enough to put McCarter in a decent mood.

"After all the things I've done with James and Encizo," the former SEAL said. "I don't think it matters much one way or the other."

The Phoenix Force leader drew the Fairbairn-Sykes commando dagger from its sheath and held it above his head in a hammer grip. "Are you familiar with the British and American expression 'This is going to be short and sweet?'" he asked the man.

The mule nodded.

"Well, this is going to be short, I'll promise you that. How sweet it is will be entirely up to you." He stopped to take a breath, then went on. "There's another expression, one that parents often use before they spank their kids.

They say, 'This is going to hurt me more than it hurts you.'
Are you familiar with that one?''

"Yes," the mule whined.

"Well, don't you believe it," McCarter said. "Now,
what's your name?"

"Vendigo," the man said. "Mario Vendigo."

"Who do you work for?"

"The Monterrey cartel."

"Where's the tunnel the next shipment is coming
though?"

"I don't—" the man got out before McCarter brought
the handle of the Fairbairn-Sykes down on his forehead.

The skin broke and blood spurted from the shallow
wound. Vendigo shrieked.

"And he was doing so well there for a while," Manning
said.

"You remember the question?" McCarter asked.

The man nodded.

"Then I see no reason to repeat it. You've got three
seconds."

"But...they will kill me if I tell you!"

"This gets tedious sometimes," McCarter said. "It's like
being in a bad high school play or a B-grade movie. My
line is supposed to be, 'But we'll kill you if you don't.'
But you know that, don't you Mario? Yes, you know it. So
I see no reason to say it. You've got three seconds again."

Vendigo closed his eyes tightly. "I'm telling you the
truth!" he pleaded.

McCarter drove the Fairbairn-Sykes down onto his forehead again. The pommel struck just to the side of the first
blow, producing similar results. The only difference was
that Vendigo screamed louder this time. Lumps began to
grow above his eyes.

"Last chance, old boy," McCarter said. He waited until
Vendigo opened his eyes, then twirled the dagger into an

ice-pick grip, the double-edged point angled down. "This one's for real."

He didn't have to say more. Staring at the tip of the dagger three inches from his eyes, Vendigo shouted, "West! West of Nogales!" He started to give further directions but McCarter slapped him across the face.

"Shut up!" the Phoenix Force leader said, leaning in until his face was an inch from Vendigo's. "Since you're out of a job, you can take us there." He grabbed the mule by the throat and jerked him off the rock. Turning to James, he said, "Where are the rest of the choppers?"

"Close," James said. "But we've only got three left."

"Call them in," McCarter demanded. "All three of them. Load as many of these men as you can and let's go." He raised his wrist and looked at his watch.

Assuming the shipment was on time, they had less than an hour.

THE HOUR WAS LATE by the time the Executioner returned the Chevy to the spot where he'd picked it up. Lyons had paid for all the vehicles in advance, and a hefty tip to the rental agent had insured that the man would violate the company's usual policy and retrieve the car himself. Getting out of the vehicle, Bolan left the keys on top of the right front tire and started down the sidewalk back to *Los Pinos*.

Two federal guards working the gate could be seen through the window of the small shack just inside the grounds. One of the men stepped through the door as Bolan approached. "Señor Belasko," he said, holding up a hand.

Bolan stopped just inside the gate. "Yes?" he replied.

"A package came for you while you were gone," the guard said. His eyes fell to the clipboard. "Latin America Parcel Service."

Bolan frowned. He wasn't expecting anything. "Who's it from?"

The guard squinted slightly in the low overhead light. "The U.S. Department of Treasury," he said.

Bolan stiffened. If it had come from Stony Man Farm, they would have used Brognola's Justice Department cover. "Where is it?" he asked the guard.

"I'm afraid the deliverymen had to take it back," the uniformed man said. "A signature was required."

Bolan nodded. "Did they say when they'd be back?"

The guard shrugged his shoulders. "Later tonight. They seemed anxious to deliver it to you."

Another sharp twinge of apprehension prickled the back of the soldier's neck. Slowly, it spread down his body. He glanced at his watch. "Is that standard procedure for the...what did you say was the name of the parcel service?"

"Latin America," the guard said. "LAPS. And, well, no. It hasn't been my experience that they work this late at night." He frowned slightly. "Or that they return for a second try the same day. But then I have never been on duty when a package requiring a signature arrived."

Bolan took a moment to think. There was something wrong here. Another assassination attempt? "Are they allowed access to the grounds?" he asked.

"No," the guard said. "All deliveries are received here. Bombs, you know. A dog is kept on duty during the day."

"What about at night? No dog then?"

The guard took off his uniform cap and wiped sweat from his forehead with the back of his sleeve. "He's kept in a kennel at night," he said. "Because, now that you mention it, I don't think packages ever arrive at night. At least none have ever been delivered on my shift, signature or otherwise." He started to speak again, then suddenly turned back toward the guard shack. "Sergeant Cordova!" he said, raising his voice slightly in order to be heard through the window. "Did you not work for LAPS before coming here?"

A burly unshaven man nodded through the open window. "Do they make night deliveries?"

The burly man shook his head.

The prickly feeling at the back of Bolan's neck hadn't gone away. If someone—the *Marxistas* again most likely—had sent a bomb, wouldn't they have gone to the trouble of finding out about the procedure surrounding the receipt of packages at *Los Pinos?* Maybe the federal bomb-sniffing dogs weren't any more competent than many of the guards themselves. But a night delivery that was bound to draw suspicion? And wouldn't they know that all packages were received at the gate rather than inside? He could understand addressing the package to him—anything sent to Fierro Blanco would come under the highest scrutiny. But the rest of it didn't make sense.

The Executioner looked up at the guard again. "If I had been here when it arrived," he said. "What would you have done?"

"Phoned inside for you, of course. You would have been required to come to the gate to receive it and sign."

Bolan caught his jaw tightening. That didn't make sense either. In order to kill the president with the bomb, it would have to be near him. How could they be certain that Bolan would be close enough to the man, and have the package with him, after he took the package back into the building. Regardless of what detonation mechanism they planned to use—remote, timer or trip wire—they had no insurance that Fierro Blanco would be close by.

There were only three feasible answers: The *Marxistas*, or whoever was behind the bomb, were incompetent in their planning. Or the package wasn't a bomb.

Or the bomb wasn't meant for Fierro Blanco at all. It was meant for the Executioner.

This made the most sense. The *Marxistas* hadn't proved to be unworthy enemies by any means. And with Bolan out of the way, Fierro Blanco would become a much easier target for assassination.

"I'll be inside," the Executioner told the guard. "Let me know as soon as they return."

Bolan crossed the lot and entered the building. He met Captain Juanito Oliverez getting off the elevator as he was getting on.

"*Buenas noches,*" the captain said.

"*Buenas noches,*" Bolan returned. "Everything quiet?"

"Yes," Oliverez said. "But *el presidente* has gone missing once more."

The Executioner nodded. "Appears to be a little game he likes to play. I'm sure he's fine."

Oliverez's eyes narrowed slightly. "You're beginning to sound like General Razon," he said. "We have discussed his mysterious absences before, and they always concerned you. What has changed?"

Bolan smiled inwardly. The ineptness he had found in so many of the guards didn't extend to their captain; Oliverez was sharp. But should the Executioner tell him about his president and Margarita Felice? He saw no reason to do so. While he trusted Oliverez more than any other man in Mexico, the need-to-know doctrine had always been one of his primary dogmas. And Oliverez had no need to know.

"Just a hunch," Bolan said. "He's done it enough times now without getting killed that I'm assuming he can do it again. Wherever he goes, he's apparently safe."

Oliverez chuckled. "Perhaps that is where he should stay then."

"I suspect he'd like that."

Oliverez gave him a quizzical look that told the Executioner he knew there was more to the story. "As you wish, Belasko. I shouldn't have asked."

Bolan rode up to his floor, got out, and saw General Razon standing in front of his room. The fat man's hand was on the doorknob. He turned quickly as the elevator door opened, a look of both surprise and guilt on his face.

"Do you need something?" Bolan asked bluntly.

Razon cleared his throat in what was an obvious stall for time; he needed to come up with a story. When the story didn't come fast enough, he leaned forward in a fake coughing spasm.

Bolan waited, mildly annoyed at the childish ploy.

A few seconds later, the general straightened and said, "Please excuse me. Allergies, you know." He coughed once more, then said, "I had wanted to discuss some new ideas I have had for *el presidente's* security but—" he glanced at his watch "—I see it's later than I thought. We can speak tomorrow." Without waiting for a response, Razon spun his bulky medal-and-ribbon-covered body away from the door and waddled off down the hall.

Bolan waited until he had rounded a corner, then looked down at the door to his sleeping quarters. The thread he had left between the door and jamb was still there.

But not quite in the same place where he'd left it.

Sticking his key into the door, the soldier entered the room. At first glance, everything appeared as it had when he'd left. But as he moved around the room, little things pointed to the fact that someone had been inside. In the bathroom, the tube of toothpaste was beneath the other items in his shaving kit. He had brushed his teeth last, and remembered tossing it back inside the case. On top. The shower curtain was open—he had closed it after taking a shower so it would dry.

Moving back into the sleeping area, Bolan walked to the bed. Someone had looked between the mattress and box-spring—a corner of the fitted sheet had come unhooked and the elastic had snapped it back. He had taken the chart he'd made of Fierro Blanco's absences with him but now he tapped the breast pocket of his jacket to make sure it was still there. The soft rattle of the paper met his ears.

Returning to the door to the hall, Bolan cracked it open
and looked up and down the doorjamb. There were no signs
of tool marks. Whoever had been in the room had either
skillfully picked the lock or used a key. That someone had
to be Razon. He hadn't been about to knock on the door
as he had suggested just now, he had been caught leaving.
And it would be no trick for him to get access to the master
keys of the mansion. The soldier knew that Razon had been
in the room. He needed no concrete proof. But he got it
anyway when he turned on the lamp and looked down at
the nightstand.

There, next to the bottle of wine he had opened earlier,
was a curly tinged hair. The kind that came from a
beard—a short reddish beard such as Razon wore. He
hadn't seen it until he turned on the lamp, and Razon
wouldn't have noticed it either.

Bolan sat on the bed, pulled the cork from the bottle of
Beaujolais, and poured the glass half full. He was about to
drink, thought better of it and set the glass back on the
nightstand. What was the general looking for? Whatever it
was, he hadn't found it. The soldier had taken the chart
with him and left nothing in the room that might suggest
his mission was anything more than what it appeared on
the surface—that of an executive protection specialist from
the United States on special loan to the president. So what
was the portly medal-covered man after?

Bolan lifted the wine glass, held it in front of the light
and looked through the dark-red liquid. It looked no different than it should. He held it to his nose. It smelled no
different, either.

Which meant nothing.

Rising from the bed, Bolan poured a few drops of the
wine into an ashtray on the nightstand next to the lamp.
Walking swiftly into the bathroom, he added water. He set
the mixture on the table by the balcony while he slid open
the door, then picked it back up and stepped outside.

Bolan held the ashtray carefully in both hands as he descended the iron stairs into the moonlit courtyard. The first lady's cats, which had been fighting earlier, had made up and they slunk out of the shadows and walked toward him as he reached the bottom. Setting down the ashtray, the soldier stepped back.

The Siamese was the faster of the two. He ran forward and lapped up the mixture of water and wine.

A moment later, the animal shivered and lay down next to the ashtray.

Bolan squatted next to him. There hadn't been enough alcohol mixed into the concoction to have had much effect. The cat's breathing was steady, his eyes open and alert. He would live, but he was sick.

The Executioner lifted the ashtray and returned to his room. Carefully, he rinsed it out in the sink. Returning to the bedroom, he poured the wine that remained in the glass back into the bottle, replaced the cork and returned it to the nightstand. Remnants of the red liquid from the glass he had consumed earlier—before Razon had poisoned the bottle—had been in the glass before he'd poured more. He left the few drops that remained where they were to dry and look the same.

When he wasn't dead tomorrow, Razon would wonder why and might return to the room. Bolan didn't want the general knowing he was on to him. Therefore everything around the bottle and glass had to look the same. It had to appear that Bolan still lived out of pure dumb luck—because he simply hadn't been in the mood for more wine that night.

The phone on the nightstand rang and Bolan lifted it to his ear. "Yes?" he said.

It was the guard at the main gate. "The LAPS truck has returned, Señor Belasko," a voice said.

"Tell them I'll be right down."

Bolan hung the phone back up and drew the Desert Eagle. He checked to make sure both chamber and magazine were full, then did the same with the Beretta. Striding quickly to the closet, he opened a case and replaced the magazines he had used during the fight at the hotel. The Applegate-Fairbairn folder was still in the horizontal sheath on his belt, and he started to leave.

His hand was on the doorknob when some instinct caused him to turn back. He wasn't sure why, but he found himself returning to the weapons case. Opening the lid again, he reached inside and pulled out a .22 Magnum North American Arms mini-revolver and an Applegate-Fairbairn covert folding knife—a miniature version of the folding dagger he already wore.

The small knife went into his underwear against his spine, the mini-revolver into the left side pocket of his jacket. Even if he didn't understand them, the Executioner's instincts had saved his life far too many times over the years to let them go ignored.

Bolan left the room and started toward the elevator. During the last thirty minutes, he had questioned the reasons behind both the mysterious package from LAPS and General Razon's clandestine visit to his room. He didn't have all the details yet, but he would. In the meantime, at least he knew what both parties wanted.

Him.

10

The trio of AH-64A Apache helicopters took off in unison, rising into the night at exactly 23:14 hours. McCarter knew, because he was looking at his watch. The fact was, he had looked at his watch every minute or so during the time it took to get the choppers loaded and off the ground.

The pilot was a dark-skinned young man with black hair and Mideastern features. He had remained silent while McCarter, Manning and Mario Vendigo crowded onto the Apache. But as they rose into the air he said, "What's my course, sir?"

"Just follow the border," McCarter said over the whir of the chopper blades. "We're going somewhere west of Nogales." Snatching the radio microphone from the control panel, the Phoenix Force leader held it to his lips and thumbed the red button on the side. "Phoenix One to Two and Four," he said. "Come in, Two and Four."

"Two here," Calvin James said over the airwaves.

Rafael Encizo followed a moment later with, "Four. Go One."

McCarter looked out the window to the mirror mounted on the side. He could see the chopper in which James rode a hundred feet behind, and farther back, the helicopter carrying Encizo. "Tell your pilots to keep at least a quarter-mile or so between us," he barked into the mike. "We're cutting it close. I don't want to spook these guys back into the tunnel." He let up on the button, dropped his hand to his lap, then lifted it again, re-keyed the mike, and added. "We don't have anybody in the tunnel or a cave-in at the other end to stop them this time."

The air convoy flew on, carrying them along the border between Mexico and the United States. They soon passed over Douglas to the north, Agua Prieta to the south. McCarter sat back and tried to relax. He and the other Phoenix Force warriors had been a long time without sleep. But he was too keyed up to rest now so he began to plan his attack.

If the mule train of drug runners was anything like the one they had just encountered, the three helicopter loads of men would be vastly outnumbered. Better to keep to the air, he decided, and take advantage of the chopper's weapons. They'd allow the mules to load the trucks so they couldn't turn back into the tunnel, then swoop in and destroy the vehicles. Apache helicopters were armed with McDonnell Douglas M-230 30 mm multibarrel guns and could each carry up to sixteen laser-guided Hellfire antitank missiles. With a range of 3.7 miles, the Hellfires could penetrate the armor of any known battle tanks.

The former-SAS officer caught himself smiling. Which meant the Hellfires wouldn't have much trouble with the drug transport trucks.

A few lights still glowed at the twin villages of Naco, Mexico, and Naco, Arizona, as the helicopter caravan flew between them. Straddling the border, they sailed on through the night. McCarter glanced at his watch again. The chopper was pushing its maximum airspeed and they were moving along quickly.

But so was the time.

A few miles later, the Phoenix Force leader looked down to see the shadowy outlines of the Coronado National Memorial. Just to the north, he could barely make out Miller's Peak in the moonlight. San Fernando and Santa Cruz came next, both on the Mexican side of the line, and then they reached the two cities both known as Nogales.

McCarter twisted in his seat to look at Mario Vendigo, who was seated next to Manning. "All right then, chappie," he said. "Time for your show to go on. Where next?"

Vendigo looked out through the window. "Do you know Vado?" he asked.

"Mexican side," McCarter said. "Maybe ten, twenty, miles south?"

Vendigo nodded his head. "The tunnel begins north of there. A mile from the border."

"I don't care where it begins," McCarter shouted over the wind and the whir of the helicopter blades. "By now they'll be inside. Where does it come out?"

Vendigo glanced between the seats. McCarter knew he was trying to get a look at the Fairbairn-Sykes dagger sheathed on his leg—the butt of which the Briton had used to raise the ugly swelling now evident on his face. With a trembling voice, Vendigo whispered, "I don't know."

McCarter reached though the seats and grabbed the man's throat. "What do you mean you don't know?" he demanded. "You said the tunnel was west of Nogales!"

Vendigo spoke with the speed of a man trying to save his life. "I said the tunnel was west of Nogales and it is!" he choked out around McCarter's squeezing fingers. "I know where the entrance is on the Mexican side but I don't know where it comes out!"

The Phoenix Force leader shoved the man back against his seat and faced forward.

The pilot had heard the encounter and turned to him. "What now, sir?"

"Keep flying while I think."

The choppers flew on as McCarter stared out through the glass into the night. He could complain, loudly or silently, as much as he wanted about Vendigo's deception, but it wouldn't do any good. What he needed to do was spend his time figuring out how to locate the tunnel exit. And when he'd thought about it for a few seconds, he decided it shouldn't be that hard. He was going to fight the battle from the air anyway, after the trucks were loaded. So he didn't need the exact location of the tunnel exit—he just needed to locate the trucks. And spotting the headlights of a half-dozen or more large vehicles in this isolated area should be fairly easy.

"How are we fixed for gas?"

"It was full when we left, sir," the pilot said.

"The other birds?"

"The same."

McCarter picked up the microphone and filled in Encizo and James on the new developments. "We're going to break this area up and search it from the air," he said. "The central focal point is the border directly north of Vado—they aren't going to want to dig any farther than they have to. James, have your pilot fly a pattern two miles east of the central point. Encizo, the same to the west. We'll fly the whole area and widen the search if anything catches our eye."

"Roger that," James came back.

Encizo seconded with an "Affirmative."

The Phoenix Force leader looked again at his watch—23:47 hours.

The Apache flew on through the night, finding the central focal point of the search and passing over it. McCarter knew there was always the possibility that the drug shipment had come early; the trucks could have already come and gone.

The pilot reached the two-mile point and turned back. Making another aerial U-turn just north of Vado, he started to repeat his course. McCarter looked below and suddenly saw tiny lights moving across the ground.

The pilot saw them at the same time. "Trucks," he said.

"I've flown this course in the daylight. There's a road down there if I remember right. Want me to buzz them?"

"Negative," McCarter said. "Fly on. They're heading south which means they haven't loaded yet." He turned in his seat to face Vendigo. "What kind of pickup trucks are they using?"

The frightened cartel employee cleared his throat. "Big ones," he said. "If they are the same ones that came when I was there. What you call, I think, tractor-trailers."

McCarter frowned. Bigger vehicles than the two-tons that had been at the last tunnel. Which meant that each could carry more but they'd go to fewer distribution sites. "How many?" he asked.

"There were three when I was there."

McCarter ripped the microphone from the dash again and informed James and Encizo. Instructing the pilot to take them out of sight five miles to the west, he said, "Let's get things ready. You do the flying. I'll operate the Hellfires."

"We don't have any Hellfires, sir," the pilot said.

"Pardon me?"

"No Hellfires, sir. Part of the president's military budget cuts."

McCarter glanced involuntarily over his shoulder. "How about the other choppers?"

"No, sir. None onboard either of them."

The Phoenix Force leader spit out a few colorful words of disgust, then regained control of himself. "Okay, we'll go with what we have. We'll have to rely on the 30 mms."

"I'm afraid that won't be possible, sir."

"What?"

"The guns were in need of repair, sir. They've been dismantled. All part of the—"

"The bloody President's bloody military budget cuts," McCarter finished for him angrily. "Tell me, soldier," he said. "Just what weapons *do* you have onboard?"

The pilot patted the Beretta M-9 in the tanker rig across his chest. "Just this, sir."

Manning leaned forward and said, "You're lucky the President doesn't know about it, kid. He'd probably take it, too." He turned to McCarter. "Makes you proud to be British, I bet, David. You know, if you guys ever wanted to take this place as a colony, this would be the time."

McCarter shook his head. "I'm sure I'll see the humor in that someday. Right now, I'd be happy just to know what we're going to do."

"Sir?" The pilot broke in timidly.

"What is it?"

"Well, if I might be so bold as to make a suggestion, like I said, there's a road down there. Actually, there are several. But only one leads all the way to the border."

"Get to the point, soldier," McCarter said irritably.

"Well, sir, that same road is the way they'll have to come back. And it crosses a wash about three miles from the border. I've not only flown over this area, I've been over that route in a supply truck. If their trucks are loaded down like ours were, they won't be able to hit more than ten, twenty miles hour tops when they come up the bank."

"Take us there," McCarter said. He lifted the radio once more to inform the other choppers.

Manning faced the pilot. "There's a future for you in the Army. But hang onto that Beretta. You're about to need it."

THE NORTH AMERICAN ARMS mini-revolver in the left side pocket of the Executioner's jacket operated by single action and had no safety. It could, therefore, be fired left-handed as easily as right. The problem was, it didn't fire quickly from either. The little .22 Magnum was a last-ditch hideout weapon and it performed that service admirably. But it lacked firepower, knockdown power and most of all speed.

Bolan waited for the elevator in the hall outside his room. The door rolled open and he stepped in.

The soldier considered the situation as the car descended the shaft. He was convinced that the Latin America Parcel Service deliveryman—or whoever was posing as an LAPS driver—was after him rather than Fierro Blanco. Was it someone from the *Marxistas*? Perhaps the man in the ball-fringe sombrero who had led the attacks on *Los Pinos* and the president's summerhouse? Since outright assault had failed, perhaps the man was changing tactics, trying deception.

The door rolled open and Bolan stepped out. He knew he was taking a chance. As soon as he walked out of the mansion he'd be out in the open, vulnerable to unseen sniper fire. But he didn't want to kill whoever was in the delivery truck. He needed to question someone. Besides, the same instincts that had directed him to take the extra knife and gun now told him that wasn't the way things would go down. If a sniper attack had been the plan, there would have been no need for such elaborate subterfuge.

Bolan left the house and descended the steps. The area around the mansion was quiet, the streets deserted and only a few vehicles could be heard in the distance. Mexico City, for the most part, was asleep. A hundred feet away he could see the main gate and the guard shack next to it. Parked just outside the gate, the purr of the idling LAPS truck engine drifted through the stillness to his ears.

The Executioner walked toward the gate, his eyes taking in every detail of the surrounding area. Two uniformed men were inside the shack, one talking to the LAPS driver though the window. Neither of the men had been on duty when Bolan arrived back at *Los Pinos* a half-hour ago. He glanced at his watch. There was nothing unusual about that. There had been a shift change ten minutes earlier.

The driver talking to the guard was a dark-skinned man wearing a faded yellow shirt. The truck was parked on the street rather than in the drive—ready for a quick getaway? Maybe the guards didn't allow delivery trucks onto the grounds. As he drew closer, the premonition that something was about to happen grew even stronger in the Executioner's stomach, heart and soul.

He was twenty feet away when the guard at the window turned toward him. "Ah," the man said. "Here he is now."

Bolan slowed his pace, reaching inside his jacket to the breast pocket of his shirt. He tapped the empty pocket as if looking for a ballpoint pen with which to sign the receipt for the package. The same hand—his left—moved unobtrusively to the side pocket of his coat where the NAA .22 Magnum pistol was hidden. Wrapping his middle finger around the tiny grip, his thumb rested on the hammer ready to cock it as he came to a halt at the gate.

The driver in the yellow shirt smiled pleasantly, then turned and spoke over his shoulder. "Santiago," he said. "Señor Belasko has arrived. Please get his package and the clipboard with the signature pad."

Another dark-skinned man, slightly younger and thinner than the driver, moved around the truck carrying a box in one hand, a clipboard in the other. But the clipboard was carried at an awkward angle and the Executioner's eyes strained though the shadows to see why.

The edge of the pistol beneath the clipboard came into view at the same time the driver extended another gun through the window of the truck and shot the guard through the left eye.

Bolan dived toward at the man carrying the package. He wanted him alive; wanted to know where he came from, whom he represented. But even as he lunged he realized he was a half-second late. The gun—a nickel-plated two-inch .38, was already pointing straight at his chest.

There was no time for his life to flash before his eyes. The soldier only had time to think how strange it was that after all these years it would end here and this way.

But it didn't. Instead of firing, the man with the .38 jumped backward.

His hand still in his coat pocket, Bolan raised it preparing to shoot through the material. But before he could cock the tiny .22 he heard a popping sound behind him and something struck him in the middle of the back. He froze in place, then suddenly, all feeling left his arms and legs. He dropped to his knees, then fell forward onto his face.

With a mighty burst of willpower, the Executioner rose to his hands and knees. The fingers of his left hand were still on the mini-revolver but the sensation was strange—like he held a lump of clay in his hand rather than the tiny pistol. He tried to cock the weapon but his fingers ignored the order from his brain. Again, he heard the popping sound behind him and something struck him—this time in the side. He fell forward once more, landing on the side that had been struck.

Above him, Bolan could see the man who held the .38 pistol and the package. An evil grin covered his face.

He could barely move his neck but he turned it enough to see that the man in the yellow shirt had gotten out of the truck. He stood over him now, an automatic pistol hanging at his side. The two men had to be brothers—the similarities were unmistakable.

Bolan heard laughter. With great effort, he twisted his neck and saw the second guard—the one who hadn't been shot—walk toward him. His vision had grown blurry but he could see that the uniformed man held a gun, too. No, not a gun, Bolan thought as he strained to cock the mini-revolver once more. Yes, a gun, but a different kind of gun. A tranquilizer gun.

Bolan closed his eyes, straining to focus every ounce of brain and willpower on cocking the mini-revolver. But all fine motor skills, and most of the larger ones, had deserted him. His fingers slipped off the tiny revolver and his limp hand came to rest on the ground, still in his pocket.

So that was it, the Executioner thought. They didn't want to kill me. They wanted the same thing I wanted—a prisoner. Someone they could question and interrogate.

Before they killed him.

Two pairs of hands grabbed Bolan by the shoulders and pulled him to his feet. To his right, he saw the fuzzy outline of a face. A sudden mustering of will brought temporary strength back to his body and he used all of it to swing his right fist at the cloudy specter. He felt his hand connect with tissue and bone but there was no force behind the blow, and the man behind the face simply laughed.

Someone's fist drove into the Executioner's gut. Something hit him over the head from behind.

"You must shoot him again."

"Yes. He's tough."

"But that's good. For soon his strength will be ours."

A moment later the Executioner heard the same popping noise he had heard twice before when the tranquilizer darts hit him in the side and back. Then what was left of his mind and body shut down. And he heard and saw nothing.

CARL LYONS PULLED the rented Ford Bronco past the bank on the corner, and turned into the center parking lot. Driving slowly past the storefronts, he scanned the signs in front of him. The large supermarket on the corner was the shopping center's main draw, with the smaller enterprises counting on the grocery to lure business. The Able Team leader stopped abruptly as a couple pushing their shopping cart cut in front of him. As soon as they'd passed, he drove the Bronco, past a Radio Shack, a hobby and craft store and an alteration shop that advertised The Fastest Seamstress in the West.

Lyons pulled into a parking space in front of a video store. "Wait here," he told Schwarz and Blancanales. "I'll just be a second."

Lyons opened the glass door to the video store, let in a

teenage boy and girl, then stepped inside. He had radioed
Stony Man Farm during the flight from Mexico City to
Houston, and learned that one of the Houston PD narcotics
detectives was a Stony Man blacksuit graduate. A call from
Barbara Price to the man's home—a similar call to the narcotics division had proved he was currently on sick leave—
and the meeting had been arranged.

The Able Team leader surveyed the store in a glance,
taking in the usual assortment of middle-aged couples looking for dramas and comedies with the teenagers jamming
the horror area. Lyons saw no sign of Houston PD Detec-
tive-Sergeant Dirk Anderson. Behind the linoleum counter
at the back of the store stood teenaged girl with a half-
dozen rings in each ear and silver studs gleaming from both
of her nostrils.

Lyons walked past the racks to the counter. He glanced
through the office door directly behind the girl, where he
could hear papers rustling. "Have you got the movie
Doc?" he asked, loud enough for whoever was shuffling
the papers to hear.

"*Doc*?" the girl asked, her eyebrows lowering in
thought. "Like in Doc Martens?"

"Like in Stacey Keach," Lyons said. "It's an old movie
about Doc Holliday and Wyatt Earp."

"Who?" the girl asked.

Lyons tapped the computer monitor between them. "Just
check, okay?" he said.

A man's head shot around the corner of the doorway.
"Don't bother, Carrie," he said. "*Doc*'s never been put
on tape." He squinted at Lyons, then stepped into the doorway. Long brown hair fell to his shoulders. He wore a huge
handlebar mustachio and a tiny gold dagger earring dangled
from his left ear. His clothing consisted of a blue sweatshirt,
faded jeans and burgundy-and-cream-colored wing-tipped
cowboy boots. He inclined his head toward his shoulder,
then disappeared into the office.

Lyons took the movement as an indication that he should return to the Bronco and pull around to the back door. He did.

Behind the shopping center, Lyons read the abbreviated signs and finally saw the door marked simply Videos. He pulled to a halt next to the sidewalk just as the door opened and the man with the long hair stepped out. Schwarz opened the back door and the man slid in next to him.

Lyons turned and rested an arm over the seat. "So, why all the secrecy?" he asked.

The ends of Dirk Anderson's handlebar turned up in a smile. "I'm twenty months from retirement and a full pension," he said. "But I'm working for an asshole captain who's doing his damnedest to make sure I don't get it." He paused, leaned onto one hip and pulled a crumpled pack of cigarettes from his back pocket. "You mind?" he asked.

Lyons shook his head.

Anderson shook a crooked cigarette from the pack, straightened it as best he could, and lit it with a Bic lighter. Inhaling a lung full of smoke, he said, "My dad died two weeks ago." The smoke streamed back out of his mouth.

Lyons nodded his understanding. "Sorry about his death."

Anderson shrugged. "It happens. In any case, I inherited this place." He glanced to the back of the store. "But I don't have the time to run it and wouldn't want to if I did. Blockbuster across the street—you probably saw them— is gonna eat us alive sooner or later. Right now they've offered to buy me out. Not a bad price, either. But it's now or never so I put in for a week's leave to get things in order. The captain turned me down." He shrugged his shoulders again and took another hit off the crumpled cigarette. "It became a matter of either catching a bad case of the flu or letting the place go under. So I'm sick."

Next to Lyons in the front seat, Blancanales laughed.

"And you thought we might be from Internal Affairs? Checking your flu story?"

"I did until I saw you," Anderson said. "Sorry, I don't remember you guys," he continued, indicating Blancanales and Schwarz.

"No reason you should," Schwarz said. "You've never met us."

"But you," Anderson said, turning to Lyons. "You taught a section on managing informants at that training school…" The cop's smile returned. "I gotta tell you, I learned more about how to handle snitches that day than in all the other training I've ever had put together." He paused and drew deeply on the cigarette. "So how can I return the favor, guys?"

Lyons ran down the situation about the cartel killings to Anderson, who was already aware of most of it from Houston PD briefings. "What we need is some local snitch who knows what's going on," he finally said.

Anderson pushed a fist against his teeth and closed his eyes. "Teddy'd be the most likely to be up on it," he said. "But he's a pro. It'll cost."

"We can pay."

Anderson nodded. "Okay, then. Let's go. You got a phone in here?"

Schwarz handed him a cellular as Lyons started the engine and drove down the alley.

Anderson tapped in several numbers, then said, "Carrie, hold down the fort. I'm gonna be gone a little while." He hung up, then leaned to the side and pulled a small red address book from his hip pocket.

The Houston detective looked up briefly. "Make a right at the street," he said. Stuffing the book back in his pocket, he dialled another number.

Lyons turned onto the street and stopped at a stoplight. Thirty seconds went by, then he heard Anderson curse in the backseat. He looked into the rearview mirror and saw the narcotics officer holding up the phone. "Answering machine," he said. "Go straight."

The light turned green and the Able Team leader drove on. "Anybody else you can try?"

Anderson didn't answer the question. He waited for the outgoing message on the answering machine to play through, then spoke into the phone. "Teddy, you son of a bitch, I know you're home. I'm on my way and if you leave before I get there, I'll part your hair with a meat cleaver next time I see you. You got that?" He hung up.

"Yep," Blancanales said, nodding his head. "This guy's definitely a graduate of the Ironman School of Confidential Informant Management."

Anderson handed the phone back to Schwarz. "He's there. Drunk or stoned or both—welfare checks came out this morning. Teddy's pretty lightweight when it comes to dope, though. Marijuana, hashish, that sort of thing. He knows if I catch him with anything heavier he goes down like anybody else."

"You don't pull good snitches off Sunday school honor rolls," Schwarz said. "If they aren't connected somehow, they don't know what's going on."

"Amen to that," Anderson agreed. He looked to the front. "So, I call you Ironman?"

Lyons nodded.

Anderson said, "How about you two?"

"Gadgets."

"Pol will do," said Blancanales. "Short for Politician."

Anderson chuckled. "Okay then, Ironman, go on up to Kelly—about four more lights—then take a left."

"Tell us about Teddy."

"Like I said, he's a professional snitch. Plays both sides of the fence but comes up with some damn fine inside info." The narc leaned forward slightly. "But like you kept saying in class, you've got to keep an eye on him."

Lyons settled back against the seat. He didn't remember

Anderson from blacksuit training but hundreds of men had gone through Stony Man. Besides, the longhaired narc in the backseat might well have been a "straight" cop and looked much different in those days. But he had gone through Carl Lyons's section on handling informants. He was proving that by everything he said and did. Anderson knew that one of the cardinal rules was to never trust a snitch.

The Able Team leader grinned inwardly. That fact of the matter was, almost everything Anderson had said into the phone sounded like a parody of himself.

Lyons followed further directions from Anderson, finally pulling off onto a side street, then down a dirt alleyway. He killed the lights and parked next to a trash can.

An unattached garage stood behind the house facing the street. Anderson led the way up the rickety wooden steps to the apartment above it. Lyons, Schwarz and Blancanales followed. The Houston narc rapped his knuckles on the splintering wood beneath the window in the door and waited.

When no response came, Anderson knocked louder. When this too brought no reaction from inside the apartment, he tried the doorknob. It was locked, but a short kick opened it easily. The Houston cop stepped inside the apartment followed by the men of Able Team. Lyons kept his right hand near the Colt Python holstered on his hip beneath his jacket as he took in the single-room dwelling.

Posters of rock bands—both new and ancient—covered the walls. Empty bottles of tequila and gin were scattered around the room. The odor of freshly smoked marijuana hung in the air.

But Teddy was nowhere to be seen.

Anderson moved into the room. He bent quickly at the waist, glanced under the bed, then opened the door to the bathroom. "Come out, come out, wherever you are," he sang. Actually, the apartment held little opportunity for concealment, and there was only one place left. Anderson ripped open the closet door to reveal two of the skinniest human beings Carl Lyons had ever seen. Both Teddy and the woman with him were stark naked.

"Well, what have we here?" Anderson said. "Hope I didn't break anything up, Teddy."

The man who stepped out of the closet wore eyeglasses with thick lenses. In one of his hands he held a hash pipe. With the other, he did his best to hide his genitals.

The woman followed. Of indeterminate age, she had mousy brown hair that hadn't seen shampoo or comb for weeks. Her breasts sagged their way sadly down her chest. Her pale white skin was spotted with bruises that matched the dirt on her bare feet.

Unlike Teddy, she made no effort to hide her private parts. She just smiled suggestively at the newcomers.

Anderson came to his rescue with, "Good God, Teddy, will you and Patticakes get some clothes on? You trying make everybody here sick?"

Teddy threw a once-white T-shirt to Patticakes and lifted a soiled pair of jeans off the floor. He spoke as he pulled them over his emaciated haunches. "Dammit, Dirk, you scared the shit out of me," he said. "I thought we was getting busted."

Anderson looked around the room. "You should get busted, Teddy," he said. "And you still could." He turned to the woman who held the T-shirt in her hands. "You too, Patti. Now cover up."

Out of the corner of his eye, Lyons saw Blancanales shudder. "Please," the Able Team psychological expert said. "Just do what he asks."

Lyons chuckled. After Pol's forced stint as chief Stony Man voyeur the day before in Mexico City, it was obvious that the Able Team warrior had seen all the ugly naked people he wanted to see for a while. The woman gave the men of Able Team a final smile before raising the T-shirt into the air to expose the large thatches of hair beneath her arms. She pulled the shirt over her head where it fell without obstruction to her bony knees.

Both took seats on the bed's bare mattress.

"You want to talk in front of her?" Anderson asked Teddy.

"I trust her," Teddy said. "We're in love. We're getting married."

"Right," Anderson said sarcastically. "I'll be best man and Patticakes can wear a white bridal gown."

"No Dirk," Teddy whined. "Really."

Anderson shook his head. "Teddy, I'm not a preacher or a marriage counselor but I don't see this as the beginning of a lifetime commitment. Is Patti going to quit working the streets?"

"Well...no..." Teddy said. "We've got to make a living somehow, don't we? And you damn sure don't pay me enough."

Anderson sighed. "Yes, Patti's life of prostitution is all my fault," he said. "Okay, listen." He repeated much of what Lyons had told him earlier in the car about the cartel wars, leaving out only the parts Teddy didn't need to know. "Where can we find these guys, Teddy? The guys doing the shooting?"

Teddy folded brittle arms across nonexistent pectoral muscles. "How bad do you want them?" he asked.

Lyons pulled out a roll of bills. He tossed two hundreds on the bed between Teddy and Patt. The informant glanced at the money on the bed but his eyes almost bugged out of his head as he looked at the roll still in Lyons's hand.

"That's a start," he said.

Lyons was running out of patience. He turned to Anderson. "Do you want a review on how to handle informants?" he asked.

"Always like to see a master at work."

Lyons dropped one more hundred on the bed. "Talk," he said.

Teddy continued to stare greedily at the roll. "You're doing better," he said. "But like I said that's just a st—"

Lyons's hand flashed out, striking Teddy across the jaw. The little man almost flipped backward off the bed. But Lyons hadn't struck him that hard, and it wasn't the first time Teddy had been hit. He resumed his seat as if nothing had happened; as if getting hit was just an everyday thing.

But Teddy got the message that more would be coming if he didn't start talking. He took his betrothed's hand. "Word on the streets is there's some heavy hitters in town," he said.

"We just told you that, Teddy."

"Okay, okay, I'm just warming up," the informant whined. He glanced nervously to Lyons. "Keep your hands to yourself, okay? The six guys who got killed last night over on Merlin Boulevard?"

Anderson nodded.

"They were with that Acapulco group. Shooters were from Monterrey."

Lyons listened. The Acapulco and Monterrey cartels had been in competition in this part of Texas for several years. "Go on," he said.

"Okay," Teddy said, finally rubbing his jaw. "The Monterrey boys are looking for the rest of the Acapulco and the Acapulco guys got a counterhit in the works." He paused, glancing down at the money on the bed. Lyons could see he was trying to decide if it was safe to ask for more yet.

Teddy evidently didn't think so. "They—the Monterrey guys that is—got ahold of Fat Jack right before the hits went down. I'm guessing Fat told them where to find their targets."

Lyons pulled another hundred off the roll and tossed it onto the dirty mattress. "And that would be?" he asked.

"They was set up in a house not far from here," Teddy said. "But that was then. They'll have moved after last night."

"Where?" The Able Team leader pulled another hundred from the roll but held it in his hand.

"I don't know."

Lyons reached forward and Teddy cringed. But instead of hitting the frail little man again, the Able Team leader pulled one of the hundreds back off the bed.

"Hey!"

"The Ironman giveth," Schwarz said.

"And the Ironman taketh away," finished Blancanales.

"I don't know where they are!" Teddy almost cried. He dropped Patti's hand and put his arm around her bony shoulders. "But I think I know where the Acapulco group is."

Lyons tossed one of the hundreds back on the bed.

"There's a house over on 4th," Teddy said. He grabbed the money off the bed and gripped it in his bony fingers. "Place where Patti used to work."

Patti spoke for the first time. "It's owned by a greaser," she said, then glanced to Blancanales. "Mexican, I mean." Her voice sounded like a woman twenty years older who had been born smoking unfiltered cigarettes.

"You talking about Gonzales's whorehouse?" Anderson asked.

"Yeah, that's his name," Patticakes nodded. "But he had us call him Lone Wolf."

Anderson turned to Lyons. "Guy's a big-time pimp with drug connections," he said. "Took his name from Lone Wolf Gonzales, the famous Texas Ranger."

"I bet the Rangers love that," Schwarz said.

"Oh yeah," Anderson said. "I got a good friend who's a Ranger and they want him bad. But so far they haven't pulled it off. You don't desecrate a Texas Ranger icon and get away with it forever, though."

Lyons pulled a pen and small notebook out of his pocket and handed it to Teddy. "Draw it for me," he ordered. "I want the chain of command of each of the cartels you're familiar with." He took five more hundred dollar bills from the roll, tossed them on the bed and stuck the remainder back in his pocket. "That's it. Don't try for more. And I want everything you know. Now."

"That's okay," Teddy mumbled under his breath. "You pay better than Dirk anyhow." He began drawing an operation chart of the cartels. When he was finished, he handed the notebook back to Lyons.

The former LAPD cop looked down at the scribbled writing. There were numerous holes in what Teddy knew about the hierarchy but that was to be expected. "Did you leave anything out?" the Able Team leader demanded.

Teddy shook his head. "That's all I can tell you."

Lyons turned to leave but the snitch said, "Hey, wait!"

The former LAPD detective turned back.

"Like I said, you pay better than Dirk," Teddy said nervously, glancing at the Houston cop. "How...uh...can I get hold of you if I get something else?"

Lyons tapped the notebook against his other hand. "This had better be all you have," he said. "If it isn't, we'll get hold of you."

The Able Team leader led the way down the steps and back to the Bronco. "Take the wheel, Dirk," he said. "This is your town."

Anderson took the keys, slid behind the steering wheel and started the engine. "To Gonzales's place, I'm guessing?" he said.

"Right," Lyons said as the Bronco started down the alley. "But there's one thing first."

Anderson turned onto the street and glanced across the Bronco.

Lyons handed him his cellular phone. "Give your Ranger friend a call," he said. "And see if he has any friends who don't mind breaking a few rules.'' He leaned back against the seat and closed his eyes. ''Besides, a little backup couldn't hurt.''

Dirk Anderson tapped numbers into the phone. While he waited for the line to connect, he said, ''Ironman, Gadgets, Politician. Colorful names. How'd you guys get them?''

Blancanales spoke. ''Gadgets is an electronics expert,'' he said. ''And you just saw Ironman's iron hand at work.''

Anderson laughed. ''Yeah, he hit him pretty good. But what about you? Politician? You get that name because you *don't* ever hit snitches?''

Blancanales shrugged his shoulders. ''I hit them when they need it,'' he said with a straight face. ''I got the name because I always apologize afterward.''

The chopper pilot guided the Apache AH-64A over the canyon, splashing the spotlight down on the rugged terrain below. McCarter stared through the window using his infrared night-vision binoculars. He could see that the pilot had been right—the road from the Mexican border dropped steeply when it reached the arroyo, and it was just as steep when it began climbing the northern side. At the very bottom, the canyon sharpened almost to a V shape. Small vehicles would have little problem navigating the sudden upward turn, and Jeeps and Hummers, McCarter knew, could crawl up and down the canyon walls like ants.

Bulky, overloaded vehicles like the Army trucks would have had to slow drastically on the way down. That meant they would lose momentum for the uphill climb and have to drop into low gears, straining and struggling slowly up the north face of the canyon.

McCarter grinned. The cartel drug smugglers in their eighteen-wheelers would have it even rougher. With the trailers attached behind the trucks, they'd be in danger of jackknifing during the brief moment when the truck started up but the trailer was still heading down.

The Phoenix Force leader dropped the binoculars to his lap and turned to the pilot. "Can you set us down on the bottom?" he asked the young pilot.

The soldier aimed the chopper's spotlight down through the night and hovered in the air. McCarter saw him squinting at the bottom of the canyon. "I can get you real close, sir," he said. "See that flat area fifty yards from the bottom?"

McCarter followed the young soldier's line of vision. "I do," he said. He lifted the radio mike. "We're going down," he told James and Encizo. "Calvin, Rafe, have your pilots follow us. Let's get it done fast." He glanced at his watch for perhaps the hundredth time. Right now the trucks would be loading. He had no idea how long that might take but they could start back along the road any moment. "Once we're on the ground," McCarter went on. "You pilots get out of sight. Don't come back until you hear our fire." He looked down at the dry scraggly trees and clumps of never-die desert grass as the pilot dropped them toward the bottom of the canyon. "Everyone understand?"

"Roger" came back from both of the other chopper pilots.

The helicopter landed on the short plateau. McCarter and Manning bailed out, hauling their M-16s, equipment packs and a very reluctant Mario Vendigo with them.

"You don't need me," the cartel man protested. "I'll just be in the way!"

Manning grabbed him by the scruff of the neck and dragged him out of the chopper. "Oh, but we'd miss your company so much, Mario," he said.

The other two choppers landed and the men disembarked. McCarter counted six task force members in addition to his men and Pug Nelson. A total of eleven. "Find the best concealment you can," he ordered the men as soon as he had assembled them. "Be careful of your lines of fire. I want men on both sides of the road but I don't want you shooting one another. We'll open fire when the lead truck reaches the bottom—just before it starts up the other side. Everybody concentrate on taking it out first—that's

essential. With the lead truck disabled, the rest of the convoy will be blocked.''

"And after the first truck is stopped?'' one of the task
force troops asked, a young man with bright red hair and
freckles.

"Shoot anybody who doesn't look like one of us,''
McCarter said. Then, turning to James, he added "Calvin,
come with me. Gary, you and Rafe take four of the men
to the other side of the road.'' He turned to where the
helicopters still sat on the ground, their blades whirling
overhead. "I thought I told you blokes to get out of sight!''
he shouted through the darkness.

The choppers rose in unison and took off.

McCarter took the youth with freckles with him and
headed for an embankment twenty feet off the road. Pug
Nelson burrowed in a few feet away, while Calvin James
took two more of the task force soldiers to a depression in
the canyon farther up the northern slope.

"Hey, David?'' Nelson whispered urgently across the
bottom of the arroyo.

"Yes?'' McCarter said. He had had little conversation
with Nelson since meeting him a little over an hour ago,
and was surprised when the man called him by his first
name.

"We haven't been properly introduced,'' Nelson said.
"I'm Special Agent Nelson. Just call me Pug.''

The Phoenix Force leader chuckled silently. One of the
most amusing, and in its own way endearing, qualities of
the Yanks he encountered was their quickness to familiarity
with strangers. "There hasn't been much time for formal
introductions...Pug,'' he said.

"No but I like your style,'' Nelson whispered back.
"'Shoot anybody who doesn't look like us.' I like that,
yeah, I do. Any chance you might take over as DEA director when this is over?''

The Briton laughed out loud this time. "Very little, I'm afraid," he said.

Nelson started to speak again but the sound of a heavy truck engine overhead to the south stopped him.

McCarter's eyes rose to the top of the canyon. He watched as a big semitractor-trailer drove to the edge of the canyon, then stopped. Another truck, just visible behind it, also halted.

The drivers got out and stood in the headlights talking. They had crossed the canyon coming the other way minutes earlier, and understood how treacherous it could be. The meeting was probably designed to build their courage.

If they only knew, McCarter thought to himself. He turned to the redheaded youth at his side. "You ready, young man?" he asked.

The man's freckled face looked frightened in the moonlight. "Yes sir," he said, his voice threatening to crack.

"Waiting is always the hardest part, son," McCarter whispered. "But it's almost over. And the fight will be over before you know it, too." He paused. The soldier was little more than a boy, and his hands were trembling on his rifle. "Remember to shoot low," he went on. "Men tend to shoot too high under stress." It wasn't stress so much as outright terror he saw in the boy's eyes but he didn't want to embarrass him. "What's your name?"

"Chris, sir."

"Where are you from, Chris?"

The youth cleared his throat. "Milton-Freewater, Oregon," he said. "It's right at the northern border, across from—"

"Walla Walla, Washington."

The man's voice brightened. "You've been there, sir?"

"No," McCarter said. "But I know where it is. Tell me Chris, do you have a girlfriend back in Milton-Freewater?" He could see the conversation was taking the kid's mind off the upcoming battle.

"Sort of, sir," the man said. "I mean, there's this girl I really like named Amanda. But she can't decide between me and this other guy, Jason. He goes to college in Walla Walla and works at the drugstore part time."

McCarter patted the young man on the shoulder as the drivers at the top of the canyon returned to their trucks. "Well Chris," he said. "After tonight she won't have any trouble deciding. You're about to become a hero, and what woman wouldn't pick a hero over a chap who sells aspirins and condoms?

The last remark brought a laugh from Chris. "Yes sir," he said. He nodded as the first truck started down the slope.

Followed by the other two trucks, the tractor-trailer drove slowly, and in the lights of the truck behind it, McCarter could see a dark shadow hanging out the open driver's door. The banana-shaped magazine of an AK-47 was silhouetted in the moonlight. "Chris," he whispered. "I'm going to aim for the front tires. Wait for me to fire. The bloke riding shotgun is yours. Take him out." He watched the kid's face in the dim light. If he was going to be a soldier, he might as well get his feet wet.

"Just...shoot him, sir?"

"Unless you'd prefer he shot you, son."

Chris didn't answer, but it was more than evident that he'd never seen combat before.

The truck reached the bottom of the canyon and stopped, getting ready to take the precarious uphill slope slowly.

McCarter aimed his M-16 at the right front tires and pulled the trigger.

A short burst of .223 rounds split the southern Arizona night as the truck's tires on the right flattened. A split second later, more explosions came from the other side of the road and the left-side tires blew. The truck righted itself but leaned forward.

Automatic rounds erupted from all over the canyon now as the Phoenix Force warriors and task force men took out the remaining rubber on the eighteen-wheeler. McCarter heard Chris's rifle pounding away and saw the man who'd been riding shotgun drop from the open door.

A second later, return fire exploded from the trucks.

Rising from the embankment, the Phoenix Force leader looked up the slope. The second semi had stopped twenty yards behind the first. It was too far down the canyon to turn back. But the third drug truck had just started the descent when the gunfire erupted and was attempting to back up the slope. Turning to Nelson, McCarter yelled, "Pug! Stay there!" He grabbed Chris by the arm. "Let's go, son!" he shouted into the youth's ear.

McCarter and the young soldier started up the steep slope on foot, their boots sliding in the loose earth. The whirring blades of the helicopters arriving sounded overhead, and spotlights suddenly shot down through the darkness to illuminate the trucks. McCarter and the kid fired at the drug smugglers in the second semi as they passed. But their rounds were meant more for cover than anything else. The Phoenix Force leader glanced at the young man as he ran.

The fear had left Chris's face as soon as the battle had begun. He fired easily and well, taking what time he needed, but no more, to aim each burst from his M-16. In fact, a thin smile even curled his lips.

The two warriors reached the top of the canyon just as the rear truck backed over the edge. Below, they could hear the ongoing battle as the M-16s of James, Encizo, Nelson and the others battled the AK-47s of the cartel men. McCarter dived to his belly just below the slope and lifted his rifle over the edge. Dropping the barrel on the front of the semi, he squeezed the trigger and sent a volley into the engine. At least one of the rounds punctured the radiator, and water began to fall between the front wheels. At the same time, Chris opened fire to his side and the tires flattened.

The Phoenix Force leader rose and sprinted toward the

driver's side of the truck. "Stay low!" he shouted to the freckle-faced man who was running toward the passenger's side. Dropping to a knee next to the driver's door, McCarter angled his gunfire upward and drilled holes into the metal. Through the glass, he saw the head and shoulders of the man behind the wheel jerk spasmodically. On the other side of the big rig he heard Chris's rifle sputtering more .223 slugs. But 7.62 AK-47 rounds also exploded on that side, and as the driver slumped over the wheels, he saw the man riding shotgun returning fire at the kid from Milton-Freewater.

In his peripheral vision, McCarter saw a shadow appear at the rear of the trailer. He turned that way a split second before a burly shadow with Kalashnikov got the barrel lined up on him. A multiburst dropped the cartel man to the sandy ground, but another rifleman stepped around the trailer to take his place.

McCarter leaned into his weapon to curb the recoil, letting the brass fly to his side, glinting in the moonlight as it arced to earth. Another cartel gunner fell to the desert floor, and the Phoenix Force leader let up on the trigger. Swiftly, he changed magazines and then walked cautiously forward as rounds still exploded on the other side of the truck and in the canyon below.

Reaching the corner of the trailer, McCarter dropped to one knee and peered around the side. A cartel man with a shotgun faced the other way. He was in the process of aiming his weapon at some unseen target on the other side of the truck.

Unseen, perhaps. But not unknown. The target had to be Chris.

The Phoenix Force leader pulled the trigger and a steady stream of gunfire zipped from his rifle. The semijacketed hollowpoint rounds started at the small of the drug guard's back, moved up his spine, and finally drilled through the long hair falling from the back of his head.

The firing below in the canyon continued as McCarter stepped over the bodies and moved to the other corner of the trailer. Peering around the side, he saw the freckle-faced man sitting spread-legged on the ground. His rifle stock was at his shoulder and moved back and forth across the width of the truck and trailer.

Blood dripped from his face.

As the shots in the canyon began to die, McCarter cleared his throat. "Chris!" he shouted around the corner of the big trailer. "It's me and I'm coming out." He gave the youth a second to let it sink in, then stepped out into the open with his M-16 hanging from its sling.

Chris swung his rifle toward him.

"Easy, son," McCarter said. Slowly, he walked forward and reached out, lowering the rifle barrel toward the ground. "Are you okay?" he asked.

For a second, Chris couldn't speak; his first words choked in his throat. Then he found his voice and said weakly, "I don't know, sir. I think I took a round in the face. It knocked me down."

The automatic fire in the canyon had stopped and excited voices drifted upward. One of the helicopters flew over, casting its bright spot down on McCarter and Chris as the Phoenix Force leader knelt to examine the young face in the moonlight.

A round had skimmed across his cheek, barely breaking the skin.

"Am I okay?" the kid asked nervously.

"You're fine, son. Barely nicked you."

"Will I have a scar?"

McCarter laughed. "A small one. More like a trophy— a dueling scar."

The young man grinned. "Do you think Amanda will like it, sir?" he asked.

McCarter looked at the young man and suddenly felt

very old and very tired, but very happy. "I don't see how she couldn't, son."

THE DREAM, LIKE MOST dreams, was wild, crazy and disjointed—and probably full of symbolism he didn't understand or care about. And it was one of those dreams where the dreamer knows he's dreaming.

As the fractured images flashed through his sleeping brain, Mack Bolan saw himself arriving in Mexico on his dual mission of protecting President Don Juan de Fierro Blanco and secretly investigating the man's honesty. He saw himself meeting General Razon for the first time on the hog hunt, and he went through the many assassination attempts that had been made on the president over the last few days. The attack on both *Los Pinos* and Fierro Blanco's summerhouse ran through his mind at the speed of light, and for a moment the Executioner felt the same nausea in his stomach and ache in his heart he had experienced when he'd thought the president, the first family and Captain Juanito Oliverez had been baked alive in the basement beneath the house.

And while he dreamed, he felt something hard biting into the small of his back.

As the slumbering visions continued, Bolan saw the man in the ball-fringed sombrero escape after the attack on the beach, and then the scene shifted to the two men and their diving performance at the Hilton's swimming pool. The grenade came sailing through the window at him and the men of Able Team again, and a moment later they were engaged in the battle at the hotel. He listened to the words he had said when he sent off McCarter, Manning and Hawkins to join James and Encizo in the search for the tunnel and Able Team to battle the cartel hitmen killing each other in the U.S. He followed President Fierro Blanco to the man's clandestine rendezvous with Margarita Felice, and he rekilled the camouflage-clad man sneaking up on the summerhouse. In the strange way that dreams sometimes combine events, he tested the poisoned wine on the Mexican first lady's Siamese cat at the same time as he chased the *Marxistas* who had fled the summerhouse after the attack.

But throughout the dream, he *knew* it was a dream. And through it all, he could still feel whatever it was that kept poking him in the spine.

As the end of the dream, he called Stony Man Farm and talked to Barbara Price. He told her he'd had no success in his investigation at *Los Pinos*, and was leaving to pursue another angle. Price promised to send someone to take his place guarding the president.

The sleeping soldier suddenly awoke knowing that part of the dream hadn't taken place. Yet.

Bolan watched the bouncing ceiling above him. It looked like the roof of a van or delivery truck and he remembered the Latin American Parcel Service vehicle. His eyes moved achingly to the sides of the sockets as if stretched tight on the ends of rubber bands, and he saw brown paper-wrapped packages piled high on both sides of where he lay on his back.

He was in the LAPS delivery truck, and it was bumping along a road. His head felt as if it had been pounded by a baseball bat and his guts threatened to expel everything he had eaten in the past twenty-four hours. Whatever it was that had dug into his back during the dream still did so, and his still-foggy brain guessed he must by lying on top of something—perhaps a small package not yet delivered—that had fallen to the floor beneath him.

In the cab of the truck, through the open curtain, he heard voices speaking softly in Spanish.

The memory of the men at the guard shack came racing back into the Executioner's brain, and his headache intensified. He remembered the man in the yellow shirt and his partner—his brother—and suddenly saw them wearing bathing suits and diving into the pool at the Hilton hotel. The truck hit a bump in the road and sharp knives stabbed his temple. He closed his eyelids and the world seemed to swim behind them.

As the truck bounced on, Bolan remembered the guard with the tranquilizer gun. The other uniformed man at the gate had been shot pointblank in the face, and it became clear now that the second guard had been an imposter. Or perhaps he was a real federal guard who, like so many other Mexican officers and politicians, had fallen victim to the bribery that was taking over the country.

The thing in his back dug deeper and Bolan tried to shift his weight away from it. Suddenly, he remembered the North American Arms .22 Magnum pistol. He could feel his coat still on his shoulders and arms, and he tried to reach for the pocket. His hands, which had refused to cock the hammer of the mini-revolver after the tranquilizer darts had struck, moved now. But only a little, and he realized for the first time since waking that his wrists were tied behind his back beneath him.

Was that what was causing the pain at his spine? His own hands? His hazy mind wasn't sure but didn't think so.

Bolan heard movement at the front of the truck and opened his eyes in time to see the thinner of the two men appear at the curtain. He closed his eyes again quickly as the man moved into the cargo area. Foul breath invaded his nostrils as the man knelt at his side, then reached under him to check the restraints. He jammed a finger into Bolan's carotid artery and held it there.

"Is he all right?" came a voice from the front of the truck.

"Yes," said the man next to the Executioner.

"You're certain? I have never seen anyone require so much tranquilizing. It was like trying to put an elephant to sleep."

"His pulse is strong."

"Good," the driver called back. "Mama would kill us if he didn't arrive in shape for the sacrifice."

Bolan continued to feign unconsciousness as the man stood, and returned to the front of the truck. Mama? Sacrifice? What were the men talking about?

The truck bumped on, and the Executioner listened, trying to get his bearings. It was light outside the truck. He could hear other vehicles passing, and horns honking. They were still in the city—Mexico City? How long had he been out? He had no way of knowing except that night had turned to day. Was it the next day? They could be anywhere on the continent for all he knew.

A horn suddenly blared and the man in the yellow shirt must have stomped on the brake, because the LAPS truck jerked to a halt. Bolan fought the natural urge to resist being thrown forward, let himself go limp and slid along the floor of the cargo area. His legs flew through the doorway to the cab, and his feet slammed into the console between the two men as the driver screamed curses and threats in Spanish. Bolan kept his eyes closed, as any well-drugged man should. His head struck something and he felt blood begin to seep from the wound as the truck teetered back and forth, then settled on its axles once more. The pain in his head doubled now, making him want to scream like a victim of cluster-migraine headaches. His abdomen churned, but he tightened his jaw and remained silent.

"Asshole!" the man in the yellow shirt screamed out the window.

Bolan lay still.

The man in the yellow shirt said, "Check him again."

"He hit his head on the seat. But he's still out."

"He's not dead?"

Bolan's pulse was taken again.

"He's fine."

"Then take him to the back again."

The Executioner sensed the other man step over him. An

arm wrapped around his chin and dragged him back to the cargo area.

Having narrowly avoided an accident, the delivery truck started through the traffic again. The thing poking into Bolan's back was still with him after his slide, although it had shifted. It couldn't be a package, he realized, and at the same time he remembered the Applegate-Fairbairn covert folding knife he had dropped into his underwear.

Slow, the Executioner told himself as the excitement in his chest began to rise, go slow. Take it slow and easy—your brain still isn't working well. He strained his hands against the straps again, and found that at least partial dexterity had returned. His fingers felt numb, and the orders sent to them by his brain seemed to take a few seconds to arrive. He spread his fingers, then closed them into fists. But when he tried to extend an individual finger, he found his brain incapable of performing the more complex task.

Could he get to the folding knife, get it out and open without dropping it? Maybe. Could he cut the leather strands on his wrists without being seen or heard, or losing the knife, or accidentally severing his own arteries? He didn't know. But he had to try.

He was on his way to some kind of sacrifice, whatever that meant. And he had the feeling he was to be the guest of honor. Mama, whoever she was, was waiting.

Raising his pelvis slightly, Bolan strained his shoulders to get his hands up over his belt. The fire in his head and belly grew stronger and his breath came in pants. He kept his murky vision glued on at the front of the truck, ready to quit if he saw any sign that the brothers had noticed him.

The covert was his last chance. If he blew it, it was over. If they saw what he was doing and found the knife they'd pump him so full of tranquilizers that he might not wake up until the...sacrifice?

What in hell did they mean by that? Who were these two strange brothers?

Finally, Bolan felt his hands creep over the top of his waistband. He shifted his buttocks again, still staring ahead, and an index finger brushed the hard plastic grip of the folding knife. It had turned sideways and fallen deeper into his black jeans, and he struggled to curl a finger around and under it.

Ahead of him, he heard the driver say, "We need gas."

The Executioner strained harder, finally getting two fingers around the knife. He forced himself to ignore the pain in his head and gut and to move slowly or risk the Applegate folder flying from his grasp to clatter out of reach across the floor. It took almost a minute to get the small weapon free, and when he had, he lay panting on the floor, praying the men in the front of the truck wouldn't turn until his breath returned to normal.

"There," the brother in the passenger's seat said. "There is a station over there."

Bolan concentrated as hard as he could, trying not to fumble the knife as he rotated it in his hands to get his thumb on the opening stud. He found the tiny protrusion and opened the blade halfway. But he didn't have the right angle or leverage to get the blade out all the way.

Bolan took a deep breath. The truck was slowing. If a move was to be made, an escape to be had, it would have to be while they stopped for gas. He had no time to painstakingly reposition the knife and take another chance of dropping it. His head feeling like someone was continually striking it with the blade of an ax, the Executioner took another deep breath and worked his thumb between the grip and the blade's sharp edge. He felt the narrow edge slice into his flesh, and beneath his back blood spurted from the wound as he pushed. But the blade opened the rest of the way, and he heard the soft click as the liner-lock fell into place.

The LAPS truck rolled to a halt. Bolan heard the driver's door open. A second later, the same man who had dragged him back after the near-collision, returned to the cargo area. Bolan watched him through tiny slits beneath his eyelids. The man took only a cursory look, then returned to the cab. A second later, the other door opened, then closed.

The Executioner worked quickly now, sawing through the restraints around his wrists. Even at the awkward angle at which he was forced to work, the serrations near the Applegate's hilt bit into the leather and popped it easily. His hands came free.

Bolan pulled his arms around to his chest and opened the fingers, then shut them again. They still didn't feel right—sluggish, as if they belonged to someone else. He rose to a sitting position with the covert in his right hand, and his head swam as if he were underwater. His stomach threatened to empty again as he reached out, trying to pull himself to his feet by grasping a large package at his side. The box shifted, and he fell to a sitting position again.

The Executioner sat still for a moment, trying to clear his head. Even with the element of surprise he would have on the two men when they returned, he knew he was in no shape to take them on. Escape was his only avenue, and considering his condition he'd be lucky to effect even that. Taking it slower this time, he rolled to his hands and knees, then stood. His equilibrium off, he rolled like a sailor new to the sea. He took a moment to let his eyes settle as best they could, then staggered forward, using the stacked packages as a handrail.

Bolan stuck his head through the opening to the cab. Neither of the brothers was in sight. Bracing a hand on the dashboard, he turned toward the driver's side and saw the man in the yellow shirt through the opening. He stood at the rear of the truck pumping gas into the tank.

The Executioner turned the other way in time to see the thinner brother rounding the corner of the service station. As quietly as he could, Bolan stepped down from the truck opposite the man in the yellow shirt. His abdomen felt like an electric blender was beating against the sides, and he leaned forward fearing he'd throw up. The immediate threat subsided, but the nausea remained.

Bolan looked around him through blurry eyes. The only direction he could go and keep the truck between him and the man in the yellow shirt was to follow the brother who had rounded the corner to the rest room. He had no idea where that pathway led but he took it, stumbling across the service station lot past a surprised customer who was entering the office area. When he reached the corner of the building, the Executioner fell forward, gasping as he caught his balance on the cold concrete wall and turning back toward the truck.

The feet of the man in the yellow shirt could be seen beneath the vehicle, still at the pumps.

The Executioner poked his head around the corner. The other brother had already entered the rest room. Wobbling forward, Bolan stepped off the sidewalk that encircled the building and across the grass, hoping his movements couldn't be heard from inside the men's room. A toilet flushed as he reeled past the door, and he dived clumsily around the back corner of the building, falling and coming to rest in a sitting position on top of a stack of garbage, wood scraps and loose wires.

Just around the corner, he heard the door open. His hand moved automatically to where the Desert Eagle should have been on his hip, but of course it was gone. The holster where his Beretta rode beneath his arm was likewise empty. He gripped the knife, and waited as footsteps left the rest room and clattered back toward the front of the station.

Bolan rose, and this time his stomach gave him no quarter. He leaned forward, his abdominal muscles seizing in pain as his belly emptied. But as soon as it had happened, he felt somewhat better. He turned his attention to the rear of the service station lot.

While he could hear the traffic on the busy commercial

street behind him, the back of the lot was adjacent to a residential area. Low-income houses ran along both sides, and directly behind the station, on the other side of an un-kempt lawn, the Executioner saw a ramshackle house with a three-foot chicken-wire fence encircling it. He stumbled to the wire, turned sideways, and got one foot over it. He was straddling the fence when he heard the excited voices shouting on the other side of the building.

The soldier tried to swing his other leg over but his foot caught on the top. He fell sprawling into a vegetable garden as the chirping barks of a dog grew louder in his ears. He felt sharp teeth sink into his ankle, and looked toward the pain to see a tiny Chihuahua holding on for dear life.

Shaking his leg, Bolan knocked the dog away and got to his feet. He zigzagged toward the side of the house, stopped and pressed his back against the tar shingles that covered the outside wall. Across the lawn, in the parking lot behind the service station, the soldier saw the man in the yellow shirt suddenly round the building and stop. The man held Bolan's Desert Eagle in his hands. The Executioner waited until he turned, then hurried to the front of the house and out of sight.

Bolan ran now, not knowing where he was going but finding his balance better when he moved quickly rather than slowly. His head still hurt, his belly felt dead and he gasped with every breath as he jolted down the street past curious men, women and children outside their houses. But none of them bothered him, and the new oxygen he was forcing into his brain slowly began to drive away the effect of the tranquilizers.

Block after block, he ran through the quiet residential streets. Finally spotting a busier thoroughfare ahead, the soldier slowed to a walk. On the other side of the street he saw a small shopping center. He realized he still held the Applegate covert knife, and smiled silently. No wonder he had gotten so many strange looks from the people he had passed. Not many men went jogging with an open fighting knife in their hand. Folding the blade, he clipped it inside the right front pocket of his jeans. For the time being, at least, it would have to serve as his primary weapon.

Bolan walked to the corner and paused, looking up and down the lanes of traffic. He saw no sign of the LAPS truck, and as soon as traffic permitted, he jogged across the street. A telephone booth stood just outside the large supermarket at the center of the strip. He opened the door, then closed it behind him.

A moment later, Barbara Price said, "Mack, your voice sounds strange. What's wrong?"

Bolan chuckled. "Just a little drug abuse," he said.

Price didn't respond.

"Bad joke," the soldier said. "I'll explain later. In the meantime, get Hal on the line, will you?"

A moment later, Hal Brognola picked up. "Striker, are you all right?" he asked in a concerned voice. "Barb said you sounded—"

"I'm fine, Hal, relax," Bolan said. He watched the early morning traffic of Mexico City drive by on the street in front of him. As briefly as he could, he explained what had happened.

"You're unarmed?" Brognola said when he finished.

"I've got the knife," Bolan said. "And my best weapon is returning."

"Your best weapon?"

"My brain, Hal, my brain."

"Okay, big guy, stay where you are," Brognola said. "I'll get a hold of Lyons or McCarter and send someone to pick you up. You can—"

"Negative, Hal. Keep them where they are, doing what they're doing."

"But—"

"No. By now, everyone at *Los Pinos* will know I was

kidnapped. They'll probably think I'm dead. I want to keep it that way."

"What do you have in mind, Striker?"

Bolan thought of the dream he'd had earlier. In it, he had told Price to send someone else to bodyguard Fierro Blanco because he was about to pursue other angles. He was talking to Brognola now, but in essence the dream was coming true. "*El presidente* will still want someone to watch his back," the Executioner said. "Send Katz down here to replace me."

"Katz helped you get rid of two people at the mansion a few days ago," Brognola reminded him.

"Yes, but nobody saw him. Send him. He's the best."

"Anything else I can do for you?"

Bolan thought of the Desert Eagle he had last seen in the hands of the man in the yellow shirt. His brother probably had the Beretta. He made a vow to get them both back, but in the meantime, he would need replacements. "Tell Kissinger to send some firepower down with Katz," he said.

"You've got it."

"I'll call back for specifics," the Executioner said and hung up.

Bolan left the phone booth, walking slowly along the street. He guessed he had run between two and three miles from the service station, and Mexico City was one of the largest metropolitan areas in the world. The chances of the men in the LAPS truck driving by were about twenty million to one.

For a moment, he felt naked without the Beretta and Desert Eagle, then he realized that what he had told Brognola was true—it wasn't the weapons that made a warrior, it was the man. And he still had his brain, the most powerful weapon of all.

Bolan saw a bus stop ahead. An old woman sat on the bench waiting, eating a tortilla. Her skin was dark and wrinkled with sun and age. Bolan took a seat next to her and she smiled.

The soldier didn't know where the next phase of the mission would lead him, but he knew he had learned all he was going to at *Los Pinos*. It made no sense to stay there spinning his wheels. He stretched his legs in front of him, and found that the feeling had returned. He thought of the man in the ball-fringed sombrero, and the two strange brothers from whom he had just escaped. Were they connected? Maybe, maybe not. His thoughts turned to the kidnapped movie star Ronnie Quartel and his friends. If either Able Team or Phoenix Force could finish their current assignments in time, he'd like to send them to Tijuana to help Leo Turrin and the two blacksuits who were currently trying to locate the hostages.

The old woman next to him broke into his thoughts. *"Señor,"* she said. "Are you injured?" She frowned in concern and pointed to his face.

Bolan reached up and felt the dried blood from the wound he'd sustained when he slid to the front of the delivery truck. "It's nothing," he said.

The woman reached into her purse, pulled out a small package of tissues and handed it to him.

Bolan took the pack and thanked her.

"Your hand..." the woman said.

The soldier looked down to see his thumb still bleeding where he had opened the Applegate folder.

The old woman smiled, then reached into her purse again, pulled out another tortilla wrapped in white paper and handed it to Bolan. "You have had a rough night?" she asked in the voice of a concerned mother.

The Executioner smiled and took the tortilla. "Pretty rough," he said as he bit into it. "But you have to expect a few bad nights in life, don't you?"